Vagabond Blue

---

a novel by

Frank Allan Rogers

Chapter One

On a Sunday afternoon, three days before he turned thirteen, Blue's two-year-old sister lay on a borrowed, corn-shuck mattress on the shack floor with a deep cough, and shivered with a high fever. Mama paced and wrung her hands.

"Get a doctor, Elmer, please." She wiped a tear with the back of her hand. "Hurry. We can't lose our baby."

"Bonnie, they ain't no way a doctor's gonna come out here from town if I ain't got money to pay him with." Elmer jerked his head and glared at her. "And you know I ain't got none."

"Maybe the widow woman will let you borrow some. Go ask her, please." Bonnie turned toward the baby on the floor, her palms up. "Oh God, Elmer, look at that poor child. If we don't get a doctor soon, she might not make it."

Elmer didn't answer. Bonnie shook his arm and looked up at him, her face drawn and tired. "I've got thirty-seven cents in my apron pocket. If you get the doctor, you can take it and bring yourself back a bottle of wine from that man you know."

Elmer took the thirty-seven cents, borrowed two dollars and a horse from the widow, and rode toward town.

On Blue's birthday, Bonnie Bailey sobbed and shivered while Blue and the widow's son threw the last shovelfuls of dirt into the grave in a small plot on Widow Benson's cotton farm. As they covered the crude wooden box, Elmer returned from town and staggered into the yard smelling of whiskey—without money, without a horse, and without a doctor.

***

The memory haunted Blue as he hopped a creek and skipped along a path through the woods. His boots, worn out and too small, scraped the calluses on his feet. Socks would help. But he didn't have any. And that was that.

In spite of it all, today he whistled. He'd told himself many times that getting out was his only hope, and one day he would make a living with his music. Take his guitar—the only thing he ever owned—walk away and never look back. Go to the camp near the railroad tracks, a place the hobos called a jungle.

The men there would likely tell him it was the worst place to start his new career, or any other career. Blue saw it as the perfect jump-start. After all, he'd have to travel to make it big. And, well… hobos knew more than anybody about traveling for free. So he'd leave the old life behind, including family.

Some called his family dirt poor. They were wrong. His family couldn't afford dirt. They had never owned a house or land. The sharecropper shacks Blue grew up in belonged to the farmers his father agreed to work for. An agreement was all a farmer ever got. Daddy wouldn't work. The family moved often.

Mama took in ironing when she could borrow an iron. She mended clothes and often cooked fatback, beans, and skillet cornbread for a crew of farmhands to bring in a few pennies. Sometimes she slipped into a henhouse at night and borrowed a chicken, a guinea hen, or eggs to feed her family.

The farmers suspected a fox or possum but never seemed to figure out how the varmint got past their dogs. That is, until a farmer waited on his back porch after dark with a plug of chewing tobacco and a shotgun. Blue caught himself grinning as he thought about it. It was kinda funny and kinda not.

The sudden bang from the shotgun set the hound dogs barking, chickens squawking, and Mama screaming. In a panic, the farmer's wife wrecked the screen door when she tore out of the house to check on the noise. The tie-string on her nightgown caught the handle of the washtub, yanked it off the outside wall, ripped off her gown, and sent the woman and tub crashing to the floor. The farmer coughed and choked on his tobacco, pigs squealed, the milk cow bawled, and mules kicked out the side of the barn while the farmer's wife flopped naked on the porch yelling, "Help me, Jee-zus."

Daddy slept right through the commotion. Mama shook him awake. The only knife in the house had a rusty blade. So, by candlelight, Daddy dug birdshot out of her backside with a fork. Blue guessed the surgery might've hurt more than Mama let on.

The farmer wanted the family out by daybreak, and he watched them while they left the shack, their only possessions hanging across their shoulders in sacks. When they got near his house, he stepped off the porch and looked at Mama.

"Missus Bailey." He took off his hat and put it back. "If I'da knowed you was in the family way, I'da been more careful. I thought it was a critter in my henhouse." He held out a dead chicken hung by a string around its ankles. Mama took the gift, smiled, and limped away.

The family moved on.

But today was the day Blue had waited for, planned for, for a long time. Today he turned sixteen, and the closer he got to the jungle, the more excited he became. He'd been there a few times before, so he might see men he knew. Or maybe not. Most hobos didn't stay long at one place.

No matter who he met, the hobos made him feel at home, and they always talked about how work was hard to find since the stock market fell last year. Blue expected to hear it again. He'd heard the same stuff from the farmers' radios more than twice, how the crash made people jump out of windows and kill themselves. And it was all Herbert Hoover's fault.

Blue shook his head as he thought about it. If a stock market was not a place where they sold cows and hogs, then he didn't understand what it was. The hobos at the jungle didn't likely know either. They never said how an outfit in New York had anything to do with milking cows or growing cotton around Possum Trot, Missouri. And if the fall didn't kill a man when he jumped out the window, did he go back up and try again?

None of it made sense. But today, he would play his guitar, sing a few tunes for the men at the jungle, and help them forget about the bad stuff they couldn't change. Maybe he'd be lucky enough to make them forget their troubles for a little while, maybe even make them smile. And if he was really lucky, Halo would be there.

Chapter Two

Everybody builds his own bridge or his own cage, and most people never learn the difference.

Blue Bailey said those words to himself as he stood in the boxcar door and watched Possum Trot, Missouri, disappear. Roads and bridges, houses and barns, fences and farms—the only world he had ever known—grew smaller.

The train left them all behind, along with people who led lives of misery. Blue pitied them, but he could no longer be a part of it. Men and women worked in the fields every day, ten hours of back-breaking labor—and had nothing. Some often dreamed of having their own farm, to be their own boss. Few ever got their wish. Most who did were tied to a farm like a dog on a chain. It didn't make sense. A dry summer destroyed crops, farmers… and field hands.

Then there were some he could not pity, who were just plain worthless, who deserved their own misery, Blue admitted. Like his own father who built his cage out of liquor bottles.

Blue brushed it all aside, and thought about how much his life changed yesterday when he and Halo sat around the fire and talked, though Blue did most of the talking while Halo listened and smoked. After Blue made a long speech about being free, he wanted Halo's thoughts.

Halo drew again on his pipe and blew out the smoke. "It's a whole new kind of freedom, lad. It's not just something you feel. You can taste it. You can smell it. And you can never let it go." He tapped the pipe on the bottom of his shoe and dumped the ashes. "One day your time will come."

Blue's eyes lost focus while he stared into the fire. Neither man spoke for a full minute. Then Blue stood and cleared his throat.

"My time has come."

The camp got quiet, like everybody had been listening. Halo drew a long breath.

"You're still young. Don't let the stuff I said make any difference."

"I made up my mind before I got here." He looked around at the men, grinned and nodded.

Some welcomed him into the circle. Not all. A tall, skinny hobo with a wine stain birthmark on his cheek stood and shook his head.

"You know what you're getting yourself into, boy?" When Blue didn't answer, the man said, "Just what I thought. You ain't got no idea how a hobo has to live."

Shorty yelled, "It'll beat you down bad. You're too good-lookin' for this kind a life, young man."

Color flooded Blue's face. "Thanks, mister, but looks don't buy the bacon."

Halo cleared his throat, and jerked his head toward men playing poker, using marbles for money.

"These men got nothing. All you have to do is look around. It's good to have a plan for your life, Blue. But… being a hobo's not much of a plan."

Blue looked around at men in filthy, worn-out clothes that didn't fit, holes in their shoes, mismatched socks, or no socks at all. He saw men with gnarled fingers, scruffy beards, pocked faces, scars, scabs, bent noses, crossed eyes, and bad teeth. Yet most had blankets, knives, forks, tin cups, and a belly full of mulligan stew. And all had stories to tell.

Blue angled his head toward them. "These men here got more than me. More than I ever had."

Halo looked him up and down and wagged his head. "Nothing to throw in the pot. Ain't even got a cup. Got any money?"

Blue shook his head. "Never had no money, but I'll figure out a way to get the stuff I need." He looked down at his guitar. "Maybe I can play a couple of songs if anybody wants to hear me."

Halo smiled. "I don't know whether to say good luck or get the hell outa here. You'd better show us what you can do."

"If you're good enough," Shorty said, "we might let you stay. If not…" he cocked his head, his eyes got large, "…we might have to send you back to mama."

Blue would play his best, but told himself he would be a hobo, no matter what.

Now, he stood in the boxcar and knew he was finally free, and the proud grin clung to his face as he listened to the rhythm of the rails. They played a song of freedom like America the Beautiful and Battle Hymn of the Republic. He was proud to be an American. Proud to be a hobo.

Still, none of it seemed real, and his mind relived the early morning, when Halo taught him how to catch a train, and he and Halo stood by the tracks while the sun turned the rails to an orange glare.

***

Blue squinted as he peeked around the tree to watch the train. He shuffled his feet, excited and anxious about his first train ride, eager to jump on board. He had a belly full of mulligan stew from a borrowed cup at breakfast, and a chest full of pride from being welcomed into the hobo jungle the day before.

Halo warned him about trying to board a jerking boxcar.

"You have to be patient and prepared," he said. "Patient enough to wait for the right time, and ready to jump and run when the time is right."

Halo stood beside him and watched the train. From the engine to the caboose, a series of metallic clunks crawled along the line of cars, the sound growing weaker as it traveled. Each car jerked forward in turn, and the repeating rhythm of clunks grew faster. As the cars began to roll, Halo hooked his finger on a chain, pulled a railroad watch from its pocket, and flipped open the lid.

Ordinary hobos did not own expensive timepieces. *Ordinary* did not apply to Halo. "Five forty-five." He snapped the lid closed. "Right on time."

"Run along behind me," he told Blue again. "After I'm in, hand up your guitar. Then grab the step on the ladder and come through that boxcar door like you own the railroad." He checked the pack on his back, looked at Blue and back at the train. "Let's go."

Blue's heart raced. Satisfaction spread through his body while he ran beside the moving train. He watched Halo catch the rung of the ladder on the boxcar, pull up, and swing inside. Then Halo lay face-down and reached through the doorway.

If that old hobo can do it, Blue told himself, *anybody can.* With his guitar held high, he moved closer to the boxcar and handed Martin, his prize possession, up to Halo. As the train moved faster, the rung moved out of reach. Blue ran harder, grabbed for the rung, and missed. He signaled Halo with his index finger, put his long legs to work and gained speed.

"Grab the guitar," Halo yelled. He held it out and yelled again. "Take the guitar."

Blue pushed himself hard and grabbed the guitar. Halo waved him away from the train, and then leaped out, running as he hit the gravel.

Blue ran to Halo and stopped. "Change your mind?"

Halo shook his head and laughed. "*You* changed my mind."

"I was gonna try again and…"

"You'da missed again." Halo looked at the train and then back at Blue. "You'd be standing here waving goodbye." Blue's eyes widened, his chin dropped as the thought set in.

"So tell me… which one would you miss the most?" Halo wagged his finger between his chest and the guitar. "Martin or Halo?"

Color rushed to Blue's face. "Well, I uh…"

Halo grinned and nodded, and slapped him on the shoulder. "Yeah, that's what I thought."

An hour later, they stood by the same tree. "We'll catch this next freight," Halo said, "and switch trains in Atlanta." He angled his head toward the tracks. "You want to be a hobo, you gotta learn to catch out."

"Catch out?"

"Yeah, catch out. Hop a train. Hitch a ride."

Blue stared at him. "That last one speeded up when I tried to hop on."

Halo shook his head and laughed but his eyes never left the target. "You got a lot to learn, friend. Get ready." The cars gained speed and rolled smoother. With a quick nod to Blue, he yelled,

"Now," and sprinted toward a boxcar with an open door. Blue snatched up his guitar and ran after his friend.

Halo swung his pack up to the door and tossed it inside. Five steps later, he reached for the rung, pulled himself up and swung his body into the car in one fluid motion. He lay face-down on the floor and stuck out his hand.

Blue matched his running speed with the train and handed his guitar up to Halo. Halo laid it to one side and stood near the door ready to help. Blue told himself he would not miss again. He would do exactly what Halo did. Blue counted five, long, powerful steps, and reached for the rung. His hand closed on the steel as if it was meant to be there, and his heart leaped as he pulled his feet up on the ladder and swung into the car. The pride showed on his face, and the two men sat on the floor, breathed hard and laughed.

Blue's face glowed. "I didn't know it would be this much fun."

"Jumping off is a bit tricky, too," Halo said without a smile. They moved to the back of the car and leaned against the wall, leaving space between them for Martin and for Halo's bindle.

***

Blue returned to his spot near the back wall of the boxcar, sat beside Halo and smiled. "You watched me the whole time I stood there, didn't you?"

Halo gestured toward the open door. "Well, whaddaya think?"

Blue laughed and rubbed his hands together. "I'm really going somewhere." He jerked his head toward Halo. "Where we headed?"

The white beard bobbed up and down as

Halo laughed. "You want to be a hobo? You jump on a train and don't even know where it's going?"

"Well, I got on, didn't I?" Blue shook his head. "Besides, every place I go will be some place I've never been."

"Well, now you're going to Atlanta. Then we'll catch a westbound to Bolling. I know a man there in Alabama, and we can get a job."

"My first real job for money." Blue's eyes grew large. "Doing what?"

"Bagging potatoes."

Blue jumped up and glared at Halo. "That's not funny."

Halo shrugged. "I'm not laughing."

"A farm job?" Blue looked away, shook his head and looked back. "Pickin' spuds out of the dirt? Chokin' in the dust all day? I been doing farm stuff like that all my life."

"All your life? You turned sixteen yesterday."

"I been a man since I was eleven. I had to take up the slack for Daddy. Slop the hogs, hoe the corn, plant cotton in the springtime, chop it in summer, pick it in the fall, till my fingers would crack and bleed. And I chopped and split firewood all year long so we could heat our shack or cook something." He shrugged. "If there was anything to cook."

Blue's eyes grew misty and he shook his head. "You and Martin are the only friends I got, and I ain't never goin' back. But I don't want to do farm work." He picked up the guitar and hugged it to his chest.

Halo nodded. "Looks expensive." Then he smiled. "Where'd you steal it?"

Blue did not smile back, but strummed his

guitar while he talked. "For two and a half years, an old man taught me how to play his guitar, and one day he told me, 'When I die, it's yours.' Guess what; he died the next day. Martin's been my best friend ever since." He pointed at the name on the neck. "Every friend needs a name."

"I bet when you got it, you practiced every day."

Blue snorted. "Sundays—the only day I didn't have to do farming. Every Sunday morning when Daddy gets out of the outhouse, he staggers into our shack with a big, stupid grin, and sings, *Oh bring back my Bonnie to me*." Blue looked at Halo. "My mama's name is Bonnie." He looked back at his guitar. "Then he orders me out of the house. Says he needs some time to play with Mama. And every time, just like yesterday, I'd stuff my guitar in a gunny sack, and go find a stump in the woods near the creek. I can entertain birds and squirrels for hours. It ain't like I ever had to be home for a meal."

Halo nodded but didn't look at him. "But you wanted to be a hobo."

Blue stared at the boxcar's rough wood floor. "When you start with nothing, you got nothing to lose."

"Well, I can tell you a thing or two about *nothing*." Halo sat up, folded his arms over his chest, and stared through the open door as he talked.

"Hobos have funny stories. They'll tell you where they've been and where they're going because it makes them feel better about this kind of life. It might sound free and easy, but they don't travel for fun, and they don't go first class. They're looking for work, for their next meal." He leaned closer to Blue and spoke in a loud whisper. "So they can stay alive another day."

Blue laid his guitar aside and stood. "Me too. I work so I can eat, so I can stay alive. But I never get to go anywhere." He shook his head and looked down at Halo. "I want to go and see things too, not just potatoes, cornfields, and cotton. I want to do things I ain't never done, maybe something I never even heard of. I want to fall asleep with a belly full of food and wake up in a place I've never been before. A place that don't stink of chicken coops, mule piss, or hog manure. Is that too much to ask for?" With his hands on his hips, he bent down and stared at Halo. "Well, is it?"

Halo stared at the floor without answering. Then he shrugged and looked up.

"Not if you got another job lined up."

Blue turned, keeping his knees bent to absorb the sway and bounce of the car. He took three steps, turned and walked back. "I won't spend my life as a spud chucker. I want to sing and play for my meals."

Halo leaned sideways and tugged a cap from his back pocket. He slipped it on his head and pulled it low to shade his eyes. Then he stuck his bindle behind him, leaned back against the wall, and let out a heavy breath. His words were slow and absolute.

"When we get to Atlanta, you and Martin can go any way you like. I hope you find what you want. I really do. Me? I'm going to Bolling."

Chapter Three

A half-hour past daybreak, Blue's bare toes broke up clods of dirt as he trudged across the potato patch to a barrel of burlap sacks. Yesterday, the first day on the job, loose dirt filled his ill-fitting shoes and left blisters on his feet. Today, he left his shoes in the shack.

Three days ago in Atlanta, Blue said goodbye to Halo and walked away from the train yard, determined to find a job playing his guitar. An hour later, he was back, sitting on a stack of railroad ties in a shaded spot. A heavy sigh escaped, and he stood and paced. *I don't know anybody here. I'm alone, with no money. Hell, I ain't even got a stew cup.*

He sat again, rested his arms on his knees, and hung his head, exhausted, barely aware of the moving train on the second track. But the whistle jolted him. His head jerked up and he watched the train pulling away. He grabbed Martin, and his chest grew tight as he ran beside an open boxcar yelling for Halo. No one appeared in the doorway.

Out of breath, Blue stopped, watched the boxcar pull away and told himself his friend caught an earlier train. Or maybe Halo didn't come to the door because he no longer wanted Blue as a friend.

When the train grew small in the distance, Blue shook his head and walked back toward the stack of railroad ties while hunger began to gnaw at his gut. Convinced that a jungle would be close by, he started away from the train yard once again. But another engine whistled and he heard the boxcars jerk forward. He turned back. He would hop aboard, be a true hobo, though he had no idea where the train was headed.

While the cars picked up speed, he walked fast alongside, looking for a car with an open door. When he found one, a man stood in the doorway of the car, and Blue wondered if he could be one of the dreaded bulls Halo warned about. "They work for the railroad," Halo said, "and they hate hobos. Look out for them." So Blue looked out, but as the car drew closer, the man waved.

Blue's breath caught, and his heart hammered in his ears while he sprinted toward the boxcar, held his guitar high and screamed, "Halo. Halo."

Halo laid flat on the floor and held out his hand. A minute later, Blue stood beside him.

The afternoon wore on with little conversation between the two hobos, and Blue curled up on the floor near the back wall. Halo didn't know Blue's thoughts brought back the conversation at the Possum Trot jungle, when the two sat on logs and Blue shared his dream of becoming a hobo, and Halo stood to smoke.

He was a big man, tall with broad shoulders. A shock of white hair and a beard made him look much older than he was. While he talked, he ran his finger back and forth along the frayed edge of the bib pocket on his overalls. He pulled a corncob pipe from the pocket, picked a twig off the ground and tapped down the half-smoked tobacco. Then he lit the twig from the campfire and held it above the bowl.

Halo crossed his eyes toward his nose to see the bowl, closed his lips around the stem and sucked the flame down into the pipe. The tobacco glowed red and he drew a long breath. When he blew the smoke through his nose, a white ring formed around his head. Halo studied it as if it held a nugget of wisdom he was about to reveal. He nodded again as another cloud of smoke rose above his head, and his voice, slow and smooth, came through the cloud.

"One day you'll leave home. A month later, you'll be sorry as hell. But a year down the road, after a hundred jungles in a hundred new towns, when you've slept and shivered in more boxcars than you can count, lived on beans for a week at a stretch, had on the same clothes every day for a month, and lived by your own wits—no matter where you are or who you're with—you'll know for the first time that your life belongs to you."

As the sun became a fine line in the western sky, darkness crept into the boxcar and sleep crept into Blue. He didn't hear Halo say, "I guess your Atlanta job didn't work out." And Blue didn't know Halo patted him on the arm and said, "Sorry, my friend."

Now, while Blue's bare feet broke up clods in the potato patch, the head of a worn-out mule bobbed up and down. Chains clinked, leather squeaked, and heavy hooves pounded the ground as the animal dragged a single-bottom plow down the field. The plow snapped roots with a loud crunch and left the earthy smell of fresh dirt turned upside down while ragged rows of red potatoes popped to the surface of the rich, black soil.

An old man gripped the curved wood handles of the plow and stumbled over the clumps of dark earth behind the mule. Long leather reins from the mule's harness ran back above the handles and looped over the man's shoulder. Blue nodded and said "mornin" as he passed. He got no reply.

The man said only *gee, haw, whoa,* and *giddy-up sumbitch.* He talked only to the mule.

Somebody said the man's name was Eustice. That was hard to remember and harder to pronounce. So the hired hands called him *Useless*. Or *Mule Man* when they wanted to be kind, which wasn't often. The dirty furrows in his face, a crossed eye, and a stained, ragged beard that never seemed to grow longer made people avoid him. And no one ever saw him wash his clothes, or his face. Or anything else.

He drove the mule. Broke new ground. Plowed up potatoes. He had the mule hitched to the plow and in the field every morning by daybreak, six days a week. When he finished a few rows, he'd bring a water bucket and let the beast drink and rest while Eustice crammed his own cheeks with plugs of Mail Pouch tobacco. Minutes later, on they went to plow again. Mule manure and tobacco spit fertilized the soil while man and mule walked the field. They were a team.

A dozen field hands scattered across the rows and gathered the crop. Each man wiped dirt from the potatoes with a rag that hung from his belt, and loaded the harvest into forty-pound sacks. The work was hard, heavy, hot, and dirty. Grunts and groans told of aches and pains, blisters, sore muscles, and aching backs. Though nothing was worse than the dust. Within the first hour, every man here would blow dust from his nose, dig it out of his ears, wipe sweat from his dirty face and burning eyes, and scratch his private parts. And he would gag and spit mud. But eating dust was just part of the job, a job Blue knew too well.

Back in Possum Trot, a ten-hour workday got him a few potatoes to feed his family, but never money. Twice a week, after the Missouri farmer made his trips to the packing house and sold his harvest for whatever he could get, he'd pay a share of the money to Blue's father. On Saturdays, Mama could buy a bit of flour or cornmeal and a pound or two of meat from the local store. His father used the rest of the money for other expenses.

Blue remembered he got two good meals each week during potato season. Mama made fatback, biscuits, and a mess of boiled poke salad she gathered from the woods. And always potatoes. That was life at its best for Missouri sharecroppers. Blue hated the job. But he and Mama worked so they could eat.

Here in Alabama, Blue tried to make himself like the job. For the first time in his life, he was getting paid—four cents a bag and two potatoes to take home at the end of the day. Yesterday, with ten hours of hard work, he filled twenty-eight bags and collected a dollar and twelve cents. *More than a dollar a day*, he'd repeat to himself. It was big money, and he was proud.

He dug a handful of sacks from a barrel and scattered them along the middle of the two rows next to Halo, who got to the patch more than twenty minutes ago. Each man fielded two rows at a time, gathered potatoes on each side of him as he worked his way to the end of the field. When a man filled a bag, he'd set it between the rows, stretch his back, and sip water from his bottle or canteen. Then he'd grab another bag and start again.

Halo tipped his canteen, rinsed his mouth and spat, and watched Blue wipe his first potato of the day. "Bout damn time."

Blue glanced at him. Halo had a full bag behind him and was working on another. "I bagged more than you yesterday," he told Halo. "I got ten cents that says I get more today."

Halo blew his nose and cleared his throat. "No bets. Just get your lazy ass to work."

Blue scowled. His face turned as red as the potatoes. But Halo laughed until Blue laughed, and the two men turned to their task.

***

At the end of another long day, field hands lined up at the big, green pitcher pump in the backyard of the farmhouse. Barefoot and shirtless with pant legs rolled to their knees, they slapped dust from their clothes and bodies with a heavy rag. When a man reached the front of the line, he'd step up on the wood platform that surrounded the pump, and wash every bare body part. He'd gasp and shiver, swear at low breath, and blame the cold water on the man who worked the handle. After a man had his bath, he'd shake and laugh, and say how good it felt, and then relieve the man who pumped the water.

Finished at the pump, Blue shook himself like a wet dog. But his hair and britches dripped, and his feet made mud on his way home.

Home was a one-room, unpainted shack he shared with Halo and Larken. The shack belonged to the farmer the hands called Boss Man, and it was the best place Blue ever lived. Larken had a coal-oil lamp that was real handy for night trips to the outhouse, and the shack held three cots, a small table, two cane-bottom chairs, and a cast-iron cook stove. And Halo had a coffeepot.

Blue figured that maybe the icebox in the corner didn't count as furniture, since the men never had ice. But right now in that beat-up wooden box, the men had groceries—crackers, sardines, cornbread wrapped in brown paper, a half tin of coffee, and enough potatoes to feed the Irish army. There was even a fly swatter the men kept on top of the box. Blue fingered the dollar's-worth of change in his pocket and wondered if this was what it felt like to be rich.

Saturday, when a downpour kept the men out of the fields, Blue played his guitar for three hours, and then lost himself in Rudyard Kipling's book, Barrack Room Ballads. Halo lent him the book while the two rode the trains to Foley. At every chance, Blue got lost in the book, and he read and reread *Gunga Din.* It became his all-time favorite poem, and when Halo shared a bit of experience Blue did not yet have, Blue would sometimes look at him and repeat the poem's last line: *You're a better man than I am, Gunga Din.*

No one worked on Sunday, and on Sunday morning, Halo and Larken sat in the shack, read a week-old newspaper, and stared at the walls. Halo had a deck of cards and wanted to play poker. But Blue had little interest in cards, and lots of interest in his guitar and his book.

Larken shook his head.

"No use to play cards less'n you gamble. I ain't much of a gambler." At least, that's what Halo thought he said. Larken was tongue-tied and couldn't say his own name.

When nobody on the farm would play cards on a Sunday, Halo shoved the deck in his pocket, grabbed his pipe, and headed for the road.

***

On Monday, Blue dragged himself off the cot a half-hour early, and wrinkled his forehead as he stepped outside. Had the rain passed? Gray clouds still hovered in the dark sky, and rainy days brought no money. He'd been here a week, caught a ride to town, bought a blanket, towel, tin cup, bar of soap, and other stuff for his bindle. And his new shoes, though not new, were the best he ever had. They fit.

Half his money was gone, and the potato harvest would last only a few more days. He wanted to pay his own way, to depend on himself on the next trip with Halo. If there *was* a next trip. Halo's bindle—his books, spare clothes, and everything he owned—lay under his cot in the shack.

Blue wiped the sleep from his face and remembered the day two years ago when he went for a walk and discovered the hobo jungle near Possum Trot. Most men there ignored him, but he and Halo struck up a friendship. Halo wasn't always there, but Blue found him twice when he went back, and they talked for a long time.

Except for a cockeyed schoolteacher, Halo was the only person Blue ever met that went to college. That by itself was a good reason to be suspicious. But Halo was different from other educated people, and Blue trusted the man.

Now, Blue worried. Not about travel. Not about rain. Not about money. The gnawing in his gut was about the best friend he'd ever known. And he told himself he had reason enough to worry. Halo left yesterday without a word. No one at the farm had seen him since.

Chapter Four

When the field hands broke for lunch on Tuesday, Blue walked past the line of trees to the road that ran by the farm. He munched crackers and sardines, and looked down the road in one direction and then the other again and again. He watched and listened for what seemed a long time.

He couldn't sleep at night, yet nodded off during the day, exhausted. This morning he'd filled only seven sacks of potatoes instead of his usual twelve. A man wandered over to him and said, "Son, I reckon you know Boss Man will give your job to somebody else if you don't get more work done." Something had to give.

A hawk screeched overhead. Somewhere on another farm, a John Deere tractor chugged across a field, and the familiar clack-clack-clack of its diesel engine carried across the open land. Minutes later, the clang of a large bell that hung on the back of the barn called the hands back to work.

Bells, birds, and tractors were not what Blue hoped to hear. He stood in front of a hundred-acre potato farm five miles from town on a road that seldom saw traffic. Still, he hoped for a car, truck, or wagon coming down the road to deliver a passenger. Or a man walking toward him, a bushy-haired man with a white beard and a pipe. Coming home.

He wanted to see Halo. Instead, he saw only what he saw this morning when he watched and waited before he went to the field, and the same as yesterday—an empty dirt road that showed him nothing but ruts left from last week's rain. His heart sank. He breathed deep and tried to rid his mind of worry. It didn't work. His friend had been missing since Sunday afternoon. So Blue would come back here again to listen, watch, and wait when the workday was done, and again tomorrow if need be.

***

In spite of blinders, the plow mule seemed distracted since the day began. Mule Man slapped the reins against the mule's backside to keep him plowing straight while the mule and the man brought row after row of potatoes to the surface.

Blue noticed a shiver in the animal's shoulder when it passed a tall weed in the field. Minutes later, the mule spooked when it passed the weed on its way back. The driver swore and slapped the mule as it moved ahead. He kept the beast under control.

Blue knew mules. He'd been around them as far back as he could remember; fed them, watered them, rode them, drove them, and cleaned up behind them. They were hard workers. They were strong and tireless, and could outlast any man who worked with them. They were often the handiest thing a farmer owned. But they were mules, half horse and half jackass, and just when you thought you had one figured out, he'd do something crazy just to prove you wrong. Something was wrong here today. Something that could be dangerous.

Blue shook his head, and refused any distractions from his job. His work had suffered for the past two days, and he turned his attention back to bagging potatoes. Still, he stole an occasional glance as the mule again worked its way downfield. But Blue jerked his head toward the sudden commotion when the mule swerved around a nest of hornets. The plow tore through the nest. The swarm attacked.

Workers stood fixed in the field, eyes wide and mouths open, and watched the animal dance, kick, and scream as hornets swarmed into his crotch and stung him again and again.

The mule bolted. Plow handles ripped from the driver's grasp. The harness across his shoulder jerked him forward. The man struggled to free himself and fought to stay on his feet while chains rattled and a shiny steel blade cast blinding reflections in the sunlight as the harness yanked him toward the plow that bounced and flipped over the black soil.

Blue's chest felt heavy. He could do nothing. The mule was out of control, and everyone on the field could be in danger if the animal ran toward them.

The mule darted left and then right. The plow tumbled and bounced, and a handle came within inches of the driver's head. The man ducked and threw up his hand to avoid the handle. The harness slid down to his waist. He lost his footing and went down on his knees. The harness pulled him through the field, his knee digging a zig-zag furrow as the dancing plow sent a spray of dirt into his face. He grabbed the harness and yanked hard. It slipped to his knee and bounced him on his backside as the mule made another wild turn. The harness slid down the man's leg and caught on his foot. He reached for his foot as he bounced over dirt and potatoes. He grabbed his boot. The harness slid off his foot. Caught on his wrist. Dragged the man across the plow.

The mule ran from the field and headed for a

pond. The plow bounced along behind, still chained to the mule. A bloody arm followed, still tangled in the harness.

A man lay in the dirt, blood shooting from half an arm. Blue's mind saw flashbacks. *A boy in Missouri lost part of a finger in a barn-door hinge, and a field-hand stopped the bleeding with a tourniquet.* Blue jerked the rag from his belt as he ran toward the man.

Two potato baggers turned away from the man on the ground, and became sick. Others gathered around as Blue knotted the rag around the stump of an arm and yelled.

"I need a stick. Now."

Three men sprinted away. One came back seconds later with a stick.

Boss Man ran to the scene. He tried to praise Blue for the tourniquet and quick thinking, but tension and dust killed his voice. His face grew red, his voice hoarse when he held his throat and forced out words to the man next to him.

"Take my horse. Get the doctor."

While the man ran toward the barn to saddle the horse, someone brought an army blanket. The men made a gurney and carried Eustice to his house. The house was little more than a lean-to built on the backside of the barn. That's where a mule man belongs, the field hands often said. They sometimes called it a stable, though none had ever seen the inside.

When the men carried Mule Man inside, Blue discovered the place was bigger than the house where he lived with Larken and… well… Halo had not returned.

The men placed their patient on a full-size bed with clean white sheets. They stood and gawked at the bed and at each other, but they jerked around and stared into a dark corner when they heard a sob and a woman's voice.

"I had a bad feeling all day. Something awful was gonna happen. I just knowed it."

Boss Man removed his hat and nodded toward her. "Men, this is Missus Hugo, Eustice Hugo's wife." The men whispered surprises when they saw the clean bed. Now they were dumbfounded as they removed their hats and nodded.

The woman placed her hand on the cold black stove beside her and pushed up from her rocker, her face now visible by the light through a clean window. Tear stains showed on her cheeks. Gray hair pulled back in a tight bun revealed the lines in her face, and pain behind the lines. When she opened her eyes and nodded at her guests, she did not look at them. Her eyes wandered while angled toward the floor, but did not focus.

Boss Man cleared his throat. "I'm sorry to say this, but your husband lost his arm when he was plowin'. Blue here…" the farmer extended his hat toward Blue, though he knew the woman could not see, "… Blue saved his life. And I sent a man for a doctor. We're doing everything we can, Ma'am." The woman nodded again. A heavy teardrop splattered the front of her dark dress.

Two hours later, the man who rode to fetch the doctor brought the horse to a sliding stop outside the house where Eustice lived. The man rushed through the door and stopped to catch his breath as he stared blank-faced at the blind woman.

"I found the doc." He shook his head. "He'll try to get here before dark. He was sewing up a man that lost a bad fight."

Missus Hugo shivered, reached back and felt the chair arm, and sat down in her rocker by the stove.

***

At one o'clock Thursday afternoon, Missus Hugo sat in a wicker chair shaded by a giant magnolia tree. The pastor from the nearest Pentecostal church spoke to the small crowd and said kind words about Eustice. Finished, he took an American flag off the coffin, folded it, and laid it on the widow's lap. The lady gripped the flag in one hand and wiped a tear with the other as she stood.

"I never met nobody here 'cept the farmer. And his wife, but she's gone to glory. Eustice was the best man I ever knowed." She sniffed and nodded. "I always been ashamed of being blind, and I didn't want him to be shamed. So I made him promise, and he never told nobody about me." She lowered her head for a few seconds as if in prayer, and then raised it again.

"We was married seven years and then he come home from that war. Had a bullet lodged in the back of his head. He wasn't never the same after that. But Eustice was my man. A good man. And I loved him." She nodded again, felt behind her for the arm of the chair, and sat down.

The preacher said a few more words about Eustice. He did not mention any nicknames, and Blue wondered if the reverend or Missus Hugo knew about Useless and Mule Man. Blue looked around in the small cemetery on the edge of the farm while he and other farm workers covered the grave. Three former field hands lay in graves near Eustice. A few yards away, a stone marked a single tomb that held the farmer's wife and infant son. The stone brought back painful memories to Blue about his own baby sister.

The preacher held the widow's arm with one hand, carried her chair with the other, and escorted her back home as people left the cemetery. Boss Man asked his workmen to stay for a meeting. The men sat cross-legged beneath the big magnolia and waited. They didn't talk, but their faces said they knew what was coming.

"Y'all missed a day o' work last week when it rained, and another today," Boss Man told them. "You'll miss another day tomorrow when I have to drive into town and hire a new plowboy. That is, unless someone here wants the job."

He rubbed his chin, walked back and forth and watched faces. No one responded. He stopped and threw up his hands, and raised his voice.

"There's no work for nobody till somebody runs a plow over the next patch of spuds. Must be somebody here that knows how to do that." He rested his gaze on Larken.

Larken's eyes grew small and he drew back his head. Then his eyes popped wide. He pointed at Blue and spoke in his best tongue-tied speech. "Blue can. He tol' me."

Larken grinned. Blue squirmed.

***

Blue reached for the doorknob, but jumped back at the sound from inside. Someone or something was in his house. He moved to the side of the house, shaded his eyes and stuck his face against the window. He jerked back and rubbed the dirt from his eyebrows. With his sleeve, he scrubbed away a layer of dirt from one of the panes. But the house was dark inside. The scrubbing did not help. Blue went back and pounded on the door.

"Hello, anybody in there?"

A faint groan came from inside, and he backed away. Near the woodpile, he picked up a heavy stick Larken kept for killing snakes, though he'd never seen a snake near the house. Blue held the club in one hand and opened the door with the other. Light filled the room.

Boss Man didn't mention any new workers, but a strange man lay on Halo's cot. A blanket covered all but his swollen face, a face with a battered nose, a face bruised and beaten and filled with stitches.

Blue rested the stick against the wall and stepped close. "Who are you?" The eyes opened, sad and painful, and searched the room. Then they found Blue, and looked at him.

Blue stared back. A gnawing sickness crawled from his gut to his throat. His chest grew tight as he shook his head. He let out a loud gasp.

"Oh, God. Oh my God. Halo, is that you?"

Chapter Five

With a last, gentle swab at the stitches, Blue stepped back and looked at Halo's face. "It's healing up good." He set the salve and cotton balls on the floor beneath Halo's cot. "Good thing the doctor gave you this stuff."

Halo rubbed the side of his face and grunted. "Don't tell anybody I'm here. If Boss Man finds out I'm living here and not working, he'll throw me out."

Blue opened the ice box that never saw ice. "You said that to me and Larken three days ago. I won't tell if you'll explain how it happened." He glanced at the window. "It's almost dark. You want some baloney before it goes bad?"

Halo wrinkled his nose, and groaned again from the pain. "I had that for breakfast."

Blue held it out toward him. "Me too. How much you want?"

"It was a fight."

"You told me that already." He cut two thick slices from the tube of bologna and removed the ring from each slice. "I kinda figured you lost." Blue frowned and shook his head. "Either that, or you punched the other guy damn hard with your face."

"It was dark. They jumped me when I came out of the outhouse after the poker game." Halo struggled to take off his boots while he talked. "I could've beat the hell out of any one of them. But three?" He wagged his head.

Blue handed him the bologna and some

crackers, and filled Halo's cup from the water bucket.

"You cheat?"

"I never cheat. Don't need to. But *they* did, and I still beat 'em. I was up six dollars when the game ended." He laid his dinner on the table and forced off his left boot. "The bastards got the money but they didn't get this." He handed the boot to Blue.

Blue's chin dropped as he pulled a watch from a cloth pocket sewn inside the top of the boot. "What the… your Hamilton railroad watch."

Halo nodded. "It's a Hamilton, but that one's yours. Mine's in the other boot."

"This one's mine?" Blue's heart beat in his throat. He clutched the watch to his chest. "It's the best thing I got since my guitar. Where'd you get this?"

"When I was here last year, I met two guys in Bolling who wanted to play poker. I won their money. When I went back a few days ago, they had a friend. Said he was a brakeman for the railroad. We had watches just alike, and he wanted to bet his against mine. He was mad as hell when he lost. I figured I better play it safe, so I stuck both watches in my boots when I was in the outhouse."

"I'm surprised they didn't take your boots."

"They would've. But a man came down the street yelling at 'em, and you could see his shotgun in the moonlight. They took off, and he took me to his house. The next day, he took me to the doctor. Without him… I'd be dead."

Blue nodded. "Yeah, I guess you would. How did you get here?"

"Shoe leather express. It's about three miles. Took me more than half a day. Had to stop and rest every five minutes."

Blue's ears heard Halo talking, but his bright face revealed that his mind and wide eyes were on the watch in his hand.

"It's like a timepiece from another planet. Looks expensive."

"It ain't just for telling time." Halo angled his head toward the watch. "It's a model 992, and they sold a few years back for sixty-five dollars. Right now, it'll bring a good twenty bucks, maybe twenty-five at a jewelry store."

"That's a lot of groceries." Blue grinned.

"Don't sell it for food." Halo stood and stretched. "You can always find a way to feed yourself. That watch might get you out of a real jam someday." Halo looked at the floor, lost in thought. A minute later, he looked up.

"While the doctor sewed me back together, a man came in and said something about a worker here getting his arm cut off by a plow."

Blue looked at him but did not respond.

Halo shrugged. "Mule Man run over somebody?"

Blue nodded and dropped his head. "Himself."

"What? How could he…?"

Blue nodded again. "It happened, Halo. I saw the whole thing. But don't ask me about it."

Halo sat again. His forehead wrinkled. He shook his head. "Think he'll ever plow again? I mean… with just one arm…?"

Blue did not look at him. "You think there are fields to plow in heaven?"

Halo leaned toward him and stared. "Heaven?"

"He died."

"Ohhh." After a minute of silence, Halo cleared his throat. "Then somebody else is plowing?"

"Yeah. Larken volunteered."

"That's good."

"No it ain't. He volunteered *me*."

Halo laughed, and then winced and touched his cheek. "It's a job, Blue. You know how many men would give their right arm for…?" Halo caught himself. Color flooded his patched-up face. "Sorry, I uh…" He went to the bucket near the door, drank a dipper of water, and scooped up a refill. He started to drink again, but instead turned to Blue and talked over the dipper.

"Speaking of Larken, I haven't seen him a whole ten minutes since I've been back. Where's he spend his time?"

Blue grinned. "He takes care of Mule Man's widow." Above the dipper, Blue saw Halo's eyebrows shoot up. "Yeah, Halo, he was married. She's blind. What Larken does for her… well, it's anybody's guess."

"The way that man looks…" Halo wagged his head, "… she'd have to be blind. Of course he couldn't look any worse than—"

Blue stood. "Halo, don't say bad things about dead people. Didn't your mother—"

"I'm sorry, Blue. You're right. I shouldn't…" Halo stiffened at a sudden banging on the door. He dropped the dipper into the bucket, grabbed the lantern, and spun around. A man pushed open the door and stepped in. His head jerked back as he looked at Halo's face in the light of the coal-oil lantern.

"You Halo?"

Halo nodded and the man said, "I heard

you've been back here three days." Halo nodded again. The man pointed at him. "Tomorrow's Monday. Be workin' in the field in the mornin'. Or…" he jerked his thumb to one side, "… be out of my house." He turned and walked out.

Halo closed the door and hung the lamp on the nearby nail. He took a deep breath, and talked to the door.

"I'm too weak to work. But thanks a hell of a lot for caring." He stepped to his cot and turned back toward the door. "I'll be gone in the morning."

Blue stood. "When you leave, I leave."

Halo looked at him and shook his head. "No. Use your head, Blue. Stay as long as you have work."

Blue stared at the wall. "Boss Man said I've got another month. Buck and a quarter a day."

"Then stay with it." Halo brought a mason jar from under his cot and held it up to the lamp. He squinted at the clear liquid. "I'm glad you and Larken left me some."

"You know Larken don't drink. Me neither."

After a long swallow from the jar, Halo gasped. Then he nodded and smiled. "You're a better man than I am, Gunga Din."

"I don't know about that, but I know it ain't smart for you to get drunk, Halo. If you trip and fall…" Blue studied the face and shook his head.

Halo set the jar on the table and dug a pair of pliers from his bindle. He picked up the jar again and cocked his head toward it. "It's for the pain." He took another short drink, and handed Blue the pliers. "The pain I'm gonna have when you yank out these stitches."

Before the sun rose, Blue and Halo shared the last of the crackers and bologna for breakfast, and treated themselves to a second cup of coffee. Now, the sun edged above the horizon and brought what Blue had dreaded. He shaded his eyes from the glare and stood in the doorway with the treasured watch in his hand and a lump in his throat while his friend left him behind.

Halo stopped at the road, turned and waved. Then he turned again and disappeared behind the trees along the shoulder. Blue took a long breath and blew it out. His chest tightened and he shook his head. It wasn't supposed to turn out this way. But he told himself he would feel better tomorrow or the next day, or maybe in a week. He checked his watch again, stuffed it into its pocket, and walked to the barn to ready the mule for another day of plowing.

Chapter Six

At the Bolling jungle, Halo pushed himself off the log he'd been sitting on by the fire, and stood, his mouth open as he stared.

"Blue? What the hell are you doing here?"

"Figured I'd find you here. Thought you'd need a few days to heal before you catch out." He looked at Halo's face and nodded.

Halo cocked his head. "Your job's over? I've only been here four days."

"Boss Man was mad when I quit, but I don't care. I waded through enough mule manure in Missouri. I don't need more of that in Alabama."

***

By six o'clock next morning, Halo pushed Blue behind a boxcar in the train yard. "Hide. That brakeman is here," he said to Blue in a loud whisper. "And he's got a big stick."

Blue's forehead wrinkled. Halo caught his breath and pointed at Blue's watch pocket. "That watch used to be his. If he sees me, I'm done for."

Footsteps came toward them. Blue and Halo slipped around the end of the boxcar and moved to the other side. They stooped next to the wheels and looked beneath the car. They watched the brakeman's boots crunching on the gravel as he marched to the end of the train. And they watched the end of the big stick swinging back and forth while he walked. When he rounded the caboose and stepped across the tracks, Blue and Halo slipped between the cars and back to the other side. They stooped near the wheels again and watched the brakeman walk past on his way back toward the engine.

"Wha-a." Blue jumped back as the engineer blew the whistle. Halo covered his mouth and laughed. The rumble of clunks jumped down the line from car to car. Coal smoke saturated the sky above the stack, drifted back, and strangled the morning air. The train began to move.

The brakeman's footsteps grew faint on the other side of the train. Halo jerked his head in that direction. "I think we lost him." Blue and Halo walked alongside the boxcar as it jerked forward. Halo talked about farming in the Midwest, and the men stepped faster to keep up as the train gathered speed.

Halo glanced at his watch and nodded. "Our train to Illinois." They broke into a slow trot as cars began a smooth roll. "Ready to go pick peaches?"

Blue shrugged. "Beats drivin' a crazy mule."

Halo gestured toward the open door. "Want to hop on first?"

Blue worried. His friend might still be too weak for this. The last thing Blue wanted was to stand in a boxcar, watch Halo struggle to get inside, and fail. Blue wagged his head. "No. Same as before."

As before, Halo sprinted beside the boxcar and tossed his bindle through the open door. Five steps later, he caught the rung, pulled up, and swung inside as if it was no more than climbing stairs.

As he ran alongside the train, Blue handed up two burlap potato sacks, his guitar tied up in one, his hobo gear in the other. Halo moved the sacks out of the way and turned back to the open door. Blue figured the footsteps on the gravel behind him meant another hobo was trying to hop aboard. But that didn't explain the look of dread now on Halo's face as he motioned for Blue to grab the ladder. Blue grabbed. And missed. The train rolled faster.

His chest felt ready to explode, his legs turned to rubber while he ran, but Blue waved his finger to assure Halo he would make the next try count. He would not disappoint his friend. He would not settle for almost. He would not fail himself.

Halo pointed behind Blue and yelled, but Blue heard only rolling thunder from the train, and footsteps growing closer behind him. Sweat soaked his hair and face and burned his eyes. No longer conscious of running or the world around him, he pushed himself harder and forced his legs to move faster while the train gathered speed. The rung drew closer, only inches beyond his reach.

"Grab the ladder," Halo yelled. His face distorted. He turned and yanked a full can of something from his bindle and threw it over Blue's head toward the footsteps behind him. Blue lunged, stretched his arm as far as it would go, and made another grab. A sigh of relief escaped his lungs. He felt the cool steel of the ladder. His fingers closed on the rung.

Stabbing pain surged through his body as a heavy stick flew from behind and slammed his hand. With a loud cry and a gasp of surrender, Blue fell. His knees plowed furrows in the gravel while the gravel dug into his hands.

Blue's chin quivered when a potato sack flew from the boxcar and crashed beside the tracks. He limped toward it while fingers bled, knees ached, and legs trembled. "Thank God," he said aloud while he struggled to lift the sack. "And thank you, Halo," he yelled at the train, grateful that his friend did not throw out the guitar, and turn it into a sack of splinters.

The brakeman picked up a square can from the gravel and looked it over. It was beat up, but not open. He grabbed a handrail on the deck at the rear of the caboose, and swung up the steps as it eased past.

Halo stood in the boxcar door, growing smaller while the car moved farther down the track. He stared at Blue and shook his head. Blue gripped the potato sack that held everything he owned, and shivered in the early morning mist—mouth open, eyes wide, a lump bulging in his throat. He raised his hand in a long goodbye and watched his guitar, his future, and his only friend head north on a train now rolling too fast for anyone to hop on. Or off.

Everything he cared about disappeared as the rumbling line of cars curved left in a long, slow arc until Blue saw only the other side of the train and the brakeman who stood and clenched the handrail. The man sneered and flashed the can of Spam. As the train moved away, he laughed, and watched Blue from the deck of the caboose, the car that Halo called the monkey wagon.

Chapter Seven

Yesterday morning at the Bolling train yard, Blue tried to catch a freight going north, hoping it would take him to Illinois. Maybe he could find Halo. But a bull stopped him. An hour later, he tried to catch another northbound. The bull chased him away again.

He guessed bulls would be watching all northbounds the rest of the day, so Blue caught the first train he could get. It took him only to Mobile, Alabama.

After two hours in Mobile, he climbed into a boxcar marked L & N Railroad. Since Louisville and Nashville were north of Mobile, Blue told himself he was on his way north. But as he watched the sun, he knew this train was headed west. With stops along the way, the short trip from Bolling had been anything but short.

Though drained of energy and tired of freight-hopping, Blue stood and watched the changing landscape from the boxcar door. Alone and lost, he wondered if he was crazy for leaving his job in Alabama. But when he thought about what he'd be doing there right now, he knew he made the right move. Potatoes didn't fit in his life plans. And never again did he want to wipe off dirt or shake hands with another spud.

The train turned south. The scenery changed from hills, forests, and farms to open flatland and sand. When the tracks curved west again, the train slowed. Blue stared wide-eyed at the blue water and white sand, and his mouth dropped open when he saw the sign: Biloxi Mississippi.

He never dreamed he'd be here. Yet, hopping the wrong train brought him to the place he'd heard about more than twice in his uncle's travel stories. Yes, Mama's brother was known to warp the truth now and again. Hell, he often told outright lies. But Blue liked Uncle John. When he came to visit he always brought groceries and candy or Cracker Jacks. Once, the man even took Blue for an ice-cream cone and a Coca Cola. That could buy a friend for life. And so far, the beauty of this place lived up to Uncle's claims. Blue jumped from the train and headed toward the water.

For a mile, maybe more, the roadside next to the beach was lined with parked cars. Blue saw Cadillacs, Packards, Lincolns, LaSalles, and other expensive automobiles he had seen before only in pictures of cars owned by rich people.

People who looked rich, happy, and relaxed strolled along the beach. Couples walked hand-in-hand showing off new bathing suits, sunglasses, and perfect hair. The breeze carried the scent of cologne from half-naked bodies that made Blue stare. That same breeze from the gulf carried the odor of fish that made him wrinkle his nose.

Blue stopped at the shoreline. He squatted, wiggled his fingers in the water, and tasted it. Salty—just like he'd always heard. He stood again and stared at the endless stretch of water that touched the horizon. And if he remembered his geography classes, Mexico was on the other side.

Short waves came toward him. Each brought a splashing sound like dumping water into a horse trough, a wave's last gasp of life before it died near his feet. Between splashes, Blue heard sounds of life passing behind him—sandals crunching sand, expensive beachwear swishing and flapping in the breeze. He heard whispers, sighs, and giggles, and a woman's voice.

"I smell a hobo."

***

A sudden shower caught him by surprise as Blue explored downtown. Seeing no rain across the street was a bigger surprise, and he chuckled as he ran across into the sunshine. He stopped and looked down at a short man enjoying a cigar on a bench outside Zeke's Place.

"You see that?" Blue jerked his head toward the rain. "I've never seen that. It's raining over there."

"You're not from around here." The man flicked ashes from his cigar without looking up.

Blue turned toward him. "You live here?"

"All my life."

"You work at Zeke's?"

Now, the man looked up as he jerked his head toward the open café door behind him. A small lamp burned in the otherwise-dark room.

"I own it." He studied Blue from his too-worn shoes to his too-long, dark hair, and then stared at the potato sack that hung from Blue's left hand.

"If you got money for a meal, I'll be done with this in five minutes." He held up the cigar to show how much was left. "But you're just looking for a job."

Blue nodded. "How'd you know?"

The man leaned back on the bench and stuck out his chin, his dark eyes so close together they seemed to pinch his nose.

"Show me somebody who ain't." He puffed on the cigar.

Blue hefted the bag to his shoulder and started to leave. The short man stood up.

"You ever worked in a café, son?"

"No, sir. Never been in one. But I learn fast."

The owner of Zeke's puffed on the cigar again, walked around Blue and looked him up and down. He stopped in front of him and looked in his eyes.

"Never been in a café? How old are you, boy?"

Blue set down his bag, stood up straight, and threw back his shoulders. "Sixteen."

The man looked down and shook his head. "I ain't hiring no more kids. The work's too hard for 'em. And soon's they get a day's pay, they quit so they can go spend it. I gotta have a body eighteen or older."

"I work hard, and I ain't the kind that quits the first day." He waited but the man did not reply. Blue picked up his bag.

Zeke's owner pointed his thumb across the street, though the rain had stopped. "It's called dew drop." He looked at Blue's puzzled face. "That two-minute rain." He puffed the last of his cigar, crushed it out with his foot, and went inside.

***

Blue spent an easy night, and shared hobo stories with the men and three women at the Biloxi jungle. His Alabama story about Mule Man was the crowd favorite, and after he entertained them with a borrowed guitar, they all wanted him to stay for a few days. He might have, but next morning the mulligan-stew breakfast didn't stay down. With no urge to repeat that for dinner, he returned to the shore. Most of the cars on the roadside yesterday were now gone, but next to a truck, Blue found a man cooking on the beach.

The man wiped his hands on a stained apron that hung down to his knees, and whistled nonstop while he stood over a cast-iron stove, dunked crab legs in butter and dropped them into a skillet. He picked up the ones that were done, dipped them in something, and tossed them on a plate.

When he saw Blue, he stopped whistling, and laughed. Then he caught a crab leg with a pair of wooden tongs and pointed it toward his new customer.

Blue leaned for a closer look. "Biggest crawdads I ever seen. Where'd you catch 'em?"

The man laughed again. Then he drew back his head and wrinkled his face. "Crab legs, my boy. Crab legs. Best ones on the beach." He held the tongs high and smacked his lips. "Had breakfast?"

"Not for long." Blue's gut growled.

"Small plate for a dime. Large plate for another dime."

Blue shrugged. "Never had one."

"Catch." The man tossed the crab leg. "Try that."

Ten minutes and twenty cents later, Blue rubbed a full stomach on his way downtown to find a job.

Items in display windows got Blue's attention as he rambled through town. New clothes, shoes, boots and belts in one store, fishing tackle in another. And tools of all types in still another. He looked at the goods on the other side of the glass at a hardware store, and started inside to check the price of scissors, *the handiest tool you can own*, according to Halo. But Blue turned around at the door. The people inside would look at him and know he couldn't afford what they were selling. If he bought scissors, he'd have to do without something, maybe food. He fingered the coins in his pocket, but didn't have to count them. Two dollars and eighty cents. Maybe he'd find another place to buy scissors. He moved on.

His breath caught and he made a sudden stop. A shiny new guitar looked back at him from the other side of the window at Downtown Music. Blue left his bindle inside near the door and walked in. Guitars, banjos, mandolins, and fiddles hung on the walls, along with harmonicas and tambourines. But the store was quiet, and no one answered when Blue called out.

"Hello. Anybody here?"

He stepped to the display window, glanced back over his shoulder and searched the store again. Then he picked up the Gibson guitar that had brought him in, smiled and nodded. He hung it around his neck and swallowed hard, missing his own guitar now more than ever.

"What the hell are you doing?"

Blue jumped when a man came through a door at the back of the room and started toward him.

"I uh… I just wanted to look at this guitar, mister. I didn't know you'd be mad."

"Oh, you didn't?" A tall man propped his hands on his hips as he stopped in front of Blue. A short red beard, and red hair that hung over his forehead, framed the man's bright eyes. The eyes did not look happy, and his breath smelled of whiskey. He dipped his head at the guitar. "You come in here, mess up my display, and you expect me to like it?"

"Well, what if I want to buy it?" Blue stood with his hands out to his sides.

The man's forehead wrinkled under the hair. "Buy it? I been in this business too long to fall for that. You know what good guitars cost?"

Blue nodded. "I got a Martin." His head dropped. "But a friend of mine's got it right now."

The owner backed up, shook his head and laughed, his teeth reflecting the light through the window.

"A friend's got it, huh? The last musician in here who owned a Martin traded it to one of them nasty gals in town. That's what musicians do around here I guess—trade anything they got for ten minutes with a whore." His eyebrows shot up. "You a musician?" Blue stared back at him, but did not answer.

The man stepped forward again, his eyebrows lower. His voice softened as he spoke.

"I seen a hundred like you, son. You boys come in here and pretend you want to buy something and pretend you can play while you leave your dirty fingerprints on everything in sight. You're not here to buy. You're here to waste my time." The man looked him over and shook his head. "I'm guessing you ain't got a plug nickel, and couldn't play a tune on that guitar to save your sorry hide."

He cocked his head toward the display window. "Now, put that back in place, and be damn careful with it." He jerked his thumb toward the front door. "And don't forget your hobo bag on the way out." Seconds later, he disappeared into the back room.

Blue searched through his pockets and pulled out a pick. He plucked the strings and turned a couple of keys. Satisfied with the tuning, he began a Jimmie Rodgers tune. He shut out his troubles and the world around him, and lost himself in the music.

When Blue opened his eyes, the owner stood in front of him again, and glared. When the man started to speak, Blue closed his eyes again and worked his magic on the strings. If the man had anything to say, let him argue with the tune. Let him interrupt the best entertainment he's had all day. *Lots of people ask me to play. No one ever demanded that I stop.*

When Blue ended the tune and opened his eyes, the man stood in front of him, arms crossed, chin drawn, head in a slow nod.

"What's your name, boy? Where the hell did you learn to play like that? You sing too? Want a job? How old are you?"

"Blue. Missouri. Yes. Yes."

The man spread his hands, screwed up his face, and bugged his eyes. "Run that by me again."

"My name's Blue. I learned to play in Missouri. Yes, I sing. Yes, I want a job." Blue guessed the man wouldn't hire a sixteen-year-old kid. "And, oh yeah, I'm, uh… eighteen." He hooked the strap with his thumb, lifted the guitar off his neck, and stood it upright in front of him. "When do I start? What's it pay? Can I use this guitar?"

"Eighteen, huh?" The man squinted. "You don't look it."

Blue wagged his head. "Can't help that."

For the first time, the man smiled. "Nothing to help. The ladies will be charmed." He stuck out his hand. "Pleased to meet you, Blue. My name's Irish. They call me *Spud*."

Chapter Eight

The new clothes didn't feel right or look right, and the shoes cramped his feet. But Blue bought them because… "You gotta look the part, gotta please the women." That's what Spud said yesterday.

Today, Blue spent the last of his money, except for a nickel, at the second-hand clothing store so he could dress for the job. He changed in the store's closet, stuffed his old clothes into his bag, and walked back to Downtown Music. Spud said he liked the new look while he unlocked the door to the back room.

Blue's eyes adjusted to the low light as he walked behind his new boss into a room much larger than the music store. Two electric lights hung overhead, but they were off. Kerosene lamps on wall brackets circled the room, but only two lamps burned. Musical instruments in various stages of repair lay on tables along the walls. Blue followed the man to the far end of the room where a piano rested on a small stage. Spud cocked his head toward a short hallway alongside the stage.

"Outhouse… straight back… through the door." He turned right, walked to the wall, and opened a door to a small room. When the man pulled open the curtains, sunlight lit the floor and walls. Blue's eyes contracted and he now realized the bigger room was dark because it had no windows.

The boss swept his hand around the room. "This'll be yours… if you want it."

Blue's eyes widened again. His voice caught

in his throat. "Uh… mine?"

"Long as you work for me. It's my room, but I'm moving in with my girlfriend." He scratched his beard as if in thought. "And speaking of girlfriends…" he jerked his thumb toward the bed, "… not here."

Blue's forehead wrinkled. "Pardon?"

"You can't bring any girls in here. In fact—nobody." He looked at Blue and nodded. "It's yours if you want it. You can let me know later."

Blue nodded back. "It's later."

"Pardon?"

"I'll take it."

The man nodded again. "Move in anytime you like."

Blue took his turn to nod. Then he dropped his bindle beside the bed and grinned. "I just did."

***

The newest magazines in the barbershop were old. Saturday Evening Post, March 1929, went back more than a year. Blue thumbed through it and didn't care. He hadn't seen it before, and the Norman Rockwell covers always made him smile. And besides, he loved barbershops, though he'd been in one only once, years ago, with Uncle John in Possum Trot.

The man now in the chair reminded him of his uncle, the way he laughed and how he couldn't talk without moving his hands, even under the barber cape. Blue remembered the clean smell of the shaving soap as the barber swished the brush around in the mug and painted the back of the man's neck.

Blue felt ready for his haircut. He took a real bath before coming here. His new room had a bathtub at one end. He'd never been in a real bathtub, and he was excited. With water heated on the stove. his bath was even better than he expected. For a half hour, he scrubbed everything he had with a soapy rag, and would have stayed in longer, but the water turned cold.

When Blue took the chair, the barber talked nonstop as he worked the scissors and clippers. He asked Blue his name, where he was from, and what brought him here to Biloxi.

A small bell tinkled. In the wall mirror, Blue watched a big man walk in, nod at the barber, and pick up the magazine Blue left on the table. He frowned, threw it back, and took a seat.

The barber took off the cape, shook it and pinned it on again. He smiled at Blue in the mirror. "Lookin' for work, I suppose, like everybody else."

Blue grinned. "Not anymore." He breathed deep to catch the smell of the shaving soap once again, and felt the coolness as the man swabbed the back of his neck with the brush. The straight-razor made the sound of a muffled bark as the barber whisked it back and forth across the leather strap that hung from the wall.

"No? You giving up? Or you telling me you found something?"

Blue waited while the razor shaved his neck.

"I start tonight at ten."

The barber stepped back and looked at him. "A night job?"

"Playing guitar and singing at Downtown Music."

The big man who waited for his haircut made faces, and shifted on the small chair. He shook his head, stood and rubbed his backside, and sat again. He looked up.

"Where did you say you're working, young man?"

Blue watched him in the mirror. "Downtown Music, sir. If you take Magnolia Street to—"

"I know where it is," the man interrupted. He cleared his throat. "I hear tell that's a blind pig."

Blue found the barber in the mirror, but saw no expression. He had no idea what the customer meant, but had no reason to show his ignorance. He looked at him again.

"I just play the guitar and sing, sir. Don't know much about the business."

The shop grew quiet. The barber didn't talk again until Blue left the chair.

"That'll be eight cents, please."

Blue searched in his pocket for the dime Spud gave him just an hour ago.

"You need a haircut before the show tonight," Spud had said, shaking his head. "Go see my barber. You can get a good cut for ten cents."

"Uhm…" Blue's face lost color while he fumbled through his pocket, though he already knew what was there. He looked at the floor as he held out his hand to show Spud a solitary nickel.

"That's all I got."

The boss came up with a dime and slapped it in Blue's hand. "He charges eight cents. I always give him a tip."

Now, Blue gripped the two coins in his pocket, let the nickel drop, and handed the dime to the barber.

"Keep the change."

"Thanks." The dime made a soft clunk as it struck nickels and pennies when the barber dropped it into the Mason jar on a shelf, the jar that held his income for the day. He shook the cape, then turned and nodded at the big man who waited.

***

While a black man practiced a piano tune on stage, the boss told Blue, "Take the chairs out of that room." He pointed to an open door at the end of the big room. "Then clear the tables and put all those instruments in that room. When you're done with that…" he motioned at the piano player, "… Lucas will show you what to do." He started to walk away, then turned back and tapped Blue's chest with his finger.

"Don't tell anyone what you see here tonight. Don't talk to anybody about this place. Nothing. Understand?" Blue nodded.

Lucas finished his tune, introduced himself to Blue, and helped clear the tables. They left two tables near the wall and spread the others across the floor to create a dining room.

Lucas wore a large grin. "'Bout eight o'clock, the womenfolk will bring in the vittles." He swept his hand in front of him. "Lots of 'em, and they'll set it all on them tables by the wall. When the crowd shows, they'll grab a plate and hep themselves." He pointed at Blue and then at himself. "You and me, we got to entertain them."

Blue pointed at Lucas and then himself. "Spud said you and me get to eat too." He looked around the room.

Lucas smiled. "The boss is gone home. But he'll be back. You and me? We get to eat first, soon's they get all the stuff in here."

While they worked, Blue and Lucas talked about music and found they liked a lot of the same tunes. Finished with the dining room setup, they went to the stage to rehearse, and Blue discovered he had a lot to learn. He'd always worked alone. Now he had to make his timing, harmonizing, and everything else fit with the piano man. But Lucas was patient, and started over as many times as necessary.

Blue's gut rumbled and his eyes popped wide when six women showed up in a truck with more food than he had ever seen.

After the ladies loaded the two large tables along the wall with food, a woman brought in two boxes of cigars and a metal box of ready-rolled cigarettes.

"Grab a plate, Blue." Lucas motioned at the stack of dishes as soon as the women were finished.

Blue stood and stared at the dinner in front of him. "This must be like going to heaven."

"It's just like going to a restaurant," Lucas said, "except here, they don't bring your food to the table. Just take what you want."

Blue turned a blank face toward him. "I ain't never been in a restaurant."

Lucas nodded. "Well then, just do what I do. Everything'll be fine."

With loaded plates, the two sat at a table across from each other. Lucas liked to talk while he ate. Blue liked to eat while he listened. So Lucas told him of his background, how he learned to play the piano when his father worked at a music store in New Orleans. He performed his first solo when he was thirteen, and he knew then that he wanted to make music his life.

"I played ragtime, jazz, blues, everything you ever heard of and some things you never did. Did gigs with some big names in 'Nawlins." He shook his head. "This ain't the big time, Blue, but it's a job." He looked down at his plate. "And the food ain't too bad neither."

Blue nodded. "Yeah, best food I ever had." He shrugged. "Of course, most of this stuff I never had before." Blue cleared his throat. "Uh… Lucas, before the boss left, he told me not to talk about this job to nobody. What's wrong with me telling people where I work?"

Lucas dropped his head and stared at his plate, his mouth moving as if forming words, but nothing came out. He looked up.

"Well now, Blue, he told me the same. So it's best if I don't say nothin'." He stood and picked up his plate. "But before this night is gone, you gonna know full well."

Blue stood too, and picked up the plate. "What if I don't?"

"You will."

***

The bed was the best Blue ever slept in. In fact, it was the only real bed he'd ever slept in. Still, he spent a restless night while thoughts about the past few hours blocked out sleep.

An hour before the party began Blue and Lucas moved a china cabinet that hid a door to a liquor closet. They brought out six cases of beer and fifty-three bottles of wine and liquor. The boss stood by the door, and unlocked it for each of his wealthy customers. Dozens, maybe a hundred, came for the big party, and he ushered in anyone who had enough cash and whispered the passcode Spud created earlier that day: *I know Blue Bailey.*

He and Lucas worked well together and played to a full house. The customers came in their fancy clothes to socialize, to show off, to have a good time. And they let no chance escape. The crowd clapped and cheered, and sang along with Blue and Lucas. They danced and laughed, puffed cigars, pipes, and cigarettes. In a room hazy with smoke, they ate mounds of rich, delicious food, and washed it down with bottles of expensive, illegal booze.

Living with a useless, alcoholic father had made Blue hate the notion of dealing with drunks, especially when they were breaking the law. But… the more booze they swallowed, the better they tipped. Blue smiled as he thought about the $2.32 he collected in tips—in one night. Now… if he only had a girlfriend. Maybe that would be the next goal.

A minute later he was dead asleep.

Chapter Nine

The job at Downtown Music had gone well for three weeks. Blue and Lucas entertained the night crowds, and they practiced two hours every day before they performed. They kept their tip-jars separated, and neither knew how much the other collected. They didn't talk about it, but both understood that it would help maintain the close friendship they had formed.

Blue's tips averaged more than two dollars a night. And three days a week, when the dining room was converted back to a repair shop, he made ten cents an hour replacing strings, keys, and pick guards on instruments customers brought in for repairs. Sundays were no-work days. Blue had money, and time to spend it. But when he strolled around town, *closed* signs hung on many business doors. Most stores were closed on Sundays, but many were closed for good, with nothing left behind but vacant buildings. Yet, some businesses seemed always open.

"Hey, handsome, want a date?" That was the standard line when Blue walked by a vacant building on a quiet day or night, and a woman would pop from the doorway. They all looked the same in their wild hair styles, too much makeup, and not enough clothes. A woman twice his age would cock her head, chew gum with her mouth open, and tell him he looked lonely. "If you got a dollar, we can have a good time." She'd reach for his arm and nod toward the door. "I can take away all your troubles."

They were right about lonely. He often felt

that way. Two weeks ago, a good-smelling woman pulled him inside one of those vacant buildings. She pushed her body against him, caught his head in her hands and kissed him. "What's your name, big man?"

"Blue."

"Aw, Baby Blue. By the time I'm done with you, you'll be lucky if you can walk." She leaned back. "But first, I need to see the dollar." She opened her hand.

Blue's hand sweated as he rammed it into his shirt pocket and yanked out four folded dollars. He peeled off one for her, and put the others back. She unbuttoned her blouse, kissed him again, and unbuttoned his shirt. She spun him around, took the shirt off his back, and hung it on the doorknob. "You ready for some real fun, Blue?"

He nodded.

"Well, then…" she angled her head at a door behind him, "… slip into that room right there and close the door. Take off all your clothes, and I'll take off mine. When you say *okay*, I'll come in and do anything you want." She licked her lips. "Maybe twice."

Blue still shuddered when he thought about how stupid he'd been. After saying *okay* a dozen times, he opened the door… and walked home without a shirt, without his money, and without his pride.

He told Lucas, and hoped the man would say everybody's a fool once in a while, or something to make him feel better. But Lucas laughed.

"I heard of people that would give you the shirt off their back. You're the first one I met." Lucas laughed again.

But that was two weeks ago, Blue reminded himself. He stood the guitar on a stand after practice, stepped off the stage, and went out the back door for fresh air. He still had two hours till show time.

Today was Saturday, the biggest night of the week for the party crowd, and the whole area around him, including across the street in back, would be covered with luxury cars like the ones he saw near the shore. Blue guessed that many who were at the beach during the day wound up here at night, and he wondered if the woman who said, "I smell a hobo," might be one of them.

It didn't matter. They tipped well. He'd entertained them, talked to them, listened to them, and watched them. Blue laughed and joked with the men, flirted with the ladies and told them how nice they looked, because the men they came with never said that.

He learned about his audience, about the people here on vacation. They came to have fun, to do things they would not, or could not, do at home. In a few days, they would be back to their everyday lives, but the night here would likely be their favorite.

Each night brought new faces and new names. A few would sit in a smaller room where they drank booze, smoked cigars, and gambled on poker. But most guests would gather in the party room, eat too much, smoke too much, and drink too much. They would dance and sing, laugh and joke, spend too much money, and stumble outside to lose their dinner.

Blue sat on a bench and checked the time. His railroad watch always reminded him of Halo, and he wished his friend was here. Would he still be picking peaches in Illinois? Did he still have the guitar, Blue's precious Martin? Would he take good care of it? Learn to play it? *Will I ever see it again*?

And what about Mama? Would she be proud of her son, making a living with his music? What would she say about his new clothes? His room? If she was here, he would give her money for groceries. Maybe buy her some perfume or candy, or a new dress, or shoes. If she was here, would she be happy for her son's new life? Would she wish him well wherever he went? Or would she cry, and beg him to come home?

And his father? What would he say and do if he was here? Blue didn't think about it long. He knew. The old man would say little, if anything. Talking cut into his drinking time. He'd latch onto a bottle and wander off. Blue and Mama would find him passed out in some doorway along the street, still clutching an empty bottle.

Blue hated thinking of the man as a *father*. He'd never been one. And today was not the first time Blue wished the man was dead. He stopped feeling guilty about that wish a long time ago. Mama would be better off without him. She would never say that, but she must have thought about it a few times. And maybe she'd be ashamed of thinking that, not wanting her son to grow up without a father. Blue snorted. What the hell's the difference? That's what happened anyway.

Blue stood and gazed at the empty buildings across the alley behind Downtown Music. But the buildings were little more than a blur. His mind was elsewhere. He started back inside while he played with the coins in his pocket, and tried not to think about the heartache he might have caused for the one who loved him the most.

He remembered standing in the boxcar door on that first day, watching his past life disappear, and telling himself he would never miss it. Now, for the first time since he left Possum Trot, Missouri, Blue missed his mother.

***

A loud crash broke open the door to the big room, and a battering ram thundered to the floor. Women screamed. Men swore. Lucas jumped up from his piano bench. Blue took off his guitar, and stared as three men with guns bolted in.

Spud whirled and jerked a pistol from his jacket. But another crash broke open the back door, and his gun clattered to the floor when a bullet struck his arm from behind. Three more men stormed through the back door, guns drawn.

"Treasury," one shouted, holding out a badge for all to see. Another pointed his gun at the crowd, and yelled, "Everyone… on the floor. *Now*."

The room erupted as if hit by a bomb. Dropped cigars and cigarettes sent tiny explosions of fire as they hit the floor in the smoky haze. Silverware bounced and clanged. Dishes, glasses, and bottles shattered as everyone screamed, dove for cover, turned over tables and stumbled over chairs.

When he was twelve, Blue discovered a moonshine still in the Missouri woods. A shotgun fired, and a man appeared from behind the trees. "Sorry," he said when he saw Blue. "I thought you was one of them revenuers." Blue didn't know what a revenuer was then. Now, he understood. A revenuer rushed at him, grabbed his guitar, and screamed in his face. "Get the hell out of here." Blue shook as he looked at the man. Somehow, the angry face looked familiar, but Blue's mind was a blur, and he could not imagine where he might have seen him.

Blue and Lucas yelled when the big man smashed the guitar down on the piano top. Lucas fell backwards over the bench. Blue jumped from the stage and ran, but there was no place to go. Men in dark suits and hats, in white shirts and shined shoes, men with badges and guns, blocked the doors.

Blue fell to his hands and knees, and crawled toward the front of the room as he worked around scattered shards of glass. He passed two women who cried and clung to each other under nearby tables. He watched while a man on the floor next to them struggled with his jacket.

The man sat up, and screamed, "Rotten bastards." He jumped to his feet and pointed a gun at the nearest Treasury man. Two agents fired. Again the room filled with screams. A large red blotch showed on the man's chest, another on his shoulder. His bloody gun discharged, and the bullet took a chunk out of the wall above Blue's head. The gun clattered to the floor.

The man cried out, grabbed his chest, and fell back on a table. The table collapsed. Man and furniture crashed to the floor on top of the gun. Blue gasped. Blood splattered on his face, and the sharp smell of gun smoke burned in his nose.

He did not understand what was happening, and refused to think about what might happen next. He kept his eyes on the floor as he moved. But his ears could not shut out the wailing sirens now outside the building. And it seemed strange to him that his mind could not shut out the last book he read before he left home, that he would think about it now. When the school library got a copy of *A Farewell to Arms*, his teacher recommended it. Blue was the first to check it out.

Was this like war? With howling sirens again and again? People falling, screaming, and crying? People trying to fight back, and being shot dead? If this was like war, would he get out alive? He shivered. Kept his head down. Kept crawling, fighting his way to the front wall.

Blue's head struck the wall before he knew he was there. He reached out and touched the wall just to be sure, and then turned left. In spite of the chaos, he now knew where he was. He crawled faster toward the side wall. But he jerked to a stop when another gunshot exploded and the screams started again. He looked toward the sound. An agent's smoking gun pointed toward the ceiling. The man's radish-colored face distorted.

"Shut up. Everybody shut the hell up. You're all under arrest, and I want silence."

Seconds later, Blue put his head down and crawled again, and prayed he would not be noticed. He reached the next wall and turned again. Only ten feet to the door of his room. He'd have to stand up to open the door when he got there. What to do? He crawled slower now, and tried to plan.

At the door, he sat up and turned to see the agents on the other side of the room. With his back to the door, the people now stood facing away from him. They no longer looked like a party crowd. Instead of catering to them, agents arrested them. Instead of drinks, they got handcuffs. And a shove out the back door was the new dance. Women pleaded and begged. "I have children. I have to go home."

Revenuers showed no mercy.

He would have to work fast to get through the door behind him before the crowd thinned out. With a slow and deliberate move, his hand went up, rubbing against the door. There it was. He breathed deep. He could reach the knob without standing.

With his hand on the doorknob, Blue watched the agents and the crowd, and waited. Waited and thought. If he could get into his room without being noticed, maybe—just maybe—he could go out the window.

The man who approached him on the stage told him to get the hell out. Did that mean he had permission to leave? Was he too young to be arrested? He didn't know, but he knew he could not just walk up and ask the man.

Sweat ran down his arm. His heart pounded. His mind buzzed. A plan formed. That's what he needed A distraction… He looked at the kerosene lanterns that hung along the wall, and dug a nickel from his pocket. Could he throw the nickel and hit the globe hard enough to break it? While sitting down? If he missed, the nickel would hit the wall, fall to the floor, maybe hit a table, or somebody in the crowd. He told himself it was a bad idea. Unless…

Again, Blue dug in his pocket, and pulled out nickels and pennies. At close range, a shotgun was always better than a rifle. Again, his heart pounded in his throat. He cocked his arm—and fired.

Chapter Ten

On Monday morning, the 6:45 rolled out of Biloxi, right on time. Blue checked his railroad watch to make sure. The man beside him in the boxcar whistled.

"Holy smokes. I've seen them in catalogs, but I ain't never seen a real one. A Hamilton?"

Blue smiled. "Never seen one? A lot of railroad men carry these."

Sledge grinned. "About the only time I see a railroad man is when he's chasing me with a club. I never get a good look at his timepiece."

Blue told him the story behind the watch. He also told him about getting separated from Halo, and about Martin. He said nothing about the music store where he'd worked. He'd grown to like Biloxi, and Downtown Music gave him a chance he'd never had before. But he didn't like the chance of going to jail. When he escaped Saturday night, he grabbed his bindle, went out the window of his room, and ran for the hobo jungle as fast as he could move.

He met Sledge at the Biloxi jungle, and they found each other easy to talk to. Sledge was headed for El Paso, Texas.

"It's where the best jobs are," he said. "If you've never been there, you ought to go with me."

Blue wanted to get away. The county sheriff or the Feds may be looking for him. In his mind, he saw the face of the Treasury man at Downtown Music, the man who told him to get the hell out during the raid. Now, Blue remembered—the face belonged to the customer at the barbershop three weeks ago. He'd asked Blue about a blind pig. That man kept him from being arrested. So Blue would get the hell out of town on a train headed west.

While the boxcar rumbled west, Blue wondered about Lucas, and hoped his friend was okay. Remembering all the great music he and Lucas made together helped Blue pass the time on the trip to New Orleans. He checked his watch twice more on the way. He was excited, and the trip seemed much longer than it was.

Sledge said they could catch another train in New Orleans, about two hours away, and another in Texas. But Blue had learned that a southbound hobo may have to catch a train going north to find one heading south, or one headed south to catch one going west. They may have to catch a dozen trains to get to El Paso. Blue didn't care. He got to see more of the country.

The New Orleans train yard was the largest Blue had seen, and when he and Sledge left the boxcar, he found it confusing. He followed Sledge toward a long line of cars on a track in the middle of the yard, with no engine or caboose.

Blue shook his head. "That's stupid. They're in the way of everything."

Sledge grinned. "Maybe for the railroad, but not for us. Follow me." He looked around for bulls, and then ran toward the disconnected boxcars.

Blue stepped inside. "What're we doing in here? This ain't even a real train."

"No, but that one is…" Sledge angled his head at the line of cars two tracks over, "… and when it takes off, the bulls will be watching up and down for hobos. They won't see us in here. Soon as they walk away, we'll jump out and catch our ride."

Blue didn't like the plan. But twenty

minutes later, they were rolling west, just like Sledge had said.

Sledge sat by the door with a newspaper he picked up in New Orleans. His lips made the same whistle as when he first saw Blue's Hamilton watch.

"You won't believe what happened Saturday night, Blue. Take a look at this." Blue sat next to him and picked up the paper.

Treasury Raids Biloxi Speakeasy

Blue's mouth hung open while he read. One man was killed in the raid, four people injured. Local jail could not hold all 67 arrested. Some were being held inside the building at Downtown Music. His breath caught in his throat when Blue saw the last line. *Two men escaped. No names have been released.*

***

The trip from Biloxi had been long and slow, and many Texas towns seemed to get in the way of the journey to El Paso—towns like Texarkana and Houston.

For a hundred miles, Blue and Sledge complained about being hungry, and they left a train in Texarkana to find a meal. They stood by the tracks, shaded their eyes from the afternoon sun, and looked back and forth across a hayfield.

Blue shrugged. Then he pointed. "I think I see a barn about a half-mile down that road. Maybe more. So maybe there's a farmhouse, and maybe we can get a bite to eat."

Sledge shook his head. "That's a lot of maybes for such a long walk. I'd hate to hike all the way back on an empty gut."

"Okay, let me hear *your* idea." Blue cupped

his hand around his ear, and leaned toward Sledge.

Sledge turned and looked at the forest on the other side of the tracks. Then he turned back and looked again at the hay, where stalks of grain swayed in the breeze like waves on the ocean. And like that ocean, they seemed to reach the horizon. He lifted his bindle, swung it on his shoulder, and started toward the trail that led through the hayfield.

A half-hour later, the two rested on a stack of bales. Sledge tilted his canteen and took a long drink. "I guess a half mile is a lot longer in Texas." He turned his head away from Blue, and grinned.

Blue drank from his own canteen, and stood. "The barn's closer now than it was. Get off your lazy ass, and let's go." He turned his head away and grinned.

Sledge grinned and stood. "Even if we live long enough to get there, how do we know we can get some food?"

Blue jerked his thumb toward the side of the road. Sledge smiled and nodded when he saw an X inside a circle painted on a large rock. The sign lifted the spirits of both hobos, and they walked faster toward the barn.

A rail fence formed a corral that surrounded the barn. Blue lifted the gate latch and the two men entered. They saw an empty corral, and no one about the farm, but Blue closed the gate behind him. It was the right thing to do. A hundred yards past the barn, a farmhouse sat in the shade of large oak trees.

Blue and Sledge crossed the corral, and climbed over the fence to the front yard of the home. Chickens squawked and flapped, and scattered across the yard. The hobos walked up the steps to the front porch. A lady opened the door and stuck out her head.

"I know you've had a long walk, gentlemen......" she shook her head, "... but I ain't got much left."

Blue's heart sank to his stomach as his gut growled. Sledge frowned and groaned.

She spread her hands. "I could let you have some hot dogs. I just baked some fresh buns, and I got chopped onions and homemade mustard to go with them. But... I gotta get a nickel apiece for them. I'm running awful low on grocery money."

The hobos looked at each other and laughed. Blue pulled a dime from his pocket. "I'll take two, Ma'am."

Sledge's eyes grew bright as he brought out two nickels. "Me too. Are they ready?"

She smiled. "I'll be out in five minutes."

The men filled their canteens with cool water at the pump, and sat on the porch. After wolfing down the food, they thanked the lady for the world's best hot dogs, and started back, hoping to reach the tracks before dark.

When they approached the run-down barn, a man jumped out, a cap low on his forehead. He pushed an open bag toward them. With his other hand, he slashed the air with a pocketknife as he glared, showing a scarred and dirty face and a mouthful of rotten teeth.

"Gimme everything in your pockets, or I'll slash your filthy guts out."

Sledge's leg twitched as if he wanted to run. Then he looked around. They were back inside the fence. He pulled folded dollar bills from his shirt.

Blue's mind went to the scissors he carried behind him, the scissors he bought the day before the raid in Biloxi, the big pair Halo said he needed.

He wore them on his back like a weapon, wedged between his britches and belt, with the blades pushed down into his back pocket.

When the robber turned his attention to Sledge's money, Blue yanked out the scissors. He opened them, waved them at the man, and spoke from the side of his mouth.

"Hey, Sledge. I castrated a lot of pigs with a butcher knife. You wanna see me castrate this pig with a pair of scissors?"

The ten-inch blades caught the sun's reflection as Blue lowered the scissors and pointed them at the man's crotch. The man's face paled, his mouth fell open, eyes popped wide, nostrils flared. The knife hand trembled. A dark wet spot grew on the front of his britches. He whimpered, turned, scaled the fence, and ran into the hayfield.

And ran.

On their way back to the railyard, the two shook their heads in silence. Blue felt exhausted, and his head ached from the tension in the back of his neck. He breathed deep to quiet his nerves. After a while, Sledge cleared his throat.

"Blue, you think that guy was just a little bit scared of your scissors? By the time he disappeared into the hay, I almost felt sorry for him."

Blue smiled, and then laughed. Sledge laughed. Then they laughed together, and the tension was gone.

Blue nodded. Halo had been right about the scissors.

***

Houston railroad bulls chased Blue and Sledge all over the train yard, determined to stop them from catching out. The two spent the night under a bridge when they didn't find a jungle. Blue got little sleep.

Next morning, the bulls were after them again. While they ran, Blue's bindle slipped from his hand and crashed to the gravel beside the tracks. His supplies scattered.

"Get the hell outa my yard," a bull screamed behind him, and drew back his big stick.

Sledge ran ahead. "C'mon Blue. Follow me."

Blue didn't follow. His breath grew short, his heart raced as he started back for his bag. He snatched up the tin cup he bought in Alabama, the new cup that was now full of dents.

The bull yelled again and ran toward him. The stick nicked Blue's ear as it flew by. Out of habit, Blue's hand went behind him and closed on the scissors. He ran with the cup in one hand, scissors in the other while a flashback darted through his mind, and he heard his mother say, "Never run with scissors."

He stopped, glanced back, and moaned. A pair of boots—heavy, black, rugged, railroad boots with leather laces that went halfway to the knee—stomped the bag again and again, mangled his fork and spoon, broke the small mirror he'd found and kept wrapped in a rag, and crushed the jar of jam and the tiny jar of sour pickles, gifts from the blind lady in Bolling. The boots destroyed the bindle he'd worked so hard to put together. His heart sank when the bull picked up his club and smashed everything the boots might have missed.

Sledge had run ahead. He cut between cars of a slow-moving train, a dangerous move. Did he jump that train? Or did he get crushed beneath it? Blue only knew that was the last time he saw his new friend.

At sundown, Blue walked back to the bridge

where he spent the night before. This time he had nothing to carry. When he found the gloves and canvas bag someone left behind, he draped the bag over his shoulders. With one glove upside down, he kept his hands warm, but his body shivered through a long, cold night under a bridge in Houston.

Early next morning, Blue stole back along the tracks and found his bindle. The ripped-open bag showed little to save. He searched through the rubble for the one thing he hoped had survived.

The day he left home, Blue sneaked a picture of his mother out of the worn-out, pocketbook her sister made for her from a flour sack. The dyed blue bag was the closest thing to a purse the woman had ever owned. He remembered the guilt when he stuck the picture in his shirt pocket, but swore to himself that he would return it to her when he came home, whenever that was.

Blue found only a torn scrap of the picture. Tears formed when he turned his head and imagined the wind scattering the torn pieces over the land beside the tracks. It was his mother's only picture of herself. And the pocket-size frame he bought for it in Biloxi was now only splinters.

"I'm sorry, Mama." His head dropped again. A tear splattered on his shoe. He wiped a sleeve across his eyes. Then he raised his head, took a deep breath, and left it all behind.

His chest felt tight, his stomach churned as he walked alongside the track in Houston, alone. But he laughed when he thought about the would-be robber, and how Sledge found the whole scary event so funny. Blue felt better after he laughed, and better still when he spotted a woman selling slices of Spam and onions on biscuits for seven cents.

An hour later, he hopped a freighter to El Paso. This time, he knew where the train was headed. He shared a boxcar with two other hobos also headed for El Paso. Neither had heard of Sledge.

***

As the train rattled and slowed in El Paso, Blue bailed out of the boxcar, clutching the worn-out canvas bag that held his faded extra shirt and two right-hand gloves with heavy stains. He hit the gravel hard. The heel broke off his shoe. Pain pierced his ankle. Blue winced, limped away from the tracks and sat on a curb next to a streetlight post. He wanted to cry out in pain, but didn't dare. Hobos often had a tough time blending in with regular people. Calling attention to himself might cause some snooty bitch to get the police.

He pulled off his shoe and rubbed the swollen patch of red that now showed through the dirt on his ankle. As the pain began to ease, Blue gritted his teeth and forced his foot back into the shoe. A ragged shoelace snapped. He pulled it from the shoe and tied the ends together, but the knot would not fit through the eyelets. He left the shoe untied.

A man in a gray suit strutted along the sidewalk, glanced down at the curb as he passed, and wrinkled his nose.

"Whew." The man mumbled something about keeping filthy bums off the street.

Blue's bum ankle was his biggest concern, and he ignored the insults and looks of disgust. He sat alone, leaned against a light post, and hoped he could land another job playing music. He knew nothing about El Paso, nor what his chances would be here. But he knew that making money with his music would be much tougher without a guitar.

Maybe he would find another music store.

Blue's gut rumbled when the smell of frying bacon wafted past and reminded him of the last time he ate—yesterday. He didn't know if the smell came from a café or a nearby home. But he knew he had to find a meal. Gobble some groceries, as Uncle John used to say.

But where to go? He was in El Paso now, another place he'd never been. Glad to be there, but not glad to be there alone, and wished Sledge was there too. Sledge had been riding the rails for a long time, was good company, and a handy person to have around. He'd traveled most of the country, and knew which trains would take him where he wanted to go next. Blue was learning. Or so he told himself.

He spun, wrapped his hands around the light post and pulled himself to his feet to take a look at El Paso. When he picked up the bag, his ankle reminded him he could get there only if he could walk.

Chapter Eleven

After a night in the El Paso jungle, Blue walked back to town. The twisted ankle still hurt, but the swelling was almost gone. He tried hard not to limp. People always noticed a limper, and they would call him *gimp*.

Four times, he asked people on the sidewalk for directions. But he found Mills Avenue in spite of their help. An hour later, he rubbed the back of his stiff neck while he gazed up at the new Conrad Hilton Hotel. The radio news he'd heard in the past said it would be nineteen stories tall when it was done. Blue had to see it, but he really came here to ask for a job. That was before he got dizzy watching the construction workers on top of the steel frame that seemed to reach to the sky.

He felt the four dollars and six cents in his pocket. It was all he had, but as he walked away, he decided he could survive a few more days without working up there. Besides, he smelled food cooking somewhere.

A block from the hotel, the rumble in his gut made Blue stop where a kitchen window opened to the street. While he waited in line, a man inside worked fast over a stove, with a big basket of eggs, a stack of sliced bread, and a bowl of butter. Blue felt the four dollars and six cents in his pocket again when he read the sign by the window. *Fried hen-egg on buttered toast, 6 cents.* It was meant to be.

"Perfect," he mumbled as he walked to a small park nearby where he could enjoy a hot sandwich washed down with cool water from his canteen.

Last night, he slept well. This morning, the mulligan stew had a bit of hamburger mixed in, and it made for a tasty breakfast. He liked El Paso, and wondered how long he'd have to stay here to be a Texan. He'd read books about Texas, about the Alamo, about Sam Houston, Jim Bowie, and Davy Crockett. They were real men. Strong, brave, and proud.

He laid his scissors on a shaded bench, sat beside them, and dug his meal out of the bag. Blue had licked his lips when he watched the cook sprinkle on salt and black pepper while the egg fried, just the way Blue liked it. He could still smell the goodness through the newspaper wrapping, and his gut rumbled again as he held it under his nose. He breathed long and deep, and yanked off the wrapping. His mouth watered as he chomped down on a corner and tore off a mouthful of the hot egg and buttered toast. Life was good.

A light breeze rattled the leaves overhead while he chewed. Blue looked up. A man in a tan suit stood on the other side of the park, sun glistening on his dark, slicked-back hair. He propped a foot on a bench, leaned forward, and rested an elbow on his knee while he smoked a cigarette and stared at Blue. Blue stared back. The man did not look away. Blue turned his head.

Down the street, on a sidewalk just outside the park, another man with a cigarette stood and watched. His dark hair was also slicked back, but he wore a brown suit. When Blue looked back again a moment later, the man was gone.

Blue rushed through his meal and took a big swallow of water. As he stood and hooked the canteen on his belt, the man across the park came toward him. Blue slung the bindle on his back and reached for the scissors.

From behind, a strong hand reached over the back of the bench and grabbed Blue's wrist. Blue looked down at the sleeve of a brown suit.

Tan Suit stopped in front of Blue, opened his jacket and showed a badge. His nose lifted.

"Lieutenant Bowman, El Paso City Police." He jerked his head toward the scissors. "Drop the weapon."

Blue felt the color drain from his face. "It's not a weapon. It's just a…" He moaned and lost his breath as the man behind him punched him in the ribs. Blue dropped the scissors. His knees buckled and he sat on the bench.

Brown suit came around the bench, yanked the bindle off Blue's shoulder, and opened it. A smirk crossed his face as he looked at the beat-up tin cup. He pulled out the faded shirt, wrinkled his nose and threw it back in. The bag dropped on the bench with a clunk.

"You call that a bindle?"

Blue did not answer.

"You a hobo?"

"I am."

"Where you from, boy?"

Blue looked up, read the name tag on the man's jacket, and said, "I didn't do nothing wrong, Lieutenant Garcia."

Tears popped into Blue's eyes when Bowman stepped forward, caught Blue's hair and yanked his head back.

"Lieutenant Garcia asked where you're from, boy. Answer the question." He pulled Blue's head farther back, and leaned close. "Or we might have to stop being nice."

Blue tried to talk with his head pulled back, but his voice caught in his throat. "I uh… I'm from… Missouri, sir."

Bowman released his grip as Garcia chuckled. "Missouri? What the hell is a Missouri?"

Blue rubbed his throat, but did not answer.

Bowman picked up the scissors and waved them at Blue. "You got any more weapons?"

"They're not… uh, I mean… no sir."

"Stand up. Put your hands behind your back." When he stood, Garcia caught Blue's arms and pinned them back. Blue winced at the pain in his shoulders, and felt the clutch of steel handcuffs close on his wrists.

Bowman kicked Blue's feet apart and patted him down. He tapped Blue's shirt pocket, pulled out the folded dollars, held them up, and grinned.

"Well, well. Look at this, Lieutenant Garcia. This young man's got money."

Garcia grinned and looked at Blue. "Maybe we underestimated this man. What's your name, boy? Rockefeller?"

"Blue."

Garcia cocked his head. "I didn't ask your favorite color, smart ass. What's your name?"

"Blue, sir. Blue Bailey."

"And your age?"

"Uhm… eighteen."

"Got any identification?"

"No."

"Ever been in jail, Blue?"

Blue shook his head. "No, and I never want to be."

Bowman moved to Blue's right side and looked him up and down. He untied the leather chain from Blue's belt, and yanked the watch from its pocket. His eyes grew wide, and he glanced up at Garcia, the taller of the two, and then back at the watch.

"You know what this is?" He dangled the watch in front of Garcia. "A railroad watch." His voice slowed. "A Hamilton... Railroad... Watch." Bowman looked at Blue and shook his head. "Our friend, Blue, here... has been lying to us. He said he's a hobo. But... a few minutes ago, he bought himself a hen-egg sandwich, and..." he waved the money, "... he still had four dollars in his pocket. And then we found this expensive watch in another pocket." He turned back to Garcia. "You ever see a rich hobo?"

"Hobo? No. But maybe that stuff belongs to somebody else." He put his mouth near Blue's ear. His words came out soft and slow.

"You stole the money and the watch." He backed up, lifted Blue's chin and turned it toward him. "You stole them, didn't you, Blue?"

Blue jerked his head free. "I never stole anything. I worked for that money." He dipped his head toward the watch. "And I got the watch from my friend, sir."

Garcia nodded as he looked down at the watch. "From a friend, huh?" He looked up at Blue with a broad grin. "Now why didn't we think of that? Let's see, your name is Blue. So what's your friend's name? Purple?"

"Halo."

Garcia chuckled. "Halo? Somebody from heaven came down and gave you that watch?" Garcia looked at Bowman. "I believe him. Don't you, Lieutenant?"

Bowman moved in front of Blue while he swung the watch back and forth on the chain. "You think we're stupid, don't you, boy?" He nodded at the bench behind Blue. "Sit down."

"No, I don't think you're stu—" A jolt of pain ripped through Blue's body. His mouth fell open. A loud gasp came from all the way down, and his knees buckled again as Bowman's knee slammed like a sledgehammer into Blue's groin.

"Sit. Down."

Blue stumbled backwards and fell to the bench. He sat and leaned forward with his face against his knees, his hands cuffed behind him… and moaned as his lunch came up and splattered at his feet. All his life, he'd heard you have to be tough to be a real man. And everybody knows grown men don't cry. Rudyard Kipling wrote about what it takes to be a man, and the words from the poem Blue trusted so much flashed through his mind. '*If you can keep your head when all about you are losing theirs…*' He wanted to be a real man, but… his mind became a blur. In spite of all he wanted to be, and tried to be, he shivered. The pain was too much. Blue did not feel tough. He felt cheated. Defeated. Ashamed.

Blue cried.

Chapter Twelve

He stood in line at the booking office, wrists handcuffed in front of him, and gripped a white cloth bag, *El Paso County Jail* printed in black on the side. The bag held a tin cup, a faded shirt, and items from his pockets—a half book of matches he'd found near the Conrad Hilton, a smooth throwing-rock he picked up near the tracks in Houston, and a guitar pick.

A woman waited in line behind him. She looked lost, alone, and afraid. Her wrists sported the same style bracelets that Blue wore, but she carried no jail bag. She reminded Blue of his mother. Not the same face, but about the same age, tall and thin, and hair the same color.

Lieutenants Garcia and Bowman leaned against the wall at one side of the room, smoked cigarettes, and watched Blue. Before he reached the records-room window, Lieutenant Bowman approached and whispered in Blue's ear.

"Don't mention the money or watch, and we won't charge you with stealing. Understand?" The officer stepped back, made eye contact with Blue, and shrugged. Blue nodded and moved up in line.

When he stepped to the Dutch door of the records room, a man inside with a Joe Shafer nametag on his shirt tapped his finger on the counter.

"The bag."

Blue hoisted the bag and set it down. Shafer grabbed the bottom of the bag and dumped the items on the counter.

"First time?"

"Pardon?"

"Your first time here?"

"First and last."

"Heard that a few times." The man held each of Blue's possessions in his hand while he wrote a description on a form. Then he dropped each item back into the bag. He looked at the guitar pick and nodded; then held it between his thumb and finger and looked up. He spoke just above a whisper.

"Nice pick. You play guitar?"

Blue's eyes brightened. "Yes, sir. You too?"

"I like the banjo. Play it whenever I get the chance."

He picked up the half book of matches and looked past Blue at the people in the room, then back down at the shelf. He placed the guitar pick inside the match book and said, "You're gonna need these." He leaned forward and stuck the matches in Blue's shirt pocket.

Blue nodded a *thank you*. The pick was worth more to him than that man could know, his only gift last Christmas. Mama had saved 15 cents, and bought the pick when Daddy was not with her.

Shafer picked up the throwing stone last, rolled it around in his fingers, and shook his head while he studied it. His forehead wrinkled as he looked up.

"About as big as a goose egg. This some kind of good-luck charm? A paperweight?" He cocked his head, and held out the stone. "So, what do you call this?"

"A rock."

The man's eyebrows dropped as he glared. "A rock?"

Blue nodded. He kept the rock in case he

needed it against a mean dog, but saw no reason to explain.

The man shook his head. "Smart-ass punk."

Blue heard the rock bounce off his tin cup when the man threw it back into the bag without recording it. One more ding in the cup wouldn't matter.

The man jerked his head at a counter to his left. "This stuff yours?"

Blue leaned forward and looked in. His scissors lay on top of his bindle bag. "Yes, sir." He looked at the counters on each side of the man, and whispered, "Is my watch and my money back here?"

The records man wrote on the possessions list, and dropped the bindle bag and scissors into the jail bag.

"This is it. For anything else, see the man that brought you here." He spun the form on the counter and laid his pencil on top of it. "If you want any of this junk back when you leave, sign here."

"How long will that be?"

Shafer lowered his head, shook it, and rolled his eyes up at Blue. "It ain't up to me, son. It ain't up to me."

Blue raised his cuffed hands to the counter and signed the paper. Another hand tightened on his arm. Lieutenant Garcia stepped beside him. The woman who had waited behind Blue stepped up to the counter, and he turned to look at her. Garcia yanked Blue's arm and led him toward the stairs.

***

"All rise."

Everyone in the courtroom stood as a man in a long, black robe entered. He wiped his brow with a white handkerchief while he walked toward a dark, wooden desk with a sign that identified him as Honorable Charles Martin. He sat, folded the handkerchief, stuffed it into his pocket, and told everyone to sit.

For the past two days, Blue lived in a cellblock with twenty-three other men and waited for his turn in court without knowing when that would be.

"The morning judge will go easy on you," some of them said. "But that afternoon judge is a real bastard. May as well just plead guilty to rape and murder no matter what the charge is." Blue worried. But an older inmate who'd been in that jail twice before told him, "Don't pay any mind to these jailhouse lawyers. They're worth just what you're paying them."

Now, Blue was here in afternoon court, sitting on the front row with five of those men, and they stared at the polished hardwood floor and waited to see if the judge was a real bastard.

Judge Martin shuffled through the stack of papers on his desk. Then he scanned the people on the front row of the courtroom below him, and talked loud.

"Miss Larson." He glanced at the paper again. "Misses Louella Larson."

Blue recognized the woman who stood. He sat up straight and stared. The judge shook his head at the creature in front of him—the dirty blonde hair that hung like frayed ropes down to her shoulders; the worn and wrinkled dress of navy blue that clung to her sweating body as she fidgeted; the once-white socks drooped around her ankles above black shoes, scuffed and damaged. He pulled his black-frame glasses down on his nose and looked over them.

"Is it miss, or misses?"

She looked up, her voice faint. "Misses."

"So you're a married woman?

"Yes, sir."

"Do you understand what you're being charged with, Misses Larson?"

She covered her face, hung her head, and nodded.

"You have to say it out loud, Misses Larson. You're being charged with soliciting. Do you understand what that means?"

The judge watched her and waited. The crowd behind her also watched and waited. The woman started to speak, but stopped and shook her head. The judge leaned toward her, his words harsh and absolute.

"Misses Larson, you're being charged with prostitution."

A whimper escaped. She trembled and shook her head again, sniffed, and wiped her nose on her sleeve. "No. I'm not…"

"Do you plead guilty or not guilty?" The woman did not answer. "Where is your husband, Misses Larson?"

"I don't know. He, uh…" She took in a long breath and let it go. "He left about a month ago."

"Left?"

"Yes, sir. He lost his job. Said he couldn't support our family anymore. And he… he went to be a hobo."

The judge rubbed his chin as he looked down at her. "A hobo?"

"Yes, sir. Left me with three children, and…"

"Have you been to the local mission?"

She nodded. "They're full. There's nothing

they can do right now. Said I could try again in a week." Tears dripped off her chin when she looked up. "The oldest is nine, and… I'm just… uh. Don't you understand, Mister Judge? I have to feed my babies. That's why I…" She hung her head and sobbed.

Blue squirmed.

Judge Martin removed his glasses, wiped his eyes with the handkerchief, and put it back.

"Misses Larson, I'm going to sentence you to a twenty-dollar fine or sixty days in jail. Since this is your first offense, I'm going to suspend that sentence. But if you turn up here again with the same charge, I'm going to be rough on you. Do you understand?"

Misses Larson nodded.

Judge Martin motioned the bailiff to the bench while he reached inside his robe and pulled out a small book. He wrote on one of the pages, tore it out, and folded it. He handed it to the bailiff and whispered. The bailiff gave it to Misses Larson, who shook when she looked at it. She wiped her eyes on her sleeve and looked at the judge.

"Oh, thank you, sir. God bless you, Judge Martin. This is more than enough, Your Honor."

Judge Martin nodded at the bailiff. The bailiff stood next to her and faced the crowd and talked loud.

"Ladies and Gentlemen. When you talk to Judge Martin in this courtroom, address him as *Your Honor*. Not *Judge*, not *Mister Martin*, not *Sir*, but *Your Honor*." He turned, took Louella Larson's arm, and led her out.

"Mister Briggs. Mister Bobby Joe Briggs." His Honor pulled the glasses down on his nose again as a young man stood. "What are you doing here, Bobby?"

Bobby grinned and made a backhand motion at the bailiff. "Well, judge, I heard what that man said, but you and me, we uh… we know each other. Can I just call you Charlie?"

Judge Martin scowled. "In this courtroom, you will address me exactly as the bailiff instructed. Is that clear?"

Bobby nodded.

"Now, I'll ask you once more." The judge leaned forward. "What are you doing here?"

Bobby shrugged. "Well, I got picked up for selling a sewing machine."

"You've been charged with selling stolen property. Do you plead guilty or not guilty?"

"I'm not guilty. I got the machine from Spencer's Warehouse, and I was gonna pay for it after I got the money."

"I happen to know that your uncle owns that warehouse. Did you have anybody's permission to take that machine?"

"My uncle knows that I…"

"I didn't ask what your uncle knows. I asked if you had permission to take that sewing machine."

The defendant didn't answer. The judge raised his voice. "When I ask you a question, Bobby Joe, I expect an answer. Did you have permission to take that machine?"

Bobby stood up straight, and yelled, "No, Your Honor." Then he lowered his voice. "I just needed some time to think about my answer."

Judge Martin wrote on the paper in front of him, and looked up at the defendant. "Okay, I'll give you time to think about it." He rapped his gavel. "Sixty days in the county jail."

Bobby's lip curled. His face reddened as he lifted his cuffed hands and raised both middle fingers. "You lousy bastard."

Judge Martin rapped his gavel again. "*Ninety* days in the county jail." He yanked off the glasses and leaned forward again. "Have you anything further to say… Mister Briggs?"

Bobby's mouth opened and his lips moved. Nothing came out, and he looked down and shook his head.

Blue hoped he would be called last so he could learn what to do or not do. Maybe he should tell Judge Martin about his guitar named Martin, and… or maybe not. Blue felt a knot in his gut as he watched the bailiff lead Bobby Joe Briggs out of the courtroom.

"Mister Bailey. Mister Blue Bailey." The judge stared at him as he stood. "Is Blue your real name, son?"

"Yes, Your Majesty."

The judge's face wrinkled. "Majesty? They don't pay me enough to be a king."

Snickers broke out in the courtroom while the bailiff stepped toward Blue and yelled, "Your Honor."

"I'm sorry. I meant to say, *Your Honor*. I'm kinda nervous."

Judge Martin shook his head and chuckled. "I am too, now." The whole courtroom broke out in a laugh, and people made comments. The judge rapped his gavel for silence, and then looked at Blue. "I take it you're new in town?"

"Yes, Your Honor. I'm a hobo."

"A hobo? How old are you, boy?"

Blue took a deep breath. He'd heard that lying in court was against the law. But he had told

Bowman and Garcia he was eighteen. "I'm uh, eighteen, sir. I mean, Your Honor."

"Is that so? What year were you born?"

"Nineteen..." the color left his face, and Blue's mouth went dry. "It was June twenty-first... nineteen... twelve."

"Very well, Mister Bailey. You've been charged with vagrancy. How do you plead?"

"I don't know what vagrancy means, Your Honor, sir. I don't think I ever did that to anybody."

"Here in El Paso, you're considered a vagrant if you do not contribute to the community, have no visible means of support, and have less than ten cents in your pocket. Do you have a job, Mister Bailey?"

"Sometimes. I get jobs wherever I go."

"I see. Did you buy anything after you got into town?"

"Yes, sir... uh, Your Honor. I had me a hen-egg sandwich."

"Did you get any kind of receipt?"

"Receipt?" Blue shook his head. "I just got the sandwich."

"And money? Do you have any money?"

Blue looked across the courtroom where Garcia sat near the door. But the man did not look back. "I had four dollars in my pocket."

The judge looked over as Garcia held up a folded paper. The bailiff took the paper to the judge for a quick glance, and then took it to Blue.

"Is that your signature, Mister Bailey?"

"Well, Your Honor, I..."

"Yes or no?"

"Yes."

The bailiff returned the paper to the judge, who looked over his glasses at Blue.

"This is a list of items you had when you came in. There's nothing here about money."

"Lieutenant Bowman took it out of my shirt pocket. I don't know where it is now."

Garcia jumped to his feet. "Your Honor, may I approach the bench?" The judge motioned him forward, and the two whispered back and forth. Garcia returned to his seat. The judge looked at Blue.

"Mister Bailey, are you suggesting that a police officer stole your money?"

"I'm just telling you that Lieutenant Bowman took the money out of my pocket, and Lieutenant Garcia was right beside him."

"Before this gets out of hand, I'm going to find you guilty of vagrancy. The fine is ten dollars or thirty days in the county jail. If you were under eighteen, I would dismiss the charge. But you've already stated your age."

"Well, Your Honor, the truth is I'm only…"

The judge rapped his gavel. "I don't want to hear it, Mister Bailey. When you first entered this courtroom, did you not place your right hand on the Holy Bible and swear to tell the truth, the whole truth, and nothing but the truth, so help you God?"

Blue swallowed hard. "Yes sir, Your Honor."

"Well then, you'll pay the ten-dollar fine or spend thirty days in jail."

Blue's mind flashed back to Bolling, Alabama, and Halo's words; "Someday that watch could get you out of a real jam."

"Your Honor, can I use my watch to pay the fine? It's a Hamilton Railroad watch, and it's worth a lot more than ten dollars."

"A Hamilton?" He looked again at the

possessions list. "You signed this paper. It's not on here. Let me see the watch."

"Lieutenant Bowman has it."

"Lieutenant Bowman?"

"He took it off my belt in the park."

Garcia curled his upper lip and shook his head when Judge Martin looked at him.

"Lieutenant Garcia, would you contact Lieutenant Bowman, and ask him to step into the courtroom, please?"

Garcia stood. "Your Honor, Lieutenant Bowman is out of town today working on a case. And I don't know anything about a watch."

"You know I had it." Blue stared at the man. "You even asked me where I got such a fine watch, and I said from a friend." Garcia stole a quick look at his prisoner and then looked away.

Blue's voice got higher and louder. "He's lying like hell, judge. They stole my money, and now they're trying to steal my watch."

The judge rapped the gavel. "Take it easy, young man, or I'll find you in contempt of court."

"I'm not in contempt of the court. I'm in contempt of somebody stealing my stuff." Blue raised his cuffed hands and pointed at Garcia. "He's crooked as a snake, and a damn liar."

"I warned you, Mister Bailey." The judge whipped off his glasses and waited.

"Well, it's true, Your Honor. And Bowman is a crook too. They're in it together, and you shouldn't trust either one."

The gavel sounded again. "Sixty days in the county jail. Are you finished, Mister Blue Bailey? Or would you like to try for ninety?"

Blue's chest puffed out, color flooded his face as he stared at the judge, and then at Garcia. "I just…" He looked at the floor and shook his head.

Chapter Thirteen

Residents of the El Paso County jail lived in large cages called cellblocks, with two cellblocks on each floor, one on the east side of the building, another on the west. A row of cells with gray steel walls lined one side of a block, each with a toilet, and a sink with a water fountain. Shallow steel boxes mounted to one wall of each cell made up bunk beds for two inmates.

Outside the cells, the concrete floor offered a courtyard with picnic tables where residents gathered to eat, play cards, and trade true stories about the women and fortunes they left behind in another state. At the far end of the courtyard, a shower stall with no soap, towels, or door got little business.

Twelve cells made up Cellblock 5 West. A new man got his pick of empty cells, and bottom bed or top. He always chose the bottom bed. Each new inmate brought his four-inch thick mattress and two army blankets he picked up in the supply room on his way in. One blanket covered the mattress; the other covered the inmate during chilly Texas nights. Upon release, a man took his mattress and blankets back to the supply room on his way out. According to the turnkeys, mattresses and blankets were cleaned and deloused in the jailhouse laundry before they were used again.

Blue didn't mind that he got the top bunk, and he understood how it all worked. But it didn't work for him. When Garcia brought him in the first day, Blue was assigned to 5 East, and he got his mattress and blankets. When the lieutenant brought Blue to 5 West after his day in court, he forgot the supply room. Every morning, Blue asked the turnkey about a mattress and blankets. Every morning, Blue got the same reply, "I'll see what I can do." After a week, he found it hard to get up at the 6:30 wake-up call when the cell doors opened with a bang.

He dragged his exhausted body off the bed, stiff and shivering, teeth chattering. His bones ached from the cold steel bottom of the bunk. He gave his shoulders, arms, and legs a brisk rub. Yet he knew it would take an hour, maybe longer, for his joints to warm up, to move without pain.

But Blue also knew that *late* for the seven o'clock breakfast—two slices of stale bread and a cup of bitter coffee—meant no breakfast at all. Someone would eat it for him, no matter how stale the bread might be.

One man who never shut up was fond of saying, "The bastards pick me up for panhandling on the street corner. And then they stick me in here and give me a chunk of bread hard enough to be a deadly weapon. So I ask you, gentlemen, which is the bigger crime?" Some inmates would groan. They'd heard that a dozen times. But Baldy could always count on laughs from the new arrivals.

When an inmate dipped the thick slices in his coffee and wolfed them down, Baldy nodded. "Everybody bitches, but everybody eats."

Nobody disagreed with him. It was the only thing going into the belly until the afternoon meal at 3:00, a metal plate of pinto beans with a spoon chained to the plate. And always two slices of bread and more coffee.

Sunday dinners brought a real treat. Along

with bread and coffee, the guests of the county got potatoes, and meat they called jackass roast or armadillo steak. Without knives, the inmates' teeth and jaw muscles got a workout, but they never left a bite on their plates.

Sundays also brought the preacher. According to guests who'd been here for months, he delivered the same sermon every week. While men on their best behavior devoured dinner, picked their teeth with their fingernails, and belched, the preacher stood outside the cellblock door with his Bible and warned them about the sins of alcohol, tobacco, stealing, and bad women, though not always in that order.

Blue figured the sermons must be working. The men here had little to steal, they smoked only when they had tobacco and papers, and he'd seen no alcohol or bad women in the cellblock.

***

On Monday morning, the turnkey's voice boomed through the big cage, his boot heels echoed on the shiny concrete floor as he strutted toward 5 West. A prisoner trustee in a jailhouse uniform walked beside him, and turned a clipboard toward him as they stopped at the cellblock door. The turnkey glanced at the clipboard and cleared his throat.

"Blue Bailey. Blue Bailey, front and center."

Blue gobbled the last bite of bread, washed it down with his coffee, and carried his cup toward the door. When he stopped, the turnkey peered through the bars and looked him up and down.

"Blue Bailey?"

"Yes."

"Bring your mattress and blankets."

"I don't have any."

The turnkey rolled his eyes, then looked into the cellblock. "Cell number?"

Blue nodded toward his cell. "Number five. Top bunk."

Most turnkeys did not require all prisoners to be in their cells every time the cellblock door opened. This one did. He leaned, peered around Blue and screamed, "The rest of you maggots crawl back in your cages."

With every man in a cell, he jerked his head toward cell five and opened the door. The trustee entered, checked the cell, and came back shaking his head. Blue handed the trustee his cup. The turnkey handcuffed Blue, and pulled him out.

Cellblocks were busy communities. Two or three new residents arrived every day. Others left—released, transferred, taken downstairs for questioning or their day in court. A lucky few would go downstairs to a waiting visitor. Yet, an open cellblock door always captured the attention of everyone in the cellblock, a welcome distraction from the stink of sweat and urine, from hot, endless days around picnic tables with worn-out jokes, amateur card tricks, reading month-old newspapers for the third time, and waiting… always waiting for the next bite of food.

The door slammed with a boom and metallic clunk of the lock. The echo of boot heels faded, and all eyes were on Blue as the turnkey led him away.

***

"Turn right."

Each man wore a number sign around his neck while he stood in line under the glaring lights, his hands cuffed behind him. In the dim light of the floor down in front of the stage, witnesses sat at small desks, each with a sheet of paper, and a pencil. They studied the men to see if one in the lineup might be the man they saw at the crime scene. An officer stood next to the witnesses.

"The men on stage can't see you," he told them. "Look at the shape of the head. Look at hair. At eyes. Ears. At noses. Then lips, chins, and necks."

Five men turned right when the officer barked the command. Blue stood first in line. He'd been warned not to look around, but from the corner of his eye, he could see number 6 at the end of the line. The man turned left. He corrected his move, but it didn't stop the officer from yelling.

"I said *right*, you idiot."

After more right turns, the men faced the back of the stage. Blue jumped as two officers came through a door in front of him. They escorted Number 6 out of the room, and Blue caught another glimpse of him between the two policemen. He didn't remember a man with a shaved head and swollen, black eye. Still, the man looked familiar, maybe a hobo he'd seen somewhere.

***

Blue woke early and told himself this would be a good day. He felt it. Yesterday was not good. He spent a long day downstairs answering the same questions again and again. "Can you prove where you were on..." He could prove it, and finally said, "If you keep records, they'll tell you I was right here in this stinking hell hole you call a jailhouse." He got a backhand slap across his face, but the questions ended.

The trip back from the line-up yesterday had a happy ending. He convinced the turnkey to stop by the storage room, and Blue came back with blankets and a mattress. No more stiffness. No more aching back. But he got back too late yesterday for the afternoon meal. Now, his gut demanded food and his mouth watered as his mind wandered to that day in the park when he enjoyed the hen-egg sandwich.

The cellblock door opened, and grabbed everyone's attention. Blue rubbed his belly, excited about breakfast. But instead of food, a new resident entered. Blue watched the new man, but the blankets and mattress hid his face as he lugged them to cell 7.

While he tried to ignore his rumbling gut, Blue stood and watched a tall man with a too-long neck and a short man sitting across from him betting on a card trick. Each man dropped a hand-rolled Prince Albert on the table, and the short man shuffled the deck. He spread the cards face-down on the table, and looked up at Long Neck.

"Okay now. I point to ten cards, and you can name nine out of ten before you turn them over? Is that the bet?"

Long Neck nodded. "That's it."

Blue heard footsteps behind him.

"Blue, what the hell brings you here?"

Blue spun around and saw the shaved head and swollen eye he saw downstairs in the lineup.

"It's me, Blue… Sledge."

Blue's mouth dropped open as he stared. A soft chuckle expressed his relief. "Damn, Sledge. Never thought I'd see you again." They shook hands and laughed. Blue glanced again at the slick head and puffy eye. "You win that fight?"

"Depends on who you ask."

"What happened?"

Sledge touched his scalp. “They shaved me downstairs. I think they wanted me to look like some bald guy that robbed a grocery store.”

“Why? It makes no sense.”

“Long story. Tell you later. How long you been here?”

“Fifteen days. Forty-five to go.”

“What the hell did you do?”

The rattle of the food cart approached the cellblock door. Every man stood and started forward.

Chapter Fourteen

Sledge held up the edge of his mattress. "I'm gonna knock that bastard's teeth out." His face flooded with color, and he nodded toward his bunk. "That's where my toast was." His upper lip curled as he jerked his thumb toward the end of the cellblock. "That damn thief in the last cell. I know he took it." Sledge's fist bounced off the mattress.

Blue cocked his head. "How do you know? He just got here yesterday."

"Yeah, but he was in 4 East when I was there. Every time he got a chance, he'd sneak into somebody's cell and steal stuff—tobacco, matches, a slice of bread, anything he found. Then he'd be wailing some goofy-ass chant all night long, driving me crazy with stupid nonsense about three stars and a half moon. Every morning, somebody swore they would bust his lip so bad he wouldn't chant for a month."

"Anybody ever do it?"

Sledge shook his head. "Nobody. They took him out of 4 East yesterday, and I figured his time was up… he could go back home to his cave. Then I get shuffled here to 5 West, and damned if he ain't here."

Blue and Sledge had talked all day. Sledge was a big man with a large appetite. Most of the day, he talked about food. His face distorted and turned red, the hair stood up on the back of his neck, and he complained about the piss-poor rations. As the men gobbled beans and bread for the afternoon meal, Sledge looked at Blue and shook his head.

"After we enjoy our jailhouse cuisine, stop by my apartment for a drink." He nodded at cell 7.

Sledge didn't let up in the apartment.

"Every morning I wake up starving like hell for two hours before they feed us. I'd eat that bedframe if I could chew it." He angled his head at the steel frame. "Although it's likely no tougher than the meat we get on Sundays."

He had saved a slice of bread from his dinner, and talked about how he could make toast if he had matches. Two minutes later, Blue returned from his own cell with the half book of matches the records-office man told him he would need.

Sledge tore a match from the book, dug his thumbnails into the torn end and separated the two halves to make two matches. He struck one and moved it back and forth while he held the bread above it. Then he struck the other match half, flipped the bread over, and toasted the other side. He wrapped his prize in newspaper and placed it under his mattress.

"That's gonna taste awful good just before lights out."

Now, a surge of red flooded his face as Sledge fumed about his stolen toast.

"Ain't nothing I hate more than a damn thief." He punched the mattress again, turned and left the cell, clenching his fists. Heads in the cellblock turned to watch. Blue followed a few steps behind. Sledge stepped through the doorway of the end cell, stopped and stared. The man Sledge hated sat on his bunk munching on toast.

Everyone in the cellblock now stood outside cell 12, and watched. When the man on the bunk looked up and grinned, Sledge's eyes grew wide and wild. His arms vibrated like a jackhammer. He threw himself forward, put his bodyweight into the punch, and with a crunching thud slammed his fist into the grin. A heavy, fog-horn groan rushed from the man's lungs as the back of his head bounced off the steel wall. Blood spurted from his mouth, and he fell to the floor. A half-eaten slice of toast landed in the sink, and a giant yellow tooth clattered across the cell.

The bleeding man lay motionless on the floor, his eyes rolled back in his head. Sledge opened and closed his fist, opened it again, and shook out the pain. He snickered as he glanced into the sink. "You can keep the damn toast."

Sledge turned to leave the cell. Only then did he seem aware of his audience. Men stepped aside. No one got in his way as he walked back to his own cell.

"Inside. On the double." The yell echoed through the cellblock as the turnkey approached, and every man scrambled to his cell. Ten seconds later, all doors clanged shut.

From morning wakeup call till lights out, echoes in the cellblock often made it hard for one man to hear another more than a few feet away. At night, while most inmates slept, echoes carried the sound. The slow drip in the shower stall at the other end of the block splattered loud and clear.

The sudden, uneasy silence now in the cellblock had nothing to do with respect for the turnkey. Any man here would laugh at that suggestion. But every man here needed to hear what every other man would say to the turnkey.

The turnkey and his trustee entered the cellblock and inspected each cell. At cell 12, the turnkey found the right key from the big ring on his belt, and opened the door.

Minutes later, two trustees entered the cellblock with a gurney. As they passed his cell on the way out, Sledge watched while the man on the gurney wagged his head back and forth, and babbled nonsense.

The turnkey stopped in front of cell 1.

"Who the hell is behind all this?" He chewed the inside of his cheek and glared at the men inside. When neither man spoke, the turnkey pushed his head forward and asked again.

One man shrugged and looked at the turnkey's nametag.

"It ain't me, Fred." The other man copied. Fred glared at them while men in the next cell snickered.

He moved to cell 2, stepped close and grabbed the door. "Tell me what happened, or this door won't open tomorrow for breakfast." He glared at one man and then the other. The two men looked at each other. Neither spoke. The turnkey smiled and shook his head. "You're gonna starve your damn guts out."

He backed up, and one man shouted, "I heard that somebody stole something. That's all I know. I swear."

The turnkey looked at the other man. "I suppose that's all you know too."

The man shook his head. "I don't know nothin' about nothin' at all."

Fred worked his way down the line of cells, but got no answers. At cell 7, he stood and stared at Sledge without talking. Sledge stood and waited for a full minute, and then sat on his bunk and looked away.

The turnkey looked down the line of cells and then back at Sledge, and stared at the cut and swollen right hand.

"You ready to tell me what happened?"

Sledge spread his hands and looked up. His voice was loud.

"All I heard was that some crazy bastard fell off his bunk while he was playing with himself."

The cellblock exploded. Inmates went insane from laughing. They needed relief from tension, pent-up emotions, worry, stress, and—most of all—boredom.

They found it.

Purple-faced Fred found nothing funny. He turned and walked to the cellblock door. When the door closed after him, he screamed, "Throw your mattress and blankets outside. Do not leave your cell. Everybody. Now."

He threw the switch to open all cell doors, and watched while mattresses tumbled out onto the floor, and blankets came flying after them. Cell doors clanged shut, trustees took out all bedding.

"You'll get 'em back when somebody talks." His head bobbed back and forth as he yelled. "So go ahead… laugh your ass off." His own laughter and the pop of his boot heels echoed through the cellblock as he walked away.

Blue stared through the bars and shook his head, not believing his fate. He had a mattress and blankets for one night. Now they were gone again.

Chapter Fifteen

The empty boxcar tossed him side to side and rattled his bones as he lay on his back. A breeze through the doorway cooled the car and made the odor inside easier to handle. But the breeze amplified the clackity-clack noise from the tracks, along with dinging bells and the whistle from the engine at every crossing.

The front of Blue's mind told him it was the reason he couldn't sleep. The back of his mind knew better. More times than he could remember, he slept in boxcars where the ride was rougher, noise louder and, as Sledge often said, the odor could make a polecat puke. If the hobo life was a measure of what a man is made of, Blue figured that, in the past two and a half years, he'd earned every right to be called a man, and a hobo. A damn good one.

After three days in boxcars trying to get to Florida, he felt drained. He needed rest. But his thoughts would not let go of El Paso, of Sledge, and the cantina where he and Sledge scored a gig that lasted nearly a year.

***

From the Mexicans in jail, Blue learned that Ciudad Juarez, a town just across the river from El Paso, hosted nightclubs for Americans who crossed the border for cheap meals and legal booze. They enjoyed the Mexican food, but most customers wanted American music for entertainment and dancing. That was the only jailhouse chinwag Blue could remember that turned out to be true. He also learned that Sledge could sing.

The El Paso County jail released Blue two days before Christmas, and he spent the holiday at the El Paso jungle wishing he could be with his mother. A few days after Blue's release, Sledge showed up at the jungle, and the two headed for Juarez. The owner of a cantina called Casa de Lobos would rent a guitar for Blue. And a new duo, *Blue Sledge Hammer*, was born.

Blue found that the tip jar in Juarez didn't fill as fast as the one at Downtown Music in Biloxi. A three-hour show often left the duo with less than a dollar each. But the job beat farm work or jail. Besides, for the duo, meals were free, and included a glass of Jose Cuervo. Though he liked the tequila, Blue drank very little. Every sip reminded him of his father. Sledge never left a drop in his glass, and often drank what Blue left behind.

Blue started every show the same. "Sit back and relax or get up and show 'em how to shake it. Get ready for the driving force of Blue Sledge Hammer." The duo would lead off with a fast tune that made people sit up, come alive, and dash for the dance floor.

For more than ten months, Blue Sledge Hammer played every Thursday, Friday, and Saturday. The crowd continued to grow, and the owner asked the duo to add a Sunday night show.

On their first Sunday night, a man in a hat and short-sleeve shirt sat alone at a table, drank tequila, and stared at Blue and Sledge. Blue forgot the words of his song, and struggled near the end of the show.

The duo quit ten minutes early, and walked to the cabin behind the cantina, where the owner allowed them to sleep after a show. Monday morning, they would go back to the El Paso jungle, and come back here Thursday.

Across the room from Blue, Sledge turned back the covers of his bunk. Then he spun around, wrinkled his face.

"What the hell happened to you? That's the worst show we ever did."

Blue nodded. "That man at the table by himself? He kept staring at us, and I finally recognized him."

"Anybody I know?"

"Remember the cop I told you about? Bowman?"

"Oh damn. I should've known." Sledge's face paled. "I was standing by the front door when he first showed up. I asked him for the time. He pulled out a watch just like yours."

"I wonder if he recognized me."

"I don't know, but I hope he shows up again." Sledge nodded and chuckled. "I'll get your watch back."

Blue shook his head. "He'll throw you back in jail if you mess with him."

Sledge leaned back and crossed his arms over his chest. "We're in Mexico. Remember?"

On the following Sunday, Sledge stepped off and disappeared behind the stage without a word, and left Blue to finish the last two songs. Blue walked alone to the cabin, thinking Sledge hit the tequila a little harder than usual. Maybe he ran to the outhouse.

A half-hour later, Blue worried. Sledge was not in the cabin, not in the outhouse, and didn't answer when Blue walked around outside and called him. But something else bothered Blue more.

Bowman had showed up again, sat at the same table, and stared at them most of the night.

Blue knocked on the back door of the cantina. Two minutes later, he knocked again.

"Cerrado," the owner yelled through the door. "Closed."

"It's Blue. I'm looking for Sledge."

The bolt slid with a squeak and a clunk. Hinges creaked, and the odor of kerosene lamps, tobacco smoke, fried onions, and stale beer smothered Blue as a cloud of smells scrambled for an exit. He stepped back as Pablo peered out at him.

The man seemed a mixture of old and young. Sometimes he looked thirty-five. Other times, sixty-five. Blue saw him as a good businessman who worked too hard for too many hours, and his ten-year-old daughter, a retarded child, wanted his constant attention. Once, on a slow day, Pablo wiped tears while he shared the story of how his wife died when his daughter was born.

"Now, Aunt Lolita cares for her much of the time. But Angela loves being with me. And I love spending time with my daughter."

Blue nodded. "I could tell, just watching you two together. I could see it in your face."

"Si." Pablo shrugged. "My family always told me my face tells the story of my life,"

Blue smiled. "Your family is right."

Pablo's face exaggerated everything he said. Forehead, cheeks, eyes, and brows had a routine that told his thoughts and how he felt about them. Lips, chin, and neck jumped into the act, changing shape and color like actors changing costumes.

Blue told Pablo about his life on the farm and why he became a hobo. The big, gentle man shook as he laughed about the name Possum Trot, Missouri.

Last Friday before the cantina opened, Blue returned to the club from the barbershop, and saw Angela playing out front with a ball. She spotted a kitten in the street, and ran after it. Truck tires screeched as the driver braked, and Angela screamed. Blue ran to her, grabbed her arm, and yanked her from the path of the truck. Pablo ran out in total panic. He too screamed as Blue carried his child back to safety. Minutes later, Pablo bawled and slobbered.

"I owe you my life, Señor Blue. You saved my daughter. I owe you everything."

"You owe me nothing, Pablo. I'm just glad I was there."

Pablo shook his head while his face disagreed with Blue. "I owe you more than I can pay." But his face brightened, danced, and grinned when he said, "It is a small gift, but I give you the guitar."

"The guitar? But—"

"I will pay the owner, Señor Blue. You must keep the guitar."

Now, at the back door, Pablo's tired face crumpled as he shook his head.

"Sledge is not here. I lock the front door. He yells at a man by the street."

"About what?"

Pablo shrugged.

"You haven't seen him since?"

Pablo shrugged again. "When I look out later? Nobody."

Out of habit, Blue felt behind him for the scissors, still amazed that the El Paso police gave them back. At the corner of the cantina, he looked around the front. Nothing moved, nothing made a sound on the dark street. Blue ventured out to the edge of the road for a closer look, but found nothing. When he started back, something from a few yards away caught his attention. Did it move? He stopped and waited. Was that a groan?

Blue stood, watched, and listened. While a shiver crawled up his spine, he insisted that his eyes focus better in the darkness. Someone across the street lit a lamp near a window. "Thank you," he mumbled, and stared harder at the form, or shadow, or whatever it was. Another groan? Yes. He eased closer, and the object moved. Blue called with a loud whisper, "Sledge?"

After another five steps, he bent over the moving, groaning form. "Oh God, Sledge. Are you okay?"

"No."

Something moved, and blocked the flicker of light from the window across the street. Blue sprang up, his hand closing on the scissors. A man approached, stopped three feet away, and slid his hand inside a pocket.

A half-hour later back in the cabin, Blue tended the knots on his friend's head.

"What the hell did he hit you with, Sledge?" Sledge groaned and mumbled while Blue washed blood from the scalp. "If it makes you feel any better, Bowman has a bigger knot on his noggin than you do. Scissor handles make a loud pop." Blue leaned closer to his friend. "I went through Bowman's pockets, but didn't find my watch."

Sledge answered only with another moan.

***

Next morning at the first hint of sunrise, a steady pounding on the cabin door dragged Blue from a deep sleep. With his eyes almost open, he stumbled to the door and leaned on it.

"Yeah?"

After a short argument, he opened the door for Pablo. The cantina owner spoke English with a heavy accent, but he knew the language well.

"Señor Blue, you must get out of Juarez. Go now."

Blue half turned, and motioned at Sledge in bed across the room.

"I'm not leaving him."

"El Paso policía and Federáles will come today. Go now. Or die in a Juarez jail."

"Sledge can't walk yet. I won't leave him."

"Señor Sledge will stay at mi casa until he is well. You must go." Pablo nodded at the corner of the room. "Take the guitar. Por favór."

***

Though he was in the boxcar alone, Blue sat up, unable to sleep. He talked aloud to himself.

"Why the hell am I going to Florida?" He shrugged and answered. "Because there is work there in the cane fields, in Belle Glade—at least that's what I heard. And because winter is coming."

The answer didn't sound convincing. But he was convinced the six dollars in his pocket wouldn't last through winter, and he told himself he couldn't hibernate. Maybe he'd like it there in Belle Glade.

"Maybe I'll get another job making music." He picked up his guitar. "Thank you, Pablo."

In two other boxcars on the way here, he entertained. Most rides were tiring and boring.

Hobos slept to pass the time. But Blue's boxcar concerts turned the trip into a party. Hobos clapped and cheered and whistled. He found the best audience he ever had.

Now, he knew one thing for certain. The next time he climbed into a boxcar, he'd pick one with people in it. In the years he'd been a hobo, he could remember only a few times when he traveled in a boxcar alone. With no one to talk to but himself, he slept more. But too much sleep made his mind feel fuzzy. When he had a good book, too much movement or too little light in the car interfered with reading. His mind wandered in every direction, and his thoughts often turned to women. What would life be like if he had one of his own? Traveling alone was good for only one thing—driving a man crazy.

Blue watched three hobos leap from the boxcar ahead as it passed the Belle Glade sign. He waited. After the long and tiring trip from Texas to Florida, he wanted to step down easy instead of jumping into the gravel. He saw no bulls from the boxcar doorway where he'd stood for the past half-hour and surveyed the countryside.

The wind through the door blew warm and humid. December in Belle Glade felt like June in Possum Trot. Blue mopped his brow with his sleeve while his gut told him this town was not like any place he'd been. The air became a strange combination of smells, some good, some not, like a fresh-baked apple pie too close to the barn.

On nearby tracks, burned stalks that looked like bamboo spilled over the tops of open train cars waiting for an engine. Children scrambled around the cars and chewed the fallen stalks. Away from the tracks, wreaths of red and green hung on a fence around the lot where a man sold Christmas trees. Alligators lay on the banks of canals that ran into the distance farther than Blue could see, and he promised himself to not go near them as the train rumbled to a stop.

***

An hour later, the wooden rails on the sides of the truck bed swayed and rattled as the truck stopped at the unpainted concrete-block building. On the way here from the downtown recruiting office, the truck driver yelled back at the men in the truck bed, and explained that it's *first come, first served* for the bunks in the barracks. Now, five men grabbed their suitcases, and jumped from the truck. Two trotted toward the building to get a choice bunk. The other three walked fast behind.

Blue didn't follow. He snatched up his bindle and guitar, jumped out of the truck, and stepped up on a stack of lumber to get a better look at the field where he assumed he would be cutting cane tomorrow.

Back home, he'd worked in corn crops where a single field might cover twenty acres, and stalks grew six to seven feet tall. A farmer would stand with his thumbs hooked in the straps of his overalls, sway back and forth in slow motion while he gazed at the crop he planted, hoed, and nurtured. He'd worried about too much rain and not enough rain, and dreaded an invasion of corn worms. He prayed for a healthy crop and, if you stood close, you would notice a nod of thanks to the Almighty. You'd see a twinkle in the farmer's eyes and a faint smile of pride on his face.

Blue figured the farmer had a right to be proud. But Blue had never seen a field like this, where stalks of cane grew ten to twelve feet high, and the rows stretched on for a quarter-mile. The field he stared at would cover thirty to forty acres.

***

Somebody banged on a bell that hung outside the barracks near Blue's bunk. He covered his ears and swore at the bell ringer for jarring people awake in the middle of the night. Men grunted, groaned, rubbed their faces, and sat up.

"3:45," a man mumbled. "Time to go."

On his first morning here, Blue learned why the men chose certain bunks and avoided others. In this bunk, he could expect the same alarm clock every morning, like someone screaming in his ear. Minutes later, he also knew his bunk was farther from the breakfast line than most others.

Blue heard men bragging about breakfast, about the scrambled eggs, salt pork, biscuits, and coffee. They had expected much less. He watched the clock on the wall as he stood in line twenty minutes to get his food. The wait left him barely ten minutes to finish his breakfast before rushing out to one of the trucks or trailers that would take him and sixty or seventy other men to the field.

They sat on the flatbed trailer, a few men wide awake and talking, others dozing, still others gazing at nothing or the morning's first hint of orange in the east, their hands in their pockets, with a leg resting on their cutting knife on the trailer floor. When the tractor pulled the trailer past the field near the barracks, Blue motioned at the field and spoke to anyone near him.

"I figured we'd be working there today."

A big, black man turned and looked at him. "Your first day on the job, huh?" Other men looked at Blue, laughed and nodded, and the man shook his head.

"I feel sorry for you, boy. You ain't never worked like you gonna work today."

Blue dug his hat from his back pocket, and put it on. He stared at the man.

"You don't know nothin' about me."

The black man put on his own hat, nodded slowly, and stared back.

"I know you ain't never cut cane. And you don't know what hard work is till you do."

Chapter Sixteen

The trailer stopped near a field of cane, and every man grumbled as he grabbed his knife and lunch bag, and slid off. Blue gazed at the stalks. They showed burn marks, and stood without tops and leaves that would get in the way of the harvest.

After ten minutes of instruction for cutting cane and stacking it the right way, Blue began to chop. He told himself the job was much easier than the man on the trailer claimed. An hour later, he brought the file from his pocket, and sat on the ground to sharpen his cane knife. The knife looked like a thin machete with a hook at the end of the blade. The cutters would chop a standing cane about four inches above the ground. With the hook, they'd pick up the fallen cane. Then they would cut it into smaller pieces and stack the pieces on the ground to be loaded onto a truck or trailer. The hook spared a lot of bending for the cutters. It also made the job faster and the boss happy. But the knife was not free.

Blue spent more than four dollars on the trip from El Paso, and checked in at the recruiting office in Belle Glade yesterday with less than two dollars in his pocket. The company charged a dollar for the cutting knife and fifty cents for the file, but agreed to deduct the charge from his pay. They would also deduct for meals, and he hoped he'd have money left each week after deductions. His mind drifted while he sharpened the knife.

Don't wanna hear 'bout aches and pain.
Get off yo' ass, and cut that cane.

The sharp words came from a man called the *pusher*. Blue heard about men like him from other cutters. The pusher walked the field and yelled at cutters to make sure they did the job right, and to keep them cutting and moving. Blue looked up and got to his feet. The tall man walked by, staring. Blue raised the large knife above his head. The pusher rested his hand on the pistol in his gun belt. Blue brought the knife down and sliced through a stalk with a soft thud. The pusher smiled, nodded, kept walking and kept talking.

Cut that cane. Mean and clean.
Stack it good. Don't let it lean.

After another four hours in the field, the pusher blew a whistle. Every man dropped his blade, dug the paper bag from the cloth bag that hung on his side or back, and sat on the ground to eat his Spam sandwich. Twenty minutes later, the whistle sounded again.

The cutter in the two rows next to Blue—the same big black man on the trailer this morning—drank from his canteen and peered between the stalks as Blue strained and grunted, and got to his feet. The man let go a loud belch. Then he picked up his knife, and hummed a tune. The hum got louder as he worked, and he began to sing. He turned his job into music, and swung the blade to strike the cane like a bass drum in rhythm with the song.

Blue swung the knife with his right hand while he gripped his shoulder with the other hand to lessen the pain. He'd cut a stalk in the row to his right, turn and cut another from the row to his left while he worked his way down the field that seemed to have no end. The knife felt like a twenty-pound weight. The soreness in his elbow and the cramp in the forearm made him groan each time the knife slammed into a stalk.

The ache in his neck brought tears with every turn of his head. The last time he'd been this tired was the first time he caught a train. His lungs needed more air then and now. But now, with every deep breath, the muscles along the right side of his back cried for relief.

The pusher walked in the row next to him.

Chop that cane. Johnny on the spot.
No more slackin'. Give her all you got.

Blue frowned and swung the knife. Another five hours to go.

***

Getting jolted out of bed at 3:45 was cruel punishment when pain and soreness robbed a man of sleep through most of the night. Blue jerked awake, and covered his ears to block out the bell's torment. He'd planned to be up before the wake-up call, dress in a hurry, wash his face at the pump just outside, and get near the front of the breakfast line. Maybe there'd be time for a second cup of coffee and a bit of a breather before loading his worn-out carcass onto the trailer. Without food he could not work, and now, he worried about having time to eat. He eased off the top bunk, and moaned when his feet touched the floor.

Throughout the barracks, men grunted, swore, and complained of aches and sore muscles much more than yesterday. His legs resisted. Lightning bolts of pain shot from his hips to his ankles as he forced on his pants. His arms, back, and neck put up a fight while he struggled and strained to fasten his shirt on the way to the breakfast line. Only one man now waited ahead of him.

Yesterday, men bragged about the breakfast. Blue heard none of that today. Maybe this was just a tough day to be cheerful. He grabbed a coffee, and sat to devour the biscuit with salt pork. No eggs today.

No trucks or trailers waited. Yesterday afternoon, men set fire to the field in front of the barracks, and the cutters would harvest that field today. They would need a few more minutes before the morning sun offered enough light to work the field, so they refreshed their canteens at the pump, and sat under the electric lights in front of the barracks and made their knives razor sharp. Every man wanted to earn bragging rights about his blade.

As the day wore on, Blue complained, if only to himself, convinced his right shoulder would fall off before he reached the end of his rows. His back demanded rest, but taking a break would bring the pusher, the same tall Jamaican he saw yesterday. Blue swore the man had a sixth sense about cutters when they stopped long enough to scratch. An hour ago when Blue paused to rub his shoulder, the man came marching down the next row, his hand on the gun butt. He wore a hard look and pointed at Blue while he delivered his singsong message.

Don't care 'bout sore muscles
Don't care 'bout aches
This here job ain't makin' cakes
It's burnin' cane, choppin' stalk
No time to rest. No time to squawk

***

From talk in the barracks, Blue knew the pusher would tolerate no downtime. He would tell the big boss, and the company would dock your pay in spite of the promise to pay cutters by the row. *Piece rate*, they called it. Two men swore they worked for three weeks, and were in debt to the company rather than getting paid.

After lunch—another Spam sandwich—the pusher came again. He stopped next to Blue and motioned toward the far end of the field.

"Follow me."

Blue followed. Sore muscles got a painful workout. He hurried to keep up, and questions flooded his mind during the ten-minute walk. *Was he being fired? Did he owe the company for meals? His bunk? Rides on the trailer? Wake-up service? Oh, God.*

On the road at the end of the field, the pusher motioned for Blue to join three men in the back of a truck. With Blue in, the man waved to the driver, and the truck rolled away.

Blue wanted to ask where they were going, and why. But yesterday morning on the trailer he showed his ignorance about harvesting sugar cane. Today, he would not ask.

The truck stopped at the end of a cane field when the passenger inside pointed out the window at a yellow flag tied to a stalk. The men in back stood up from the box they sat on, and opened the lid. Each man took a torch from the box. One man nodded at Blue, and then angled his head toward the other torch. Blue picked it up and followed the men to the field.

The tall, skinny man in charge bobbed his head when he walked. Blue stifled a laugh and wondered if the man's mother had been frightened by a crane.

The crane spread the other men along the edge of the field. They stood several rows apart with their unlit torches made from oil-soaked rags wrapped and tied at the end of a cane stalk.

They waited while two men at one corner of the field looked back and forth at each other and gazed at an orange windsock on a nearby pole. The sock flew straight, which told the men that the wind blew toward the other end of the field. But seconds later, the sock dropped and wiggled. The pattern repeated a dozen times or more while each man shook his head and shrugged. When it stayed straight for a minute or more, they agreed conditions were right.

Crane Man brought a box of long matches from a leather bag that hung on his belt. Blue wondered if he would strike the match with his beak, but the man struck it with his thumbnail, and lit the other man's torch. Along the edge of the field, the men met to light one torch from another and then hurried back to their places.

From his corner of the field, Blue copied the other men; set fire to the leaves on the stalks along the edge, and threw his torch into the field. Like a pile of dry twigs, the end of the field was ablaze within seconds.

"Hey." Someone from behind yelled, and Blue turned to see a man waving at him to follow the others to the truck. Blue followed, and when his feet hit the truck bed floor, the truck sprang forward.

Flames leaped thirty feet high. The windsock stood straight, and a strong breeze carried fire through the rows of sugar cane while the truck rounded the corner of the field and raced toward the far end. Faces grew hot and red. Men stared wide-eyed. Fire popped, roared, and crackled, while it destroyed leaves, weeds, and brush. Heavy gray-white clouds of smoke carried a smell like burned beans, and shut out the sun. Blue recalled a wheat-field fire from years ago, but had never seen a fire like this.

At the end of the cane field, the truck turned away from the fire and stopped. The two men in the cab jumped out, stood and watched. The men in the bed kept their seats. Everyone stared at the blaze.

"It's better than a fireworks show," one said. Another man nudged Blue.

"People around here say that's what hell is made of—burning sugar cane."

Blue half smiled but did not reply. The man pointed at the ground where the rows ended.

"Watch what happens."

Blue stared where the man pointed. "Lots of birds. They got a good reason to leave."

The man grinned. "Keep watchin'."

Blue watched. Seconds later, a small deer ran from the field. Then another. Rabbits followed. Dozens of rats and mice scurried across the ground. More birds, grasshoppers, lizards, and snakes streamed out of the blazing cane.

Blue nodded. "They all gotta get out."

The other man shook his head. "Only the fast ones."

As he said the words, a man and a woman with light brown skin, each wearing only a rag tied around the waist, ran out of the field. A cloth bag hung on the man's shoulder. Behind him, the woman ran with something bundled in her arms.

Blue snapped his head around. "What the hell?"

The man shrugged. "Everbody's gotta live somewhere."

"I know… but…"

"Ain't the first ones I've seen come out of a cane field."

"Where will they go?"

"Most likely…" the man pointed to the next green cane field down the road, "… right there. Same place as all them other critters."

"Yeah, but when that field gets burned…"

The man nodded. "Yep." He looked at Blue. "I never said any of them was smart."

Blue turned up his hands and cocked his head. "Can't we do something?"

The man snorted. "They'd kill you before you found 'em."

Blue's mouth hung open. Within minutes, the fire reached the end of the quarter-mile-long rows of sugar cane.

Chapter Seventeen

On Saturdays, the workday ended at four o'clock, and every man lined up at the front of the barracks to get paid. Two men sat at tables and handled the payout while a man with a holstered gun stood between the tables and glared at everyone who looked his way. When a cutter stepped to the table, the payer checked his name off the list and handed him meal tickets for the coming week. From the cutter's remaining pay, the company man subtracted what the worker owed from the previous week. Sometimes, a man broke even. Other times, he owed the company. But most men got a few coins to spend or waste from one Saturday till the next. Most men with coins were ready for a party.

The plantation owner had a strict rule against booze in the barracks. Most of the seventy-two residents would admit they didn't obey the rule, but said they, at least, respected it. So they hid their liquor under a bunk or in a suitcase to show their respect.

Rum made from sugar cane was cheap and easy to find. Known as Nelson's blood, kill-devil, demon water, and many other names, rum had been around since pirates brought it to the new country from nearby islands, and was often used as money.

No matter what they called it, rum was the drink of choice at the barracks, and at least half the men got drunk every Saturday night. For most, it was a happy drunk where men would slap each other on the back and yell, "Ahoy, Mate," or, "Shiver me timbers." And at least once every hour they would be singing, "Sixteen men on a dead man's chest. Yo-ho-ho, and a bottle of rum."

Blue remembered the words from Treasure Island, a favorite book he read in school. He doubted that most men here read that book, or any other book. They simply repeated what they heard from other men. But he decided it didn't matter. It made them happy until they woke up on Sunday morning.

When the preacher showed up every Sunday and yelled a sermon at them about the evils of alcohol and gambling, they'd sit bleary-eyed, nursing a hangover along with black eyes and busted lips from last night's fight, and swear to each other it would never happen again. When the preacher left, they'd cheat at card games to rob their friends of money, rings, watches, and meal tickets. And always, their rum.

Sundays with the preacher reminded Blue of the El Paso jail, except the inmates seemed easier to trust. He found little excitement in barracks booze parties, stealing money, and fighting with friends. Instead of drinking, he'd dig his guitar from under the bunk and play a few tunes for the men. They would throw tips in his cup, but they would take it back when they needed more money for poker games. After a month on the plantation, he needed to find a different crowd.

***

Everyone in Clewiston and Belle Glade knew the work and pay schedules for the cane plantations and sugar mills. By five o'clock on Saturday, a man named Billy would park his pickup truck near the barracks where Blue lived. When the truck bed filled with men, he'd give them a ride to *The Billy*

Club, a business he owned in Belle Glade. Before he left, he would yell back at the men and repeat the same line every week.

"You can get anything you want in Belle Glade. But if you get something you don't want, I ain't paying your doctor bill."

The line always made the men laugh, and put them in the mood for a party.

Blue found Saturday nights in Belle Glade unique, like everything else he'd learned about the city and the countryside beyond. Cafés, pawn shops, movie theaters, strip clubs, and bawdy houses lined the downtown streets. In any café, strip club, or cathouse in town, a customer could get a drink. In spite of prohibition, the town never ran dry, and the mayor's pockets never ran empty.

When the crowd hit town, it moved as a group, like a flock of birds moving from one tree to another. On Saturday nights, men flooded the cafés for supper, and for most men, it was the only decent meal of the week. Two hours later, the cafés would be nearly empty. The flock moved from one club to another in search of the best party, and that meant the clubs with the best entertainment.

Blue soon discovered that most singers and music entertainers in town were Islanders. They were good at what they did, but the second time he went to The Billy Club, Blue took his guitar, set up a tip jar, and performed his own kind of music for three hours. People on the street stopped to listen, walked in, spent money, applauded, and left tips.

At the end of his performance, the tip jar held more money than Blue made in a full day chopping cane. And the guitar pick weighed much less than a cutting knife.

On the following Friday, Blue worked harder than he ever had. He wanted to impress the pusher. The man walked by twice before lunch. The first time, he nodded but didn't slow down. Blue took that as a good sign. The second time, he smiled as he nodded, but still did not change his pace. When he came again two hours after lunch, Blue held up his hand. When the man stopped, Blue said, "Hope you're having a good day, sir." The pusher gave a half nod as his eyes burrowed into Blue, but he did not speak.

"Sir, I have some business in town to take care of. I need to leave today at four o'clock."

The steely-eyed expression never left the man's face. "Saturday is tomorrow. Today, we work till six."

"Yes, I know. But…"

The pusher smiled. His eyes grew wide. He shook his head, and began his poetry as he walked away.

The boy's tellin' me he's got a hot date
Wants a day off. But the cane won't wait
Come six o'clock he'll be workin' still
The cane must be cut; must go to the mill

***

Blue heard a rustle and looked up. The big black man watched him between the parted stalks of his own row. But the man turned his attention toward the pusher while the pusher laughed as he neared the end of the rows and grew smaller.

On Saturday after work, Blue caught a ride back to The Billy Club. Billy said nothing to him in front of the other men in the truck. But Blue performed again at the club, and Billy came to shake hands when Blue took a break.

"Good show, Blue. What happened last night? I was there at five to pick you up." Blue explained. Billy nodded. "I been here a long time, and I know how the plantations operate. They think they own you. And they do… if you let them get away with it."

"Hacking cane ain't my favorite hobby. If I can play here every weekend, I'll tell them I quit, and go live at the local jungle."

Billy nodded again, stopped and leaned toward Blue. "Watch your step."

After work on the following Saturday, Blue left his cutting knife and file under his bunk, and returned for his pay, making sure he was last in the payday line. The man seated at the table picked up his glasses and looked up at Blue before he put them on. In front of him on the table, a board displayed the name *Leonard*.

Without speaking, Leonard totaled Blue's pay for the week, handed him meal tickets for the next week, and eight quarters. Blue dropped the quarters in his pocket, and dropped the meal tickets on the table.

"I won't need these. This is my last day."

The man with the gun cracked his knuckles while the man at the table gazed at the paper and touched Blue's name with the tip of his pencil. He did not look up as he spoke.

"Blue Bailey." He cleared his throat and pushed the meal tickets back toward Blue. "You signed a contract that binds you to the company for another six weeks."

Blue took a deep breath and let it go. "You can't force me to work here. That ain't legal. I quit."

The man shrugged and looked up. "Your bunk number?"

"Seventy-two."

The man wrote the number beside Blue's name and looked up.

"Wait here."

He picked up his cashbox and papers, scooped up the *Leonard* sign and disappeared into the office behind him.

Blue fidgeted, muttered to himself, and glanced at the wall clock again and again, convinced the man would not come back. Blue turned to leave, but stopped and stared when he saw the big black man from the cane field who stood by the front doorway and watched him. Blue wanted to talk to the man, but as he turned toward him, Leonard came out of the office. He stopped at the table, his gaze fixed on Blue's chest instead of his face.

"You have to sign a resignation." He jerked his head toward the office. "See Miss Grizzle." Leonard left.

Blue said hello, and closed the office door behind him. He looked around and called again.

"Hello, anybody here?"

He sat at a chair in front of a desk and waited. Nothing told him who the desk belonged to, but it was the only one in the room. Minutes later, a big woman lumbered through a back door. Her heavy shoes clunked on the wood floor of the office while she trudged forward and plopped behind the desk. With the backs of her pudgy hands, she pushed her large breasts apart and looked down between them at an open book that lay flat in front of her.

"Blue Bailey?"

"Yes, Ma'am."

"Don't call me Ma'am."

"Sorry, Ma'am… I mean, uh… sorry."

The breasts slapped together as she released them. For the first time, her gray eyes met his blue eyes, but the gray eyes appeared unfocused, and Miss Grizzle's face showed no expression.

"You owe the company four dollars and sixty-five cents."

Blue leaned forward with a mixed look of anger, confusion, and surprise. "I owe the company?"

She gave a slight nod, spread her breasts again, and looked down at the book. "Cutting knife, file, bunk, clean sheets, extra meal tickets. Four dollars and sixty-five cents."

"I already paid for the knife and file. I never got extra meal tickets, and I washed my own sheets. If anything, the company owes me."

The woman's face still showed no expression. "You must pay up before you can leave."

Blue stood, leaned across the desk, and snarled. "You're out of your monkey ass mind." Then he yelled. "Ma'am."

Miss Grizzle's face now showed expression. She leaned back and grabbed at a paperweight on her desk. Blue whirled and went for the door. The steel paperweight crashed against the doorframe an inch from his head. Blue left the office without saying goodbye.

Two minutes later, the heat of anger rose from his chest and flooded his face while he stared at his bunk, stripped of everything. The mattress and sheets did not matter, but his knife and file, his bindle and guitar had disappeared along with them.

He swore and turned as the man from the pay table walked toward the bunk. The man with the gun walked beside him.

"You have ten minutes," Leonard told Blue.

"Ten minutes for what?"

"Return the mattress and sheets, or pay for them."

Blue looked around at the crowd beginning to form, and shook his head.

Gun Man gave Blue a hard look and drummed his fingers on the butt of his gun when Blue shook his fist at Leonard. Blue ignored him and yelled at Leonard. "You're crazy as hell if you think I'm gonna pay you for the stuff you stole, including my own stuff."

Leonard's big ears turned red, but he kept calm, drew out his watch and turned its face toward Blue.

"Nine minutes."

Blue smiled. He slapped his right hip. The scissors were still there, but he knew they would be gone if he'd left them at his bunk.

"Okay, I'll be back in eight minutes." He took off in a dead run toward the front door.

Chapter Eighteen

Gun Man drew his weapon and pointed it at Blue's back. Leonard jerked his head around, saw the crowd of men, and brought his hand down easy on the gun. He pushed the barrel toward the floor. The would-be shooter wore a frown while Leonard shook his head.

A buzz erupted throughout the barracks. Everyone talked at the same time and watched Blue fly through the front door. Two men waiting outside the door sprang toward him, but Blue left them behind as he darted left and sprinted toward the gate. From 4:00 p.m. Saturday till midnight Sunday, the gate for the eight-feet-tall, chain-link fence remained open, and seldom had a guard. But now, a man on Blue's left, a man he recognized as a company man, ran alongside the fence toward the open gate. He had a shorter distance to the gate than Blue, but the man looked too heavy to keep up his pace.

On Blue's right, another man ran toward the gate. Blue knew he had to beat both men. The man on the right appeared farther away, but he looked fit and confident, his long strides eating up the distance. Each time Blue looked at him, the man looked back, and each man pushed a bit harder. His face said he was measuring Blue's determination to win.

Blue couldn't know what motivated that man, but he knew his own reason to reach the gate first, and his mind flashed back to a race that now seemed so long ago. He could still see the brakeman on the deck of the caboose, the man who taunted him while the train went north without him. If only he had run faster, fast enough to catch the train on his first try, he would have been on board with his two best friends, Halo and Martin, friends he had not seen in almost three years.

Blue could not guess what would happen if he lost this race today. But, like that train, he knew there could be no second chances. Though the gate could now be no more than thirty seconds away, Blue's legs began to tire. Muscles needed more oxygen, lungs ached, and his breath grew heavier while his heart tried to hammer its way out of his chest.

The man on Blue's left limped toward the gate with one hand against the fence and the other over his chest. Blue glanced again at the man on his right. He looked to be about Blue's age, but the man was not a cane cutter. He did not have the weeks of conditioning and muscle building that cutters endured. He had no experience at the hardest job in the world. Blue saw an open mouth and red face. He saw legs moving slower. But it was the slow wag of the man's head, the telltale sign of defeat that told Blue he could win. The new confidence flooded Blue's lungs with oxygen, gave his heart new strength, shot new energy through his legs. As the other man slowed, Blue ran faster. He knew he had won.

With the gate only a few steps away, Blue's face changed from a look of victory to the fear of losing. A man from outside the gate ran toward him, grabbed the gate and swung it. Blue tried to stop fast enough to keep from crashing into the gate, but another man appeared, and a large black hand reached over the other man's head from behind, grabbed the gate and held it open.

The company men yelled at each other as Blue ran through to the other side of the fence. The black man scrambled inside the gate and slammed it shut. He looked through at Blue and pointed left.

"Run to the truck."

"Thank you, my friend," Blue called over his shoulder as he rounded the corner of the fence. His mind was a blur. He did not understand how or why the big black man got involved. The two worked side by side but seldom spoke. But Blue was now outside the fence, and he could see a pickup truck waiting in the distance, exhaust rushing from the tailpipe.

He glanced through the fence and saw a lot of commotion as he ran. People watched him, pointed, and yelled. One man clapped and yelled, "Run Blue, run." Someone hit the man with a club, and he went down. Ahead, something poked through the fence. Three seconds later, Blue knew it was a rifle barrel, and he now ran faster than he had ever moved on his own two feet, knowing a moving target would be harder to hit.

Blue's back stiffened at the sound of the rifle. A second later, the bullet thudded into the rear fender of the truck. Fear gripped him. If they could scare away the driver or cripple the truck, Blue had no chance.

The truck now moved back toward him as Blue closed in on his last hope of escape. Only a few more steps, but with the truck coming toward him as he ran toward the truck, his timing had to be perfect. Otherwise, he'd die from a rifle shot, or be crushed beneath the wheels.

At ten feet away, he leaped, caught the top of the tailgate and swung over. The truck stopped while gears made grinding noises and tires spun.

When Blue's feet made a loud thump on the floor of the truck bed, the truck leaped forward.

The rifle cracked again. The driver swore and jerked the wheel back and forth to make the truck sway. "Hang on," he screamed. He made a sharp right turn onto a road lined by tall palm trees that would shield them from the gunfire. Midway through the turn, another shot ricocheted off the rail of the truck bed, and the truck's rear window exploded. Splinters of glass showered the inside of the truck and scattered over the bed. Blue felt a sharp pain on his cheek, and screamed, "Oh damn, I'm hit."

He ran his hand across his face expecting to find a bullet lodged in his cheek. He picked out only a small sliver of glass and found a single drop of blood. He poked his head through the shattered window.

"I'm sorry, sir. Just a little piece of glass." The driver turned to look at him, and Blue said, "Billy? I didn't know that was you behind the wheel."

Billy snorted. "You know somebody else as crazy as me?" He stopped the truck and looked back. "Help me clean the glass out of this seat, and you can ride up here. I don't think anybody will follow us." He pulled a large revolver from under the seat. "If they do, I'll give them a taste of this."

Giant palm trees lined the gravel road, their trunks giving the appearance of concrete fence posts that stretched thirty to forty feet high before sprouting limbs and leaves that looked like open umbrellas. Sunlight flickered between the palms as the truck sped past. Blue had lots of questions, and Billy explained the past few days.

"You told me you were leaving the sugar plantation. I figured it would be on payday, and I knew the bosses wouldn't like it. Happy came into the Club after I talked to you last time and—"

"Happy?"

"Yeah, the big man who helped you get out the gate."

"I never knew his name."

"Well, he knows yours, and he agreed to help. But now, you've got to get out of Belle Glade. It ain't safe for you to stay."

Chapter Nineteen

The screech of steel wheels on steel rails grated down the line of cars, and the train jerked as it slowed. From the boxcar doorway, Blue searched the Possum Trot countryside and remembered his sixteenth birthday when he and Halo sat by the campfire and Halo said, "One day you'll leave home. A month later, you'll be sorry as hell."

That was three years ago. Blue never missed this place and had no regrets about leaving. But Halo also said, "A year down the road, no matter where you are or who you're with—you'll know for the first time that your life belongs to you." Like most things, Halo had been right about that.

Blue glanced down at his bindle and nodded. *A good blanket, food, and supplies.* Then he looked out at the world beyond the tracks. *Friends and freedom.* He'd had some tough times but came through them tougher and smarter. After Belle Glade, he spent a few months in Homestead, Florida. The weather was perfect there in the winter, and he found work on the huge farms. Picking tomatoes was not fun. Grading and bagging potatoes at the packing house was a tedious, boring job, but it was better than harvesting them in Alabama. His bindle was now the best ever. And… he had a few bucks in his pocket.

Life was better now except… his chest grew tight as he thought about his Martin guitar. Since it disappeared he'd played other guitars, one at the blind pig in Biloxi, and for a few weeks he had the one Pablo gave him. But his beautiful old Martin had been a dear friend, and he wondered if he would ever own another.

The train rolled slower, and Blue grabbed his bindle. He often strapped it on his back before he left the boxcar. Once he held it in his hand while he bailed out. But only once. The extra weight on one side threw him off balance, and the scars on his knees were a good reminder.

Today, he tossed out the pack and leaped out after it. Like a hundred times before, he hit the ground running, and then slowed to a walk as he turned and went back for his pack. Other hobos made thumping and crunching sounds around him as they flew out of a dozen cars and landed on the gravel.

Possum Trot brought an uneasy feeling to his gut. It had no reason to be there, he told himself. But it was. Maybe it was the guilt he sometimes felt about leaving his mother without saying goodbye. For the past three weeks, his conscience pushed him to come back, just for a day or two. She was the reason he was here.

His head hung down and he stared at the ground while he walked and thought. Tomorrow, he'd find Mama. She'd stand with her hands on her hips and glare at him. Her eyes would show the anger at her son. But not for long. The eyes would fill with tears of joy that he was back. He and Mama would sit, hold hands, and talk. He would give her a kiss and a big hug and slip a dollar into her apron pocket. He shook his head. No, he would give her the two-dollar bill he'd been saving because she thought two-dollar bills were lucky. She would treasure it.

To make the day complete, he'd tell his worthless father to go to hell, and then he'd walk back to the jungle and dine out with the boys.

Maybe that would get rid of the gnawing in his gut.

"Hello, Blue. Long time, no see."

Blue's head snapped up. A man waved and came toward him. Blue recognized the hobo not because of what he saw, but what he didn't see. The man had no more than a half-dozen teeth scattered throughout his mouth. Like so many other men, his nickname didn't earn him any bragging rights, but it was a good fit.

"Hey, Snag." Blue held out his hand. "How the hell are you? Always good to see a friend."

"Same here. But you caught me at a bad time." He angled his head toward the bindle hanging on his shoulder and then toward the tracks. "I'm catchin' out." His crooked smile showed off two teeth together at one side of his face. Then the smile left. "I'm just sorry about your reason for being here."

Blue's forehead wrinkled. "You are?"

"Yeah, I mean… about your daddy. Ain't you here for the funeral?"

"I uh, I don't know what you're talking about." Blue wagged his head.

Snag stood with his mouth open and his eyes wide. "Oh, damn, Blue." His expression changed to sympathy as he wiped his hand across his face. "I just figured you knowed about it. I'm awful sorry."

Blue squeezed the man's shoulder. "It's all right. Just tell me what happened."

"I don't rightly know. I heard that a farmer come here this morning and said your pa had an accident yesterday while he was workin'. The farmer was hoping somebody could find you and let you know. So when you showed up, I uh…"

"What's the farmer's name?"

Snag's shoulders rose and fell. "Nobody

said."

"You sure he was talking about me? About my father?"

"You the only Blue I know."

"I'll ask around."

Snag left to catch his train. Blue shook his head, and while his feet moved toward the jungle, his mind rejected the story. *A man was killed while working? Had to be someone else's father.*

The Possum Trot jungle had more residents now than Blue remembered from three years ago, but little else had changed. The cast-iron kettle still hung in the same spot, though there was no one named Shorty who tended the fire. Blue's heart felt a sudden pang. He missed his old friend.

"I'm Chigger, the kettle boss," the man by the pot said. "Our mulligan might not be the best you ever had. But it ain't bad."

"I got nothing to throw in the pot, Chigger, but I got a few coins for coffee."

Chigger pointed to the red Hills Bros. coffee can on a log near the kettle. "Just toss in a nickel or two, and we're squared away."

The two men stood near the kettle and sipped stew and coffee while other bo's came by to say hello. Blue knew some of them from other camps, but they didn't stay around to talk. When he asked, some said Snag told them about Blue's father, but that's all they knew. Most men just offered a polite hello and moved away.

When Chigger and Blue were alone again, Chigger said, "Blue, I'm filling in for Shorty at the kettle. When he's here, it's all his."

"I know Shorty. When's the last time he was here?"

"This morning. He's the one the farmer

talked to about your pa. Shorty told Snag to tell everybody. When Snag told me, I came here to handle the pot, and then Shorty took off for Dyersburg looking for you."

"I've never even been to Dyersburg."

"Me neither. If you want to talk to Shorty, he'll likely be back in the morning."

***

Blue's world had changed, and getting comfortable in his bedroll seemed a lost cause. Nagging questions plagued him during the night. Would his mother beg him to stay? Could he leave her all alone? He told himself he would stay with her a year. Then he'd see.

With that settled, he finally slept. Yet it seemed only minutes later Blue moaned and covered his eyes when early-morning sunlight penetrated his eyelids.

He forced his body out of the bedroll and rubbed his face. He'd go to the kettle, stoke the fire, make a pot of coffee, and wait for Shorty to show. But when he stumbled into the circle of logs around the kettle, he saw the fire already stoked, heard the gurgling, and caught the smell of fresh coffee. *Somebody* was an angel.

"Blue, is that you?" A short man with a stir stick shielded his eyes and poked his head around the kettle. Shorty was always up before the sun.

"That's me. Is that you, Shorty?" Blue stepped toward him and shook hands. "Good to see you."

Shorty angled his head toward the coffee pot. "I got a fresh cup o' mud for a good friend."

Blue unhooked the cup from his belt and filled it. "Just what I need. You're a saint."

Shorty laughed as he looked at the sky. “Never heard of Saint Shorty, but I’ll take that as a compliment.” The two men were silent while Shorty stirred the big pot of stew. Then he stopped, looked at Blue, and shook his head. “Well, since you’re here, I reckon you heard the bad news.”

After a long swallow of coffee, Blue said, “Didn’t know anything till I got here yesterday and caught Snag on his way out. Then I saw Chigger over here and he told me you went to Dyersburg. I’m grateful to you, Shorty.”

“You’re here. That’s all that matters.” Shorty grinned while he stirred the stew again. “Your dogs barkin’?”

Blue smiled, nodded, and rubbed his belly. “Oh yeah. Stew’s ready?”

Shorty took a small dip from the kettle, and the steam flew sideways when he blew across the top of his cup. He spooned out a sample, blew across the spoon and then sipped the stew. He nodded as he swallowed. “I’d say she’s ready.”

“Sure smells good.” Blue finished his coffee, dipped his cup into the kettle, and pulled a spoon from his pocket.

“Fuzzy helped a farmer butcher some hogs yesterday,” Shorty said, “and he brought us a coffee can full of brains. They make the stew thicker and give it a good meaty taste.”

The two men ate in silence until Shorty pulled out his watch and said, “The hungry crowd’ll be here in a few minutes.”

Blue ignored him. “Who was the farmer you talked to yesterday?”

“Johnny Rodman.”

“I know him. What happened?”

“He didn’t say. It was like he couldn’t talk

about it. Just a bad accident. But he said the funeral's today, this afternoon. I don't remember what time. Did Snag tell you?"

"No. He just said my paw got killed while he was working. I thought about it all night. I guess I'll stay with my mother for a while and then see what happens."

Shorty's forehead wrinkled. His eyes lost focus and his face went pale. He wagged his head, stepped forward and gripped Blue's wrist. "Your paw? Did Snag say your paw was killed?"

Blue leaned closer and stared. His words were slow. "That's... that's what he said. My paw was killed."

Shorty released Blue's wrist and turned away, still shaking his head. "Oh God. Blue, I'm uh... I'm awful sorry." He turned to face Blue. "Snag got it wrong. It wasn't your paw." He walked to the other side of the pot and turned his back.

"Whose paw was it?"

Shorty shook his head but did not turn around. Blue sat his cup on a log and walked up behind him.

"Shorty, what is it, man?" Blue caught the man's shoulder, turned him and saw that his eyes were red and wet. "Shorty, look at me. What's wrong?"

Shorty swallowed hard. "It wasn't your..." He drew a ragged breath. "It wasn't your paw, Blue. It was... it was your maw. Your mother." He took off his cap and ran his fingers through his hair. "I didn't know her, but... I'm sorry, Blue. I'm awful sorry."

Hot tears sprang to Blue's eyes. His face lost color as he shook his head. "My mother? My...?" He went back to the log and sat down hard. His cup and spoon clattered to the ground, spilling stew. He covered his face and shivered.

When he heard Shorty stirring the kettle, Blue uncovered his face. The silence in the jungle made him look around at the somber faces of men who stood with their arms folded, and watched him. He trembled from a sudden chill while he picked up his cup and spoon. Then he stood, shook his head from side to side and gritted his teeth. His pulse pounded in his temples.

"My mother. Why her? Why couldn't it have been my old man? Does anybody know if he's still alive?" He looked around, but saw only shrugs and shaking heads.

Chapter Twenty

The morning scattered streaks of sunlight among the trees, but most of the trail was shaded. June could be hot in Possum Trot, Blue remembered, while he picked his way along the same path he walked the day he left, when he just wanted to get away. This time, he was going the other direction. And this time he had a score to settle.

Today, Blue crawled out of his bedroll at the first hint of daybreak and changed into his spare set of clothes. He had the whole day planned. But by the time the day offered enough light to leave the jungle, the news from Shorty hit him like a club between the eyes and weighed on his shoulders like a sack full of rocks. As Blue left the jungle, Shorty stopped him, and swallowed hard. Tears formed in the man's eyes.

"Blue, I hate funerals as much as any man I know. But I'll go with you if you need some company."

Blue turned down the offer. He didn't want Shorty or anyone else to see him beat the hell out of his own father.

The easy trail gave him too much time to think of the past, and memories of his sister haunted him once again. He could never forgive the old man, and figured he was probably the reason Mama was dead.

***

The Rodman farm was an hour's walk from the jungle as Blue recalled, and he would go there first to find out how his mother died. Even if his dear sweet daddy was not involved, Blue decided he'd follow him home, or wherever, after the funeral. Before this day was over, the old man would know how his own son felt about him.

At the edge of the woods, Blue rested and looked out over the countryside. The land had not changed. But memories touched a treasured place in his heart, and he knew this land had become a part of him. He breathed deep and followed the trail through the long, shallow valley with its rolling hills of grass, the Rodman dairy farm. He paused again at the top of the third rise to take in the view of the lightning rods and tarnished windcock on the tin roof of the giant, faded red barn below, where his mother once worked as a milkmaid.

Blue never had a reason to keep track of how many cows he'd milked in his lifetime, or how many times he'd milked the same cow. But he liked the taste of the rich, foamy milk, and the farmer often sent him home with a quart for his family.

The chore had left no fond memories for him, but he always liked hearing his mother talk about her first job, and it made him feel close to her to see the gleam in her eyes.

When Blue would ask, Mama would tell him how the cows had to be milked twice a day, every day of the year. So a girl got a day off only when she brought someone with experience to fill in for her. In winter, most girls milked before school, and again before supper. They shivered in the freezing winds and snow that blew through the barn. They opened their mouths wide and breathed on their cracked and bleeding fingers to keep them warm, and they soon learned that a cow might kick if icy fingers gripped an udder.

Summers were worse. Milkmaids itched and

scratched in the heat and humidity. Sweat ran down their backs, down their legs, and down their faces, and burned their eyes.

Winter and summer, hardwood stools and heavy milk pails gave the girls backaches, leg cramps, and sore muscles. Bonnie's friend, Juanita, suffered a broken arm when a cow in a bad mood kicked her. Even one in a good mood might slap the milkmaid's face with a tail full of manure. The battle with the cows never ended. And the stink never left the barn.

"Sometimes we smelled as bad as the cows," Mama would say. She'd smile, shake her head, and wrinkle her nose. "We'd air out a bit while we walked home."

Blue loved the stories, and knew his mother didn't mean them as a complaint. They were all just part of the job, a job she was proud of because she could support herself from age twelve.

Blue also knew the old barn was part of the story of how he came to be, though that story was not one he heard from his parents. He picked it up in scattered slurs and whispers from others as he grew. By the time he was a teenager, the story was easy to put together.

When the barn boss was not around, a handsome, smooth-talking man who peddled rotgut whiskey hung out near the barn and flirted with the milkmaids. Bonnie was his favorite, and he knocked her up before she turned sixteen.

Though he was a deadbeat, and twelve years older, Bonnie married the man. Everyone agreed it was the only decent thing for a woman to do. The child has to have a name, they said.

***

Johnny Rodman stood near the steps on the back

porch of his faded, two-story farmhouse with a full water bucket and a red-and-white can of Colgate toothpowder on a small table next to him. He pulled a toothbrush from the bib pocket of his overalls and sprinkled the brush with the powder. The white foam oozed between his lips and ran down his chin while he worked the brush over and around his teeth.

Blue watched from a few feet away, not sure if Mister Rodman had seen him come into the yard. Teeth brushing was getting to be a weekly habit for some folks, most often on a Saturday morning before they went into town. Maybe this was a special brushing today because of the funeral. If that was the case, Blue did not want to interrupt.

The white foam mixed with the blood from his gums and made a pink splat when Rodman leaned over the edge of the porch and spewed it to the ground. Three chickens darted for it and stabbed their beaks into the splat. Rodman took a dipper from the bucket. His cheeks bulged when he sucked them full of water and swished it around in his mouth. He spat again, turning his head to avoid hitting the chickens. His eyes grew wide when he saw his visitor. He dropped the dipper back into the bucket, wiped his mouth on his sleeve, and squinted.

"If you're here to buy milk, young man, you'll have to come back in a couple hours. I've got a funeral to go to in a short while."

"Mister Rodman, I'm Blue Bailey. Bonnie Bailey was my mother."

"Oh my word." Johnny Rodman shook his head. Then he waved Blue forward. "Of course. Come on up." As Blue stepped onto the porch, the man offered his hand. "Ain't seen you in quite a spell. You're all growed up now." The man pulled two wicker chairs away from the wall of the house and motioned for Blue to sit.

"The missus likely knows you're here," he said. "She ain't ill-mannered, but I reckon she might be too busy to come out and say a proper greeting."

Blue knew the man was covering for her. He remembered how shy she was around everyone outside of family.

After Blue was seated, Rodman sat in the other chair and leaned toward him. "I feel real bad about your mama, Blue. God knows I do." He sat up in his chair. "She was a good woman. And I've knowed her since she was a youngun."

Blue nodded. "She always thought highly of you too. I just wish I could've seen her one more time. It's been three years."

Rodman folded his hands. He leaned forward again and stared into Blue's eyes. "Maybe I ain't the right one to tell you this, Blue, but there's something you ought to know. It about drove that poor woman crazy when you took off the way you did. Your mama didn't deserve that." He leaned back in his chair as if waiting for Blue to say something.

Blue's chest tightened. He propped his elbows on his knees and rested his head in his hands. After staring at the floor in a long moment of silence, he said, "I got no regrets about leaving but I guess I did it the wrong way. I wanted to tell her I'm sorry, but—"

"Yep. That's the way it goes, son. We always seem to wait too long to tell somebody we're sorry."

Blue shook his head, sat up, and looked at the man. "Can you tell me what happened?"

"I can. But it ain't pretty." He looked at Blue and waited.

"I really want to know, Mister Rodman."

"Well now, I ain't Mister Rodman. I'm Johnny. My daddy died before you was even born. You know what it's like trying to run a business..." he looked out over the valley and swept his arm in a wide arc, "... when you ain't but seventeen? Life got mighty testy there for a long time, and I..." He stopped and shook his head. "I don't mean to bellyache about it."

He drew a long breath and started again. "But anyhow, I was on the way to town in my truck and I seen something off the side of the road that looked like a woman on the ground. I stopped and got out, and before I even got to it, I knowed what it was. I got some trees here on the property that fell during the last bad storm we had, and your mama... she'd been out by herself and was chopping firewood. Well, she, uh... she'd split her foot wide open with that big ol' double-blade axe of hers. It was..." He stopped, covered his eyes and shook his head. After a deep breath, he dropped his hand. "It was still in her foot, and I pulled it out, but there was... there was nothing anybody could do. She was laying in a pool of blood and I think she'd been dead for quite a spell."

Rodman shuddered, and then stood and walked to the bucket. He filled the dipper and offered it to his guest. "It's good water and it's cool." Blue raised his hand and shook his head. Rodman slurped down the water, tossed the dipper into the bucket, and clamped his hand on Blue's shoulder from behind.

"I'm sorry, Blue. That's a really awful thing to happen, but it did." He moved around in front of

Blue. "The funeral's at eleven over at the church." He pulled a watch from his pocket. "A bit over an hour from now."

When Blue stood to leave, Rodman stood, cocked his head, and leaned toward him. "I'm awful sorry, Blue. Awful sorry about all this." He laid his hand on Blue's shoulder again. "It's about a mile. If you want to ride with me and the missus, you're welcome."

Blue wiped sweat from his face and shook his head. "I appreciate the offer, but I gotta do some thinking about things. I'll just walk to the church." He left the porch and headed toward the road, a lump growing in his throat, his eyes growing wet. He stopped and turned when Johnny Rodman called out behind him.

"You know, Blue, a woman oughta never have to chop a stick of wood anyhow. I don't mean to say nothin' against your daddy, but …" He shook his head as if he'd changed his mind about saying more. Then he said, "Well, your daddy should've knowed that's a man's job. A woman just ain't built for that kinda work." He turned and took the water bucket into the house.

Chapter Twenty-One

The pinewood coffin lay open in front of the stage at the Nazarene Baptist Church. Sweat dripped off the preacher's chin and soaked the collar of his wrinkled white shirt while he stood on the stage behind the coffin and played an out-of-tune guitar. Not to be outdone, his wife stood beside him, mopped her cleavage with a handkerchief, banged a tambourine against her hip, and sang *Shall We Gather at the River*—out of tune.

Before the funeral began, the preacher and his wife tried to convince Blue to sit at the front, but he sat as far from the coffin as he could get. He wanted to remember his mother alive and well, and he refused to look at her cold, lifeless body. So he sat on the left side of the church in the back pew near an open window and fanned himself with a hymnbook, wanting the service to be over, but afraid it would take forever.

The couple left the gathering at the river, and sang their next song out of tune together. Blue wondered if life could get any worse. While the duo on stage sang *I'll Fly Away*, a hornet flew through the window. Blue tried to shoo it away with his hand, but it buzzed around his head and insisted on getting acquainted. When the hints didn't work, Blue introduced the hornet to the hymnal. He swung the book hard and caught the pest head-on in flight. The hornet splattered on the book with a loud pop, and all four people in the congregation turned to look at Blue.

The Rodmans sat up front on the left. When they turned, the shy pink face of the missus seemed to apologize for looking. Lyla, a good-looking red-haired gal who was Blue's mother's cousin, sat on the right with her new husband. Blue met him minutes ago, an ox of a man with a crushing handshake. Not a man most people would want to mess with.

Blue counted himself and the song butchers on stage; that made seven. Not exactly a packed house, he told himself. But he couldn't count his dear daddy until he arrived, and Blue expected him to show up late and drunk. On time and sober just wouldn't fit.

Over the years, he heard Daddy's church story many times, always the same. Daddy tried church once, but they didn't like him. When it was over, the preacher man caught him on the way out and got downright persnickety—didn't like people laughing during the sermon, and then said Daddy couldn't bring his own wine to church, and couldn't take communion all during the service. But the worst part was when the reverend wanted Daddy to give back the quarter he took from the collection plate.

"Too many rules," Daddy said. He never went back.

Blue hoped there would be no collection today as the preacher leaned his guitar against the back wall, rubbed his sweaty hands on his britches, and picked up a Bible. For more than a half-hour, his faded blue necktie bobbed up and down with his Adam's apple while he yelled out scripture from various books, all of it saying the same thing with different words. Blue wondered why. If you believe the Bible, you only need a verse or two to say something. If you don't believe, then forty more verses won't matter.

While the preacher went on and on, Blue looked around at the rough plank floor, plastered walls, dirty windows, and empty pews, convinced that pews were designed to keep people awake, not for comfort. This church would seat about sixty people, he guessed, and wondered if it had ever been full. A small sign that faced the congregation hung on the wall next to the stage to tell everyone that nineteen people showed up for church last Sunday, and in the offering they gave two dollars and seventeen cents.

The holy man waved his Bible and got Blue's attention. He knew he should be grateful to the minister for the service, but on the way here, Blue hoped the service would be about his mother, to tell people she was a good woman like Mister Rodman said. Instead, the minister used his verses to preach about sin, death, heaven, and hell. Blue couldn't figure out which direction the man was sending his mother, since he mentioned Bonnie Bailey only once. But he talked a lot about God's mercy.

Faith in God's mercy was restored for Blue when the preacher finally ended the sermon. He left the Bible on the podium and lifted his guitar while his wife lifted her more-than-ample backside off a chair and joined him for *Will the Circle be Unbroken.*

When the song ended, the preacher set aside his guitar, asked everyone to stand, and said another prayer. The lump grew again in Blue's throat, and he turned his head away when the man stepped off the stage and closed the coffin. The reverend's wife propped open the side door of the church with a rock left there for that purpose. Worn wheels on the bier sent a loud squeak through the church as the reverend pushed the coffin toward the door, and beckoned for everyone to follow.

Outside, the preacher placed each person next to a coffin handle, except for Lyla, the smallest one of the crowd. He angled his head toward the cemetery behind the church.

"That cart'll never roll over that rough ground," he said. "We'll have to carry her." He grabbed a handle. "Praise the Lord. Let's go."

The pallbearers worked their way over the uneven surface and snaked around ruts in the make-believe road and passed tombstones of old graves. Blue hoped that when his time came, they wouldn't plant him here. But he supposed his mother would have picked this place for herself, and he believed she was now at peace. Or had been until the preacher's wife uttered a loud groan, and stumbled. She went face-down in the dirt. The coffin tilted, landed on the back of her leg, and took Missus Rodman down with it. Blue and the ox set down their end of the coffin and then held up the other end while the preacher and Johnny Rodman pulled their wives to their feet.

The crowd waited while the preacher's woman wiped dirt from her face and bloody mud from her leg with her sweat-soaked handkerchief. The embarrassed Missus Rodman insisted she was fine, and grabbed the handle again. Lyla, a much smaller woman than the preacher's wife, caught the free handle and said, "I can do this."

"She's stronger than she looks," her husband told them. No one challenged him.

Pallbearers panted, sweated, moaned, mumbled and stumbled, and lugged the coffin toward the gravesite while a plump, crippled, and bleeding troubadour hobbled alongside, waving her bloody handkerchief like a victory flag. Blue shook his head, a bit ashamed by his thought that the scene should be set to music.

Though he didn't know ahead of time, Blue didn't mind serving as pallbearer for his own mother. But he was relieved to find two men at the gravesite to handle the burial.

As if God had not heard him for the past hour, the preacher broke into another long-winded sermon in the cemetery, and gave the graveside mourners a chance to enjoy more of the summer sun. His wife wiped her sweat with a new handkerchief and said *amen* nearly every time he took a breath. Blue's attention strayed.

The last time he saw Lyla, he was fourteen and she was fifteen. She had changed. A lot. When he caught himself staring at her breasts, now much bigger and fuller than before, he was embarrassed. He was embarrassed a lot more when *she* caught him. And he knew what she was thinking when her face turned the color of her hair. While the preacher stretched out his prayer, Blue said a short one of his own—that the ox had not been watching *him* while he was watching *her*.

"Mankind cannot understand the meaning of eternity," the minister told them. Blue knew better. *Eternity was the length of a Baptist funeral.*

At the end of eternity, the man tossed a handful of dirt on top of the coffin and said, "We commend this body to the ground and the spirit to God who gave it." He uttered his last amen and looked at the people around the gravesite.

"Missus Rodman and my dear wife prepared some of God's bounty, and we hope you'll join us inside for nourishment." He headed for the church to partake of the bounty, and left his dear wife behind to limp there on her own.

When the crippled one stumbled into the church, she went to a back corner of the stage where a hundred flies buzzed in frenzy and crawled over a bed sheet that covered a treasure they seemed desperate to reach. While the men rearranged benches and chairs on the stage so the group could sit in a circle, the women chased away most of the treasure hunters with dish towels, fly swatters, and one bloody hanky. They uncovered straw baskets of fried chicken, a large bowl of fried potatoes, a pan of fried cornbread cut into squares, and a jug of tea. From the moisture on the outside of the jug, Blue guessed it had been ice-tea before the funeral.

The pink-faced missus and the preacher's wife stopped, stared at the food, then at each other. They looked around at the other people, back at the food, and then at each other again. The preacher's wife beckoned her husband.

"Thelbert, come and look at this. Somebody's done been here. They's a big scoop of taters that's missin', purt near half the chicken, and three squares of cornbread."

The minister stood over the food and shook his head. Missus Rodman stood next to him with her fists on her hips, her usual pink face now radish-red. The preacher started to speak, but froze when the missus screamed.

"What the hell? Some no-good bastard filched my chicken."

Johnny Rodman's face distorted as his head jerked forward. He backed away, his chin quivering. The preacher's wife gasped and whirled around. Her mouth gaped. Tears flooded her eyes. The ox looked confused. Everyone stared. The shock of blasphemy hung on pale faces. Awkward silence hung in the air like the smell of hog manure. Blue wanted to laugh, but didn't dare.

The preacher's eyes bugged wide and he mumbled a prayer. Then he looked at the sinner and said, "May God forgive you, sister. We all know you didn't mean them awful words."

"Well..." the sinner said, angling her head toward the food, her voice beginning to crack, "... can you explain this bullshit?"

The preacher moaned and nodded. "I got a strong notion it's the kid that lives just around the bend. It's happened before. A lot of folks is hungry these days. We have to show mercy."

The missus covered her mouth. Her mumbles sounded less than merciful.

Ten minutes later, the group sat with plates on laps while they chewed, stared at each other and swatted at flies, but didn't talk. Between bites, the preacher said they should all be of good cheer because the lady we laid to rest would want it that way. Then he told the story of The Last Supper, which appeared to cheer no one.

Missus Rodman seemed determined to get her share of the food she brought. Her attack on the chicken reminded Blue of the flies as she stuffed it into her pink face and gnawed the bones.

***

The trail back to the hobo jungle seemed longer, the hills steeper, and the sun hotter while Blue weaved his way through the herd of black-and-white cows, trying to avoid the piles, and crossed the Rodman dairy farm. At the edge of the woods, he hoped for relief, but the heat of the day had penetrated the shade, and the humidity was higher. A stump offered a place to rest.

Though he tried to enjoy the sights and

sounds of the forest, thoughts of his father would not leave his head. A half-hour ago, when Blue stood outside the church saying his goodbyes, the preacher came to him and placed his hand on Blue's shoulder.

"I'm sorry about your mother. It's a big loss. I've been there, and I know." A few seconds later, he added, "I'm sorry about your father too." The man did not show up at the funeral for his own wife, had no respect for the mother of his children, and showed no feelings for his son.

The preacher didn't know where the old man lived, and when Blue asked Mister Rodman, he said, "I met him on the road and told him about your mama the day it happened. He didn't say much, and I don't know where he was stayin'."

Blue asked Lyla about him.

"Your mama was at my wedding last fall. Came by herself. It's the last time I saw her alive. I don't know nothin' about your daddy." Her gaze grew hard, color flooded her face, and her open palm moved up and down.

"Well, there is one thing I *do* know. If I ever see that sumbitch again, I'm gonna slap the livin' hell outa him." The preacher screwed up his face, whirled and walked away. Ox grinned. Johnny Rodman's lips didn't move, but the laughter showed in his eyes.

Blue left the stump, relieved himself, and then took the cup off his belt and walked to the creek. In spite of the hot day, cool water rippled in the stream, and his cup went down for a second dip. While the water soothed his throat, something moved near the trees by the bank.

A rabbit in that brush pile? If I had my slingshot... He watched and waited, saw nothing, and headed back to the trail.

"Blue."

Someone behind him said his name. Not loud. But there it was, plain as day. His heart raced. He stopped, cocked his head and listened hard, but did not turn around. Crazy questions filled his mind.

Another hobo out here? Somebody following me? Blue felt the color drain from his face.

Ox? Oh, shit. He saw me gawking at his wife's tits, and now he's gonna...

"Blue."

Turn around? Or run like hell? Blue turned around but saw no one.

"Come over here, Blue."

The command came from the pile of brush Blue saw near the creek bank. Now, he knew the voice. His jaw tightened, his fists clenched as he walked back to the brush pile. He stopped at a crude, tarpaper shelter covered with branches that hid it from the trail. A filthy old man sat on the dirt floor in the half-dark shelter with his finger hooked in a ceramic jug handle. He wore a large grin, and peered out.

"Hey, Blue, you gotta smoke?"

Blue's jaw dropped. "A what?"

"A smoke. You got one?"

"You ain't seen me in three damn years. Do you say, 'Hello, good to see you, son?' Do you say, 'I missed you, glad you're still alive?' Hell no, you just want to bum a smoke. That's my loving father, all right."

The voice from the shelter came out calm and controlled. "Well… I ain't the one that left. Left without a word. You know what you done to your mama, boy? Took a while, but it killed her. That's why she's dead. You did it, Blue. Killed your own mother."

Blue stooped and stuck his head inside. "You lying sack o' shit. I know how Mama died. If you had a decent bone in your worthless body, you'd a been out there chopping wood. Maybe you'd be dead instead. And that would be just fine with me. I oughta drag your filthy hide out here and beat the dog shit out of you."

Elmer Bailey was silent for a few seconds, and then grinned again. His eyes got large. "Could I have a smoke first?"

Blue didn't know whether to laugh or scream. But the old man laughed. He fell over on his side, laughed and vomited. The jug fell with him and lost its cork. While the sour contents spilled in the dirt, Blue stared at the floor where the jug had covered a large pile of fresh-gnawed chicken bones and a half-eaten square of cornbread.

Chapter Twenty-Two

An awful day, Blue told himself. The death of his baby sister six years ago left a big hole in his heart. Now, his mother was dead. And his father was still alive. None of it was fair. None of it made sense. He'd wanted to kick the old man senseless, take out his anger on the one he blamed for a lifetime of poverty, for a lifetime of hurt, for the lack of a real life for himself and his family. The sorry sot deserved it. But when Blue stood in the doorway of the makeshift hut, he knew that kicking him would do nothing for his own pain. He left the old man right where he belonged, on a dirt floor in a puddle of his own vomit. Without a smoke.

The sun on the horizon, now even with the tops of the trees, told Blue that dark was about twenty minutes away. At night, the woods grew darker than anywhere else, and sleeping out here without a bedroll seemed about as much fun as diarrhea. He walked faster. Ten minutes later, faint sounds of laughter filtered through the trees. Could it be coming from the Possum Trot jungle?

In the past three years, Blue had spent many nights and too many days in hobo jungles, and he'd learned a few things about camps and the people in them. The camps were filled with men restless or bored, and often depressed and low on self-respect. They needed a distraction to keep them from going nuts, especially when they didn't find work. Most would drink liquor if they could get it. Or they'd pick on somebody to get laughs. Or start a string of jokes, most of which were worn-out one-liners that made the rounds from one jungle to another. Even so, the men laughed because they needed to laugh.

But another type of laughter, a true and easy, heartfelt kind, infected the whole camp when someone brought good food, like a big turkey or a few chickens to share with the group. Or when a long-lost friend showed up and brought good news. Blue was certain he heard that special laughter. When singing and banjo music followed the laughter, Blue's heart leaped and he started to run toward the music.

Several men in the Possum Trot jungle stood and turned as Blue came out of the woods and ran toward them. Blue's mouth fell open when he saw a tall, broad-shouldered, pipe-smoking man with white hair and a white beard.

"Halo. Oh man, it's really you." Blue ran toward him as the big man stood with arms outstretched, eyes wide, while he laughed and nodded. After a big hug, Blue pulled away and wiped his eyes, and color filled his cheeks when the men around him applauded.

"In case anybody here doesn't know this man," Blue said, "this is Halo. He's one hell of a hobo, and I ain't seen him in three years."

"I never had a better friend," Halo told him. He stepped back and looked at Blue from his boots to his hat. "You gotta be three inches taller than the last time I saw you. You've made quite a good-looking young man of yourself." Others stood by and grinned as if waiting for something to happen. Halo dropped his head and looked up at his friend.

"I brought you something, Blue." Blue's eyes widened but he did not reply. Halo angled his head toward a tree and said again, "I brought you something, my friend."

Blue jerked his head around. A guitar case

leaned against the tree. He walked toward it. "You brought me a guitar?" He picked it up and opened the case. His hands shook while he lifted the beautiful Martin guitar out of the case, held it against his chest and hugged it. His eyes grew misty again. "Oh my God, Halo. There's nothing in the world I wanted more than getting my guitar back. I never thought I'd see it again. How did you hang on to it all this time?"

Halo was all grins. "I just remembered that it belonged to my best friend."

Around the night fire, the two nursed cups of stew, sipped coffee, and swapped stories about most of the jungles they'd been to, and how many times they missed each other by a day or two over the past three years.

"You've grown in more ways than one," Halo said. "And learned a lot about this crazy hobo life."

"That's the only way a man can survive." Blue shrugged. "You learn or die. And I damn near did that too, a couple times."

Halo lit his pipe and listened while Blue told him what happened to the watch Halo gave him in Alabama. Blue expected him to be upset.

"Things happen we can't know about ahead of time." Halo wagged his head. "Life would be awful boring any other way. If you learned something from that… well, then maybe it was all worthwhile."

He tapped the ashes from his pipe, put it away, and said, "Possum Trot is a nice town with a lot of good people. I've been back here five or six times since we got separated. But I could never catch you here. I thought some of the boys here would tell you that and you'd show up once in a while."

"It's my first time back. And you probably heard… I wound up going to my mother's funeral."

Halo nodded. "Yeah. Sorry."

Blue felt his whole body smile as he picked up his guitar and ran his hands over the neck. "Halo, these are new strings. How did you…"

"Last week in Dyersburg, I went to a shop that sells guitars to look for a case. When the man saw the guitar, he bragged on it a lot, but said it needs new strings. I bought a new set, and he gave me that used case he had."

Blue tuned the guitar, played a few chords, and rubbed his aching fingertips. "You hung on to it all this time. You put new strings on it. You got a case for it. And you brought my guitar back to me after three long years." His eyes grew misty when he stood, rested a hand on Halo's shoulder, and spoke in the best British accent he could manage.

"You're a better man than I am, Gunga Din."

Halo's eyes grew misty too, but he chuckled. "What are friends for?"

He stuffed his pipe and relit it. His eyes lost focus as the smoke rose around his head. After a minute of silence, he told Blue about a girl he met in Dyersburg.

"She'd probably never go for somebody like me," he said, "but I have to find out. She's the prettiest thing I've seen in a long time."

"Sounds like you're struck, Halo. What's her name?"

"I am struck, and her name's Sherry. I'm not pretending that I have anything going with her, but a man can dream. If I had a woman like her, I think I could settle down, give up being a hobo."

"Change your whole life? That's pretty serious. But you're right. A man can dream, and I'm happy for you." Blue dropped his chin and rolled his eyes up at Halo. "So you're going back to Dyersburg?"

Halo stood, leaned and looked down. "Tomorrow. And I want you to go with me."

With a wrinkled forehead, Blue set his guitar aside and stood. "You're throwing a monkey wrench into my busy schedule, but… what are friends for?"

Halo scratched his head and frowned. "Just don't forget we're friends."

"Forget?"

"Well, maybe I'm crazy to take along some guitar-picking charmer who is even better looking than I am and a lot closer to her age. One look at you, I may not stand a chance."

The guitar picker fidgeted and blushed, but didn't answer.

***

A head full of excitement about having Martin and Halo back in his life kept Blue awake most of the night. By the time the two men caught the early morning train to Dyersburg, he was exhausted, and just wanted to sleep. Twice, he dozed off while Halo talked about Dyersburg and Sherry. But Halo woke him up and kept talking until Blue said, "You got it bad, Halo. You're in love with a gal you barely know."

"I never said I was in love with her," Halo snapped.

"You may fool yourself, but you're not fooling me."

Halo stopped talking, and Blue dozed off

again. But the worn-out boxcar jerked and rattled, and made sleep impossible for more than ten minutes at a stretch. Blue felt grateful the trip from Possum Trot to Dyersburg was a short one.

Stretched out on the floor of the boxcar, he lay with his head on his bindle and wondered about tomorrow, next week, and next year. He remembered that uneasy feeling in his gut when he jumped off the train in Possum Trot, a sense that something bad was about to happen. His gut was right, of course, but the bad turned out to be worse than he could have ever imagined.

Today, the loss of his mother began to sink in. The hurt was deeper now than yesterday, and he thought about how much she must have suffered. She did not deserve such a fate, and he wondered if she thought of him while she was dying. His father's words echoed in his head. *Left without a word. You did it, Blue. Killed your own mother.*

His conscience nagged. *How can you criticize the old man for not going to the funeral? She wasn't tormented by that. But you, Blue... you didn't go back to see your own mother even once while she was still alive*. He rested his arm over his face as if to shade his eyes, and wiped the tears on his sleeve, hoping Halo didn't notice. Halo did, and patted him on the shoulder.

Minutes later, a new feeling washed over Blue. His gut never explained anything. It just said things to him that he sometimes understood, but often did not. Now, it seemed to be saying something about Dyersburg, and a feeling that his life would change in a good way. He breathed deep and dozed off again with a smile.

Chapter Twenty-Three

They'd been in Tennessee less than two weeks, but Blue and Halo came to the square four times already. On the way from Possum Trot, when Halo didn't talk about Sherry, he bragged about Courthouse Square in Dyersburg. Blue figured the man loved it because it's in the same town as Sherry. Regardless, Halo was right about this place, and today Blue told him, "This is one of my favorite spots on the planet."

The square sat like a park in the middle of town, with shade trees, benches around the perimeter, and a drinking fountain in the center where Blue always got his fill of the cool water. He liked the Johnny Reb statue in front of the courthouse because it made strangers talk to each other. He liked the smell of the planted flowers, fresh-mowed grass, and pipe smoke. And he liked the perfume of the young ladies when they walked by, talking about shoes, dresses, books, movies, and men. Best of all he liked the tantalizing smell of bread, cookies, donuts, and rolls that wafted across the square from the German bakery. He'd tilt back his head and breathe deep. The sweet, delicious aroma seemed to penetrate everything inside him as it made his mouth water, and made his stomach beg for a taste.

A few days ago, he stood in front of the bakery with his hands in his empty pockets while funny noises came from his empty gut, and looked at all the goodies through the window. An older lady gave him a polite nod on her way in. She came out minutes later and handed him a treat.

"I hope you like warm cinnamon rolls," she said. He hoped his *thank you* was loud enough for her to hear as she walked away without a reply. If she would have stayed a bit, he could tell her that he never had one before and how much he liked it. "Cinnamon roll." He said it aloud, and knew he would never forget the name.

During the day, older men warmed the benches inside the square. Blue sat among them once, but not for long. He didn't fit.

They all seemed to know each other, but often referred to a man by the logo on his cap instead of a first name. Case, Farmall, John Deere, and a half-dozen others chewed plugs of Day's Work tobacco as they sat and whittled, making nothing, or sometimes whistles and slingshots. And always, the too-short legs of their overalls would reveal socks drooped over the top of beat-up work shoes, and uncover scarred shins that never saw the sun.

When the men didn't talk of rabbit traps, root cellars, or storm shelters, they agonized about the bad news in the State Gazette, remembered when times were good, swapped lies and pocket knives, and cussed FDR for taking everybody's gold.

By five o'clock, the bench warmers had solved the world's problems. But there'd be new ones to solve tomorrow. "Lord willin' I'll see you gents in the morning," they'd say, and then climb into their pickup trucks and head home for supper.

When the gents moved out, hobos moved in, and the benches would become beds. For those without blankets, left-behind newspapers would be their only cover for the night.

Hobos didn't count on sleeping late. At the

crack of dawn the beat-cop would rap the bottom of their shoes with his nightstick and run them out of the square to make room for regular people. Except on Sunday mornings when the regular people went to church.

Blue and Halo found farm work near Dyersburg, picking beans and chopping weeds out of crops. But a job was good for a couple of days at best. When neither had work, they came here.

Halo told Blue they might get a dollar each, maybe more, for a pint of blood. So today, they walked through the square on their way to the Red Cross blood bank. Then they would come back here and buy lunch. Then, if Blue could find an empty bench, he'd play his guitar and sing. He played here twice before. People applauded after almost every song, and some dropped pennies in his cup.

"I guess everybody had the same idea," Halo said as they walked around the corner and found a line of people outside the blood bank. "So the Red Cross must be buying blood."

When Halo got in line, Blue said, "Save a place for me." He moved away from the line, set his cup on the ground, and took his guitar out of the case. While he stood and played, people in the line clapped and whistled. No one left the line to bring money. But as a man came out of the building, he stopped and asked Blue to play Wildwood Flower.

At the end of the song, the man said, "That's my favorite tune." His nickel clattered in the cup, and he left with a happy face.

A young couple came out, stopped and listened. While Blue played a slow love song, they stood wide-eyed and stared at each other. When he finished, each dropped a penny. They held hands and walked away.

People in line to sell blood don't have money to spend, Blue figured, so he'd have to catch them on the way out. Yet five minutes later, an attractive, well-dressed young lady on her way in stopped and tossed a nickel in the cup. Blue's eyes met hers, and their gaze stayed fixed on each other while he played, made a short bow and said, "Thank you, Miss. My name's Blue."

"I like your music, Blue."

Blue looked down and then into her eyes. "I like playing for you."

A slight blush appeared on her cheeks. She smiled, looked away, and went into the building through a side door.

Halo waved, and motioned for Blue. When Blue joined him in line, Halo whispered, "That was Sherry, the girl I told you about. If you talk to her, put in a good word for me."

Inside, a lady motioned Blue to her desk. When he stood in front of her, she stared at his guitar but didn't look at him. Then, with glazed eyes and a droning voice she read to him a half-page of information about donating blood.

When Blue told her his name, the woman made eye contact for the first time and shook her head. "We cain't use no nicknames." She appeared doubtful when Blue said that was his real name, but she wrote it on the form. Afterwards, she called him Mister Bailey and asked lots of personal questions. Finished, the woman handed him a white card with a red cross on it and angled her head toward the other side of the room.

"Stand in that line till somebody stabs you."

Blue waited for a smile that never came, and joined the line, glad to see that it moved faster than the one outside. Minutes later he looked up from a cot, his sleeve rolled up and a tourniquet on his arm.

"Hello, Blue." The woman he met outside approached him with a needle. But Blue saw only her face as she stabbed him, hooked tubes to his arm, and took off the tourniquet. "Make a fist, please."

"Halo told me your name is Sherry."

Her forehead wrinkled. "Halo?"

Blue looked around and then back at her. "He came in with me, but I don't see him. A big man. White hair and beard. He says he knows you."

"I meet a lot of people. Chances are I saw him here."

"He's my best friend, and he also told me how beautiful you are. I thought he might be stretching it a bit. But he wasn't."

Her cheeks glowed while she watched the blood pumping through the tubes. "Squeeze your fist and then release it. Do that ten times, please." Sherry looked back at him. "I really like your music. You been playing long?"

"Since I was a kid. I used to sit on a stump in the woods and play for the birds and squirrels. I don't know if they liked it or not. They never clapped."

Sherry laughed. "So now you play for people and they clap. And I'll bet they stop and give you money."

"Sometimes."

"And I'll bet you get lots of girlfriends that way too."

It was Blue's turn for red cheeks. "No. Not really. I mean… I don't have a girlfriend."

Sherry kept busy checking tubes, reading dials, and filling out forms, but did not talk to Blue again until she smiled and said, "Okay. We're all done here." She unhooked him and wrapped a bandage on his arm.

"If you're feeling good, get up slow and easy. Then grab an orange out of that box over there and sit on the bench and eat it before you leave." She nodded at his guitar leaning against the wall. "And don't forget that."

"That's my friend, Martin. I won't forget."

A half-hour later, Blue caught up with Halo in the square. "What happened, Halo? You disappeared."

"They wouldn't take my blood because I was there a couple weeks ago. I have to wait a couple more months. Everything work out?"

"Yep, paid me two dollars on the way out."

"You talk to Sherry?"

Blue nodded. "While she was draining my blood. And I, uh… I mentioned you too. Told her we're best friends, and what you said about her being pretty."

"You told her that? What did she say?"

"She just blushed. But I could tell she liked it. Come on. I'll buy you a sandwich."

***

Halo found work, helping a farmer repair his barn, and said the job might last a full week. But, sorry, the farmer needed only one man. So, early the next morning, Blue left the jungle with his guitar and his cup, and whistled most of the way to the square.

He found an empty bench and played for a half hour before anyone stopped. A young man who wanted to learn to play the guitar stopped and talked for ten minutes. He dropped a penny in the cup and walked away pretending he was playing his own guitar.

After another dozen songs without pay, Blue packed his guitar, picked up his cup and headed for the blood bank. He didn't know if a crowd would be there again today, but he knew about the big shade tree in the front, and he knew he was singing for nothing at the square.

***

A sign by the door said the blood bank opened at ten. But people came early and waited in line. They turned to watch Blue set up under the big tree. The old man who taught him to play once told him, "You gotta know who you're playing for if you want them to like you." So he watched and listened. Blue had no respect and no sympathy for anyone too lazy to work for a living. His life and his father had taught him that, and he'd learned to recognize those people, often at first glance, by the way they held themselves, the way they talked, and their attitude about money.

Like so many others he saw in his travels, the people here were hard-up through no fault of their own. Just yesterday, he stood in that same line, but he had only himself to look out for. These people were here to sell their blood so they could buy flour, maybe a quart of milk and a couple cans of Spam to feed their skinny children, to survive for a few more days. Blue hoped he could make them feel a bit better with a song.

Only three people clapped when he finished the first tune, but everyone in line clapped when he ended the next one. As he expected, none brought money. But a young lady who worked there stopped on her way in. She smiled and dropped two pennies in his cup, but didn't stay to talk.

Blue massaged his fingertips, and then gave

the fingers a workout. He closed his eyes and concentrated on a tune he'd heard on radio many times from a band called The Skillet Lickers. It was an instrumental that took a lot of work, and the last tune he learned from the old man who taught him to play. "Lose yourself in the music," he said. "When you become a part of it, it becomes a part of you. And that's as good as it gets."

So many things had changed since then, and now that time seemed so many years ago. In his mind, he saw that dear old man, the patient hands that taught Blue to make the guitar become a part of his body, the eyes that showed faith in his student, and the encouraging voice that called Blue a natural.

Now Blue closed his eyes and began to play. Instinct and magic led his fingers across the strings as he drifted into that world of sound and feeling inhabited only by the music and the one who gives it life.

Loud applause began as Blue finished. He opened his eyes to see more than the people standing in line. A small crowd off the street had gathered to hear him, and a few came and dropped pennies in the cup. In front of him, with eyes wide and bright, a young woman stood and clapped.

"Hello, Sherry. You're looking lovely this morning."

"Thank you, Blue. The more I hear you the better it gets." She left another nickel in his cup, and he realized it wasn't her money he wanted, only her approval. *Was it any wonder Halo was crazy about her?* His eyes followed her to the door. A man in a necktie, with eyeglasses and a dark mustache, stepped out and held the door for her. He did not speak. He did not smile. He stared at Blue as Sherry passed by and went inside. Then he followed her in and closed the door.

Chapter Twenty-Four

Most crewmembers at the Red Cross blood bank agreed that the workday went by much faster when the days were busy. So they liked the hectic pace, and were seldom disappointed. But sometimes they welcomed a breather, a slow day that allowed time for necessary tasks like inventory and cleaning, and more time for employees to talk. Today was one of those days.

As the ladies swept, mopped, dusted, and made a sincere effort to organize things, they talked about how much they appreciated the jobs and the Red Cross. Later in the day, the conversations turned to clothes, recipes, and entertainment.

"Speaking of entertainers," one said, "that guy that's been playing out front? I don't know his name, but he's good."

"And a tall, good-looking, young thing too," another added.

Two more jumped in.

"I saw Sherry talking to him. I bet she knows his name."

"Yeah, I think Sherry's got a new boyfriend."

"Oh, you have to tell us about him, Sherry."

Sherry cleared her throat loud enough for all to hear. "His name is Blue. He is not my boyfriend."

"He's not? Well, I don't blame you, Sherry. He don't look clean to me. I think he's just a hobo. You can do better than that."

"Maybe she can. But she put money in his cup again today. I saw it."

"I dropped a couple of pennies too, but I think Sherry outbid me." The woman giggled.

"Maybe Sherry likes hobos and just won't admit it."

"Oooh, Hobo Blue and Sherry too."

A lady laughed and lost her grip on a steel pan. When it clattered to the floor, the others laughed. All except Sherry. Her cheeks burned.

"All right, that's enough. He's a nice man. He may be a hobo but you've got no right to pick on him. And for the last time, he is not my boyfriend."

"Well now, ain't you the touchy one."

Sherry heard no more talk about Blue, but whispers and snickers flew around for another hour. She knew they were talking about him. Maybe about her too. Eager to have the day over, she leaned through the doorway to see the wall clock in the hallway, but Wanda blocked her view.

Wanda, a short and squatty, big-breasted woman who moved with a sway and with her elbows held out to her side, appeared to be swimming when she walked. She pulled a strand of her salt and pepper hair back into place and fastened it with a bobby pin while she swam down the hallway and into the storage room. She stopped in front of Sherry, waved her hand to get attention from the others, and looked around. Wanda lowered her head, rolled her eyes up at them, and kept her voice low.

"Everybody see that notice on the bulletin board? Hmmm? We got a meeting in the boss's office at 5:30. Must be something mi-igh-ty interesting."

Sherry looked out at the clock, and shook her head. "We only have twenty minutes to worry about it. You know nothing good ever comes out of those meetings."

A dozen times before, the boss tacked notices on the board for such meetings, but never a hint about what he wanted to tell them. Except for a part-timer hired to lift things too heavy for the women, the boss was the only man who worked here. Sherry was convinced that the only thing the boss knew about women was that men could lift more.

A meeting notice would make the women fret, mutter wild guesses, threaten to quit, rehash old rumors, and start a few new ones. They could not keep their minds on work, and Sherry wondered if he knew how little work would get done after he posted the notice. But today at least, there was little time to wait or waste.

At 5:30 the man with the necktie, glasses, and mustache stood outside his office and held open the door. After all seven ladies filed in and stood without talking, he walked past them and sat in the big chair behind his desk. He ignored the ladies while he slid a cigarette-rolling machine to the center of his desk, placed a paper in the machine, and spread tobacco on the paper. Next, he cranked the machine, pulled out the cigarette, licked the edge of the paper to seal his creation, and fired it up. The boss blew smoke in the ladies' faces and leaned back in his chair.

"Well, girls… looks like we have a little problem. One that we have to fix before it gets to be a big one." He blew more smoke at them and stared at each one in turn.

"I know people have to have money to live, and we've been paying them for their blood, including the hobos that come here, and there's more of them all the time. But when we're done with them, we're done—and you have to tell them to leave. I don't want a bunch of filthy hobos hanging around trying to bum money from anybody. And if we put up with it from one of them, before long, the yard'll be full of 'em." He blew smoke again, and glared at Sherry. "And playing music is no excuse for it."

The boss opened a cigar box on his desk. "We got name tags now." He took out a name-tag and held it up. "Everybody take one and write your name under the Red Cross logo. Pin it on your blouse and wear it to work every day." He raised his voice. "Every day. It ain't complicated."

He tapped out his cigarette in the ashtray and looked up. "No questions? Meeting's over."

***

Sherry lay awake more than she slept during the night, and while the early morning rooster crowed, a knot formed in her stomach. Her chest felt tight before she reached the blood bank. When she left the car and walked toward the employee entrance, a man under the big tree got her attention. He stood next to a pushcart with a *Candy for Sale* sign. The man reminded her of the Saturday Evening Post with pictures of pushcart vendors in New York, but she had never seen a real one. When she stopped to talk with him, he glanced at her name tag, removed his hat, and made a slight bow.

"Best o' the mornin' to ya, my dear. I hope I have your kind permission to sell my candies here today."

Sherry nodded. "Of course. And best of luck to you, sir." The man was not a hobo or a bum. He was running a business. She would not have to tell him to leave. He even made her smile.

But Sherry knew the real reason for her

relief was what she did *not* see. When she arrived yesterday and the day before, Blue stood under the tree with his guitar. She would not have to tell him to leave today. Blue was not here. She was glad. And yet… she missed him.

Sherry was also glad the boss wasn't here. After yesterday's meeting, he told the girls he wouldn't be here before noon. Of course, when the boss was gone, the girls would play, and the teasing started when Sherry walked through the door. One got it started and the others jumped in.

"Oh, Sherry, bad news—your boyfriend's not here."

"Did you tell him not to come back, Sherry?"

"You two have a hot date last night?"

Sherry felt the heat rise in her face. She turned her back and spoke over her shoulder. "Don't start with that. I'm exhausted and not in the mood for it. Couldn't you just say, 'good morning?'"

"Well, girls, Sherry didn't say good morning to us. She's exhausted. Must've been a really heavy date."

The girls laughed. Sherry whirled and glared at them. "Okay, how about this? Kiss my ass. How's that for a 'good morning?'"

Sherry did not smile. The girls no longer laughed. The conversation died.

***

A busy morning, crazy people, and a couple of events helped keep the girls from causing more trouble. The line outside the door kept growing, and the receptionist turned away more blood sellers than she accepted. One of the rejects was a drunk and happy little man who insisted his real name was Piss Ant. When he laughed and told them he needed money for another pint, everyone in the building laughed with him. But when the crew wouldn't buy his blood, his humor disappeared. He yelled obscenities while he stomped out.

The little man shut the door behind him, but opened it again, stuck his head in, and screamed, "Up yours." He slammed the door, startled Wanda, and caused her to yank the tube from her patient's arm. Blood spilled on her, on the patient's clothes, and on the floor. A big man, who stood by waiting for his turn, fainted.

After the crew revived the man and cleaned up the mess, Sherry stuck her head into the hallway to see the clock. Again, Wanda blocked her view, but told Sherry the time.

"It's a quarter of twelve," she said, "and…" she jerked her head toward the employee door at the end of the hallway, "… I think you've got company."

Sherry stepped into the hallway. "Oh, God," came out just above a whisper when she looked through the door window. Seconds later, Blue opened the door and walked in with his guitar.

The knot in her stomach was back. Other women popped out of nowhere into the hallway behind Sherry, and whispers started again. Blue held his head high, smiled big, and waved. He stopped in front of her.

"Good to see you, Sherry, I just…"

Sherry wagged her head hard, afraid the boss would walk in at any minute. "You can't be in here. Sorry, you have to leave."

He took a step back. "Okay, but I just wanted to…"

"No, Blue. You have to leave. Now. Right now."

He took two steps back. "But, Sherry, I only…"

She pointed at the door. "Out. You can't play here again and you can't hang around here. The boss said no more filthy hobos." She gasped at her own words and slammed her hand over her mouth.

Blue's face paled as he spun around and stepped to the door. He left it open behind him, and walked away.

Wanda closed the door and watched him through the window. Sherry turned and glared at the other women. They scattered, and she stood next to Wanda.

Under the big cottonwood, a small girl in a dirty dress stood next to a tall, skinny man and wiped her tears on the back of her hand. She pointed at the *Candy for Sale* sign on the vendor's cart, and then pulled on the man's sleeve. He bent over and held out his hands, palms up, and shook his head.

Sherry could not hear them talk, but the big *Please, Daddy* on the child's face was easy to read. The man turned the empty pockets of his pants inside out while he shook his head again.

Blue hung his guitar on his back and walked around the man and the girl. He dug coins from his pocket, gave them to the vendor, and pointed to the cart. As the man brought a candy bar out of the cart, Blue angled his head at the child.

The little girl cried through a giant grin as she tore at the wrapper. Wanda sniffled, wiped a tear with the back of her hand, and shook her head.

"Such a nice young man. He'll be a great

daddy someday." She turned, edged past Sherry, and went down the hallway.

Tears, hot and salty, stung Sherry's eyes, and she tried to blink them away while she watched Blue walk down the street. A man who worked for pennies sacrificed them to ease the pain of a stranger's child. A man who shared his gift of music poured out his heart to the miserable, even if it scattered only crumbs of relief from their troubles. He stopped, turned, and glanced back at the door. Then he turned again and was gone.

Sherry licked a tear from her upper lip. A lump grew in her throat, and she stared at a blur of colors, trees without shape, streets without purpose, people without faces. Pressure in her chest forced out the words.

"Oh my God. What have I done?"

Chapter Twenty-Five

Halo's carpentry job ended. With a few dollars in his pants, and a bit more in his shoe, he came along with Blue today to enjoy the square. While Blue played, Halo wandered. While Blue sang, Halo talked to strangers. While Blue collected a few coins, Halo spent a few, buying a bit of candy and new shoe laces. He also wandered across the street, and surprised Blue when he came back with cinnamon rolls and a coffee for each of them.

"Don't take too long with that coffee, Blue," Halo told him. He smiled big. "I gotta take the cups back or they'll come looking for me."

When Halo took back the cups, Blue started a song he'd played many times and could sing in his sleep. But the words for the second verse escaped him when he looked across the square. He could not mistake the woman who came toward him for anyone else, and the guitar hung on his neck in silence while he waited.

Sherry stopped in front of him, her arms across her chest, her face drawn, her chin down. "You probably don't want to talk to me, Blue, but I hope you will, because…" she looked up, "… well… because I'm sorry about what happened."

Blue watched Halo come back and stop behind Sherry. She didn't seem to know he was there, and kept talking. "What I said was awful, but I didn't mean it."

Halo stepped forward. "Hello, Sherry."

She looked at him. "Oh, hello. I, uh… I think I've seen you before. Maybe at the blood bank? I work there."

"Yes, I know. I'm Halo. That's where we met." He shuffled his feet, stuck his hands in his pockets, and took them out again. His smile was gone.

"Oh, of course. I'm sorry. Now I remember." His face brightened until she said, "Blue told me about you. You two are best friends." She looked back at Blue. "And I hope Blue and I are still friends. I really am sorry, Blue. Sometimes my boss is not a nice man, and he said I had to tell you that you can't play there anymore."

"It's okay, Sherry. You had to do your job."

"I want you to come play at our church." She stepped closer.

Blue's forehead wrinkled. "My stuff? In church? You trying to get me arrested?" He grinned and shook his head.

Sherry giggled. "No, no. Not during a service. It's a Saturday talent show, outside. They take up a collection for the three best ones. And you can sing anything you like. Well… almost anything." She put her palms together. "Please. You're really good."

With a slow nod, he said, "I'll think about it. Do I need to sign up?"

"Nope, just show up." Sherry pulled a folded paper from her pocket and handed it to him. "If you're gonna be here on the square, I'll check back with you in a day or two." She started away, but stopped and turned. "Oh, goodbye, Halo."

Halo watched her walk away. Then he walked away. Minutes later, Blue caught up.

Walking two miles from the square to the jungle always seemed shorter with Halo along. Today, it seemed longer. Today, Halo didn't talk. After a mile or more of silence, Blue walked faster to get ahead. He stopped, turned to face Halo, and waited till he caught up.

"Okay, Halo, what the hell's wrong?"

Halo walked by. "Who said anything is wrong?"

"You been saying it all the way." Blue caught up. "It's about Sherry, ain't it?"

Halo stopped and spun around to face him. "I've been a damn good friend to you, Blue. You know I have. How the hell could you do that?"

"I didn't do anything." Blue started forward again, and Halo walked beside him. Blue told him what Sherry said at the blood bank. "Today's the first time I've seen her since. You don't think she owed me that apology?"

"It was a lot more than that. I know flirting when I see it. She invited you to her church."

"It's a talent show. Everybody's invited, Halo, including you."

"Yeah, I heard her gracious invitation. She barely talked to me. And by the way, I saw that note she passed you."

Blue fished the folded paper from his pocket and held it out. "It just tells where the church is and the time for the show." Halo glanced at the paper but refused to take it.

The conversation died until they approached the jungle. Blue tried again.

"Look, Halo, nothing's going on with me and Sherry. And I don't believe you're stupid enough to think there is."

Halo's gaze hardened as he snapped his head around. "I'm not stupid… and I'm not blind." He turned and headed into the crowd of hobos.

Minutes later, Blue stood by the kettle with his cup of mulligan stew and talked to other hobos about jobs, FDR, the weather, and women. He learned nothing new about any of those, but he hung around and waited for Halo. He waited because only a true friend would do the things Halo did. He could have sold the guitar. Instead, he protected it for three years and brought it back with a case and new strings.

Blue hoped the big man would realize his pride was the only thing wounded, and that Blue was not at fault. He waited so he could tell his friend, *I'm sorry. I didn't mean to call you stupid.* And he would set up a meeting for just Halo and Sherry. They could sit on a bench in the square, and talk. Or maybe Halo could take her hand, walk her across the street to the bakery and buy her a treat.

Blue waited because he remembered three years ago when Halo said, "If you want to *have* a friend, you have to *be* one." Blue would be one. He waited.

But Halo didn't show.

Blue snatched up his gear and guitar and headed out of the jungle. There was still enough daylight to hike across the field to the abandoned barn about a half mile away where he slept before in peace and quiet.

***

Morning brought a fine mist of rain and chilly air. Most day jobs were fair-weather work, so most bo's who would have been working today were stuck at the jungle. Another day without work was often a day without food except for the stew pot. Men crowded under the shelter next to the kettle with their cups and smokes.

No one seemed to know how long the posts with the ragged tin roof had been there or who put them up. And no one cared. They were just happy to have a roof. It offered cover from the rain, and when a slow drop came through a nail hole and splattered in a cup or put out a smoke, it always got a laugh. When a man got tagged by a drop, he'd swear, look up, shake his head, and move to a new spot. And no one would spoil the fun by warning the next man who moved in with his pipe or cigarette, and his cup of stew.

Blue's mind raced back over the last three years and how much he'd learned. On his first day as a hobo, he didn't know what to say when someone asked if he knew the recipe for mulligan stew. By the next day, he knew that hobos threw anything edible, and a few things that were doubtful, into a kettle of boiling water. That explained why the smell and the taste of the hot stew never seemed the same two days in a row.

Today, the smell, mixed with tobacco smoke under the roof, mingled and collided with the rank odor of dried sweat on filthy clothes and the stench of bad toilet habits that lingered on dirty bodies. Men often suffered from food poisoning and diarrhea with only scraps of newspaper, a catalog page, or corncobs to finish the job. And they found few places or chances for a bath or laundry.

On a street in town, people often found them disgusting, wrinkled their noses at hobos and avoided them. But the hobo lifestyle was more than tolerated in cornfields, boxcars, and jungles. It was a culture of its own, founded by men like Stretch, Booty, Slim, Shorty, Snag, Bonzo, Greaser, Goose, and Limpy. And of course, Halo, along with thousands more.

Most had nicknames, some earned, some not. The handles were not used to conceal their past lives from other hobos. Instead, they protected the people back home from disgrace, so the left-behind didn't have to associate the family name with a hobo.

All hobos had dreams of a better life ahead, and they shared stories and rumors about good times coming tomorrow, as if repeating them could make them come true. They grabbed at any sliver of hope, for they wanted only to work, to earn their own way. And the dream job was any job that would allow them to support a family.

For now, they were America's orphans. A government that promised a chicken in every pot and a car in every garage had instead dumped a hobo on every rubbish pile, and left him with only his own two feet for transportation.

Now, they were desperate men with shabby, ill-fitting clothes and mismatched shoes they'd often found in that pile of rubbish. Now, they were men who scrambled and scraped to feed themselves every day as a way of life, who often had to give ten hours of hard labor for a single meal just to stay alive.

Not all stayed alive. They died from accidents on the railroads, from bitter cold weather, from heat exhaustion, from parasites and disease. They died from cheap wine that promised short-term relief from long-term misery, relief that destroyed the liver. They died of pneumonia, suffered from malnutrition or gut-wrenching dysentery, and fell dead in a roadside ditch, a farmer's field, or outhouse.

Only a man who learned fast would survive the harsh life, and making connections in the hobo brotherhood was a big part of the self-training. To be accepted in a jungle, a survivor knew he must often lend a hand with a chore, toss on a stick of firewood, drop a nickel in the coffee fund, and accept another man's habits, quirks, personality, and even body odor.

Each man understood that he added to that overall fragrance of a hobo jungle. And though the collection of smells was seldom pleasant, it was not one most men thought of as a tolerated condition. It became instead, a common comfort like the familiar face of a dear and ugly friend—a part of their identity, a part of the culture, a language that told them they were among friends in the presence of strangers. And true friendship was what a man prized most. Or at least as much as a hot meal on a cold day.

With a dozen discussions going at once, the crowd under the roof was never quiet, and a man often yelled to be heard above the noise. After an hour or more of laughs, economic forecasts, and philosophy, Blue yelled out to ask if anyone had seen Halo today. No one had.

Minutes later, a new man joined the group and worked his way into the open spot. Within seconds, a raindrop splattered on the man's nose. The nose drop was everyone's favorite practical joke from the rain. The victim's reaction always made him look stupid. After another round of laughs, Blue asked the victim about Halo.

"Yeah," the man said, "I thought you knowed about it. I talked to him a while ago. He was catching the 6:40. Said he was making his way back to Illinois."

Blue shook his head. "That couldn't a been him."

The man answered with a quick nod. "It was him alright. I said, 'Ain't your guitar-playin' friend going with you?' I felt bad for him. He had kind of a long face and he said real slow, 'Blue found a girlfriend. I don't think he wants me around.'"

Chapter Twenty-Six

Ten minutes after the talent show, Sherry ran out the front of the church where the crowd now stood and talked to the contestants. Blue stood with his foot propped on the wooden, rear bumper of a pickup truck and played a slow love tune. Three teenage girls swayed and swooned in front of him with worshiping grins that looked to be permanent. Sherry stopped behind the girls and waited. But not long.

"Excuse me, Blue." She held up her hand. "Sorry for interrupting, girls," she said when they turned toward her. She moved between Blue and the girls.

"I've got the voting results." She stood beside him, caught his wrist, and raised his hand. "Mister Blue Bailey wins second place in our talent show." Sherry brought his hand down and placed money in it.

The three girls dropped their shoulders. One sighed, another shook her head. The other said, "We all thought he would win first prize. He was the best." The other two nodded as Sherry turned.

"Second prize is good too," she told them. "You should congratulate him."

Sherry drove Blue back to the jungle, and talked all the way.

"I'm so proud of you, Blue. You should have won first place, but I guess you really couldn't."

Blue's face was a puzzle. "Why is that?"

"Well, I know it's not supposed to work this way, but the pastor's son was in the show and a lot of people felt obligated to vote for him." She turned to look at him. "I'm sorry. But at least you won $1.05."

For the next twenty minutes, she tried to persuade Blue to attend church with her. Blue did not commit. When she stopped the car at the jungle, Blue reached over and squeezed her hand.

"Thanks for everything, Sherry. For getting me into the show..." He opened his hand and smiled. "For the money, and for the ride." He reached for the door handle.

Sherry cleared her throat. "Didn't you forget something?"

Blue shoved the money into his pocket, and reached for his guitar in the back seat. "I think I got everything."

"You mean a girl gives you money, takes you home, and brags on you all the way, and..." She shook her head. "You don't even offer her a goodnight kiss before you get out of the car?"

Blue felt his face grow warm while his eyes grew large, and he turned toward her.

"Oh, Sherry, I'm—"

She planted a big kiss on his lips, drew back and looked at him, and then kissed him again.

Blue's pulse quickened and his breath got heavy as she drew back, looked at him, and broke out a big grin.

"Okay, Blue. You can go now."

***

Blue remembered last night's kiss and how Sherry made him feel things inside he'd never known before. He did not remember the start time for Sunday School, but he heard music and singing when he arrived at the church. Maybe being late was rude. Better to make no impression than a bad one, his mother often said. He walked across the street, found a shaded stump, sat and waited.

The music died. The church sat quiet for a minute or so. Then the sounds of a piano came through the open windows with a vengeance, and it seemed the whole congregation sang as loud as it could. When the music died again, Blue assumed church was done for the day. He stood, ready to walk back across the street, when a man inside the church began yelling about sin and the fires of hell. Blue sat again and waited.

And waited.

Blue jerked awake when the church doors opened and people streamed out in endless chatter. He started to cross the street just as Sherry came out of the church. He stopped and waved. She waved back, and then stood with her hands on her hips, and stared. Blue couldn't tell if she was happy or mad as she came toward him.

"What're you doing? How long you been here?"

"A couple of hours, I guess. Just waiting for you." Blue explained why he waited outside, and Sherry shook her head.

"Mama's at home cooking," she told him. "We got company coming for a fried-chicken dinner after church. So I have to get home and help her. But I got time to give you a ride back to the jungle if you want."

The ride to the jungle was the same as the night before, with Sherry talking most of the way there. For Blue, it was all worthwhile. He got another big kiss, and tingled all inside, before he left the car.

Chapter Twenty-Seven

"Shorty, you got a twin brother?"

"What?"

"I left you in Possum Trot. But when I get here to Dyersburg, You're here too."

Shorty laughed as he stood and scratched his backside. Then he sat down again on the log where men often rested with their backs to the fire and swapped jokes about the government.

"Wish I did have a twin. But no, I got no family. I tend the pot here as long as there's a dozen men or more in the camp. When it's below that, I go back to Possum Trot. When it's low there, I come back here. It's a short trip."

Blue spread his hands. "How come you always tend the pot?"

"It's a job that needs to be done. And the pot boss always eats."

Blue chuckled, shook his head, and asked himself why he'd never thought about that. The man who tends the pot always has a meal. He looked up and nodded. Shorty was a rare hobo—not skinny.

Shorty turned and nodded at a man walking toward the jungle. "I didn't know Rev was here in Dyersburg, but it don't surprise me none."

Blue stood, shaded his eyes, and watched a long-legged man on the gravel road who walked fast with a slight limp.

"I been a hobo for three years," Blue said. "I hear about a preacher called Rev from everybody I meet. But I never met the man. Is that him?"

"The same," Shorty said as Blue sat down.

"You're about to meet a legend." Shorty laughed, and added, "Or at least he *thinks* he is. Some stories about the hobo preacher are true, but a lot of 'em ain't. A few months ago, I heard one about Rev turning water into wine at a jungle in Texas." Shorty shook his head and laughed. "Now, I got some serious doubts about that one. Don't get me wrong, Rev's a good man, and he's on a mission to save us hobos from hell.

"He plans his travels so he can be in a jungle somewhere when Sunday gets here." Shorty grinned. "And every time before a sermon, he'll dig a wadded ol' green necktie from his pocket and hang it on his neck. Everybody makes fun of him, but he wears it like a badge."

Rev stopped, shaded his eyes and stared. He rested his Bible on a large rock, and dug something from his pocket. Shorty's grin got larger.

"Yep, there he goes with the necktie. And here he comes."

As the man with the Bible limped into the jungle, Shorty shook his head. "Come Sunday, he'll preach around the kettle at breakfast. Says he can corral more souls in one place that way. He acts like he comes to do battle. And a battle is what he usually gets."

Blue's eyebrows shot up. "Yeah, but this is Tuesday, and the day's almost gone."

"It don't matter. Here he comes, and you're about to get preached at, Blue."

"Why me?"

Shorty smiled and lowered his voice. "He's cherry pickin'. Figures the young ones are easier to convince."

"Of what?"

"You're about to find out."

The lanky preacher stopped in front of Blue.

For a tall man, the tie was much too short, and it suffered stains from mulligan stew, dirty pockets, and all the times the devout reverend lifted the end of the tie and wiped his sweaty face in the middle of a sermon. He leaned and stuck out his hand.

"What's your name, young man?"

"His name's Blue, Rev, if it's any of yer damn business."

Blue turned to see a man standing by the fire who pointed his tin cup at the preacher.

"Before you start telling us that God loves everybody, how about telling us why we're living like this. A lot of folks in this country ain't got enough to eat, don't have good clothes or a decent place to lay their head. You tell God to make it all better tomorrow, Rev. Maybe then we'll buy what you're selling."

The preacher looked around at the other men and then jerked his head toward the man who spoke.

"Who cranked him up?"

No one replied. Rev held up his Bible and shook it at the man. "You're disputing God's word, mister, not mine. I just deliver the message. If you don't believe, well… you're the one that's gotta pay for that."

He turned back to Blue. "Good to meet you, Blue. They call me Rev. You believe in the Word of God?"

Blue shrugged. "Which word?"

"Uhm… all of them." He shook the Bible at Blue.

Blue shrugged. "I don't know 'em all. Only a couple."

"You ever go to church, son?"

"Yeah, I went to church a lot, but—"

"A lot? I'm proud of you, Blue."

Blue nodded. "Yeah, four times. Two funerals and a wedding thing. And then I went with my Mama's sister once for no reason at all."

"No reason? What did they do?"

"Sung and preached. Stuff like that."

Rev's jaw tightened and he rolled his eyes. "Do you believe in heaven and hell, Blue?"

"It don't make no difference what I think. It ain't left up to me to say if there is or ain't."

Rev waved the closed Bible again. "The Good Book says a lot of people are gonna burn in hell, but anybody can go to heaven if they believe."

"Anybody?"

The preacher drew up his chin and rocked back and forth. "That's right son. Anybody… if they believe. Do you believe, Blue? Tell me what you believe." The preacher's eyebrows seemed to claw for higher ground as he leaned forward and stared down at the young hobo.

Blue rubbed his chin and thought hard. He crossed his arms over his chest and looked up.

"If my daddy makes it to heaven, I believe his ass end will be on fire before he gets there."

Half a dozen men broke into a laugh. Rev shook his head and walked away.

***

All night long in the jungle, hobos coughed, wheezed, sneezed, and snored. And no matter the hour, at least one hobo would be looking for a blanket, a smoke, a place to take a leak or a spot closer to—or farther from—the fire. Though it was a half mile from the jungle, Blue loved the peace and quiet of the old barn where he slept a dozen times before. He grabbed his sack and guitar and took off across the field, worried like always that the barn would be gone—torn down, burned, or blown away. But minutes later, the rusty tin roof of his favorite refuge came into view, a silhouette in the dying sun.

Since the first time he'd seen it, the old barn came alive and cast a spell on Blue each time he came. It stood alone, a silent sentry on the abandoned farm, tired but proud; empty, yet flush with memories of busier days—of wagons and plows, horses and mules, a milk cow and a family dog. Memories of a hardscrabble life and hard-labor men, the endless chores of wives and mothers whose struggles made them old before their time, and the ceaseless energy of noisy children.

The barn held memories of a nearby house that a happy family once called home. Now, a blackened and crumbling stone chimney marked the place where the home had stood, where the family lived and loved, laughed and cried, hoped and despaired. Where they shared goals and dreams and homemade ice cream, whispered secrets on the front porch swing, and said grace before meals. The home where children grew up and parents grew old now remained only as an outline of ashes in a field of invading weeds.

Barn walls held the gentle scent of weathered wood and the lingering smell of new-mown hay. Daylight squeezed through knotholes, intruded between planks, heated the barn, and scattered ragged streaks of sunlight across the shadowed floor.

At night, streaks of sun gave way to ribbons of moonlight while the cool breeze coasted through with easy whispers. Silence would follow. Then the whispers would advance again.

Boards held no memory of paint, for decades of wind and rain had washed the sides and softened the corners while sun faded the colors and added dignity and character like the silver hair of an aging man. And like that aging man, the frame leaned, groaned in the wind, and told the story of the old barn's past—of failed crops and seasons of plenty, of droughts and floods, heat and cold, joy and tears, of life and death within its walls, and indiscretions in the hayloft.

"I wish I may, I wish I might." Blue stood with his fingers crossed and looked at the sky while he wished upon an early star that the barn would stand as long as he lived. He wasn't sure why this old building stirred feelings inside him each time he came. But he knew that feelings were stronger than thoughts, and somehow the barn seemed to hold the missing pieces of a life he'd always craved but never known. Here, he was a part of the old barn and it was a part of him. Here, he slept better than he ever slept anywhere.

He'd need a good night's sleep for the big day ahead.

***

After an early breakfast, Blue washed his cup, dug a rag out of his sack and borrowed a lump of soap from Skeeter. Behind the cardboard curtain next to the rain barrel, he dipped water from the barrel to wet the rag and scrub down, and then to rinse. He dried off with his blanket, dressed, and spread the blanket and the rag over a bush in the sun while the other men watched him.

When Blue dropped his cup back into the sack, the men nodded and whispered. And when he returned the soap, Skeeter grinned as if he wanted Blue to explain. Blue grinned back but ignored Skeeter the same way he ignored the others.

A man yelled, "Hey Blue, you got a date tonight?" Another said, "This ain't Saturday. Didn't Rev tell him it's a sin to take a bath on Wednesday?"

Blue had a good reason for a Wednesday bath. Yesterday, he met Sherry at the Red Cross station during her lunch break. She claimed she brought far too much food, so the two of them shared her lunch in the shade of a big tree. They ate and talked and laughed.

"Kinda like a picnic, huh?" Sherry said.

Blue shrugged. "Never been to one."

Her eyes widened. "I get Wednesday afternoons off, so let's have one tomorrow. Just you and me. I know a perfect spot on the river bank. I'll pack some sandwiches and pick you up about twelve-thirty in my father's car, okay?" Sherry didn't wait for an answer. She leaned close and whispered, "And bring your guitar."

When they finished lunch, Sherry gave him a bag, a little present, she called it. Inside, he found britches, socks, and two shirts, and she told him they came from her church's clothing drive. But these were new. Never in his life had Blue owned new clothes. And someone had guessed the right sizes on everything.

Now, in a jungle filled with hobos, he tried not to strut. But he was mighty proud of his new clothes.

When Blue asked for the time, two men yanked out their trusty pocket watches and argued about a one-minute difference, though neither could prove his watch was right. The exact time didn't matter to Blue. He wasn't catching the 9:05 to Memphis. He waited for the 12:30 to river bank.

A small knot formed in his gut. What if Sherry had to work past noon? Or had car trouble? Or worse. What if she changed her mind about the picnic? Anything could happen. If he told the men in the jungle he was waiting for a pretty, young woman and then she didn't show, no matter the reason… well, he'd never live it down. Besides, it was fun to keep them guessing. So he let them go about their daily chores, and told them nothing.

Skeeter sat and sipped from his cup while he cut squares from a pair of discarded overalls to make patches for the ones he wore. Next, he fitted layers of newspaper cutouts inside his shoes to cover the holes in the soles.

Finished, he put on his shoes and stood to check out the repairs. Satisfied, he sat again and dug a pack of papers and a cloth bag of Bull Durham from his chest pocket. Automatic responses came from men who watched Skeeter while he rolled a smoke and put away the tobacco. One breathed deep and rubbed his chest. Lips twitched on a couple of other men, and one held his fingers to his lips as if he was smoking. None seemed aware of his own actions. But Skeeter understood the habit. He pulled out the makings again and passed them around. The men took advantage of his offer and gathered around to smoke.

Shorty stood in the center of the men who sat on stumps or logs. They passed around a burning twig from the fire to light their smokes. Shorty held up his cigarette. "Thanks, Skeeter. You been busy all morning and ain't said a word. What's going on with Blue?"

Skeeter wagged his head. "I don't know any

more'n you do."

"Maybe you're just jealous like the rest of us 'cause we figger Blue's gonna get a lot a good kissin' and huggin' and who knows what all." He grinned big as he glanced at Blue, and then turned back to Skeeter. "I bet it's been a long time since a woman smacked you a big juicy kiss."

Skeeter wrinkled his face as the men laughed. "I ain't jealous of nothin' or nobody."

"Oh no. Of course you ain't."

"You're wrong, Shorty. Maybe I ain't a guy most women would want to kiss. But even if I was, I don't want nobody kissing on me."

Shorty's eyes grew big as he blew out a cloud of smoke. He shook his head. "Well now, I don't rightly know what to say about a man that don't like a woman to kiss him."

"I don't have to explain nothing," Skeeter told him.

The men watched him but didn't talk as Skeeter licked his fingers and squeezed the fire from his cigarette butt. Then he rolled the butt back and forth between his thumb and forefinger and sprinkled the remaining tobacco back into the bag. He put the bag away, looked around at the men, and cleared his throat. He stared at the ground.

"When I was growing up, my daddy's cousin would come over to our house all the time to bum a meal. Her name was Josephine but I called her Josa Fart. I hated her sorry ass 'cause she always wanted to kiss me."

Shorty chuckled. "And did you let her?"

"Hell no, I didn't let her. I'd run and hide ever time she'd come over. But one time, Daddy made me come out, and she chased me down. She was a ugly, bald-mouth, snuff-dippin' bitch with big ol' floppy titties, and her breath smelled like puppy shit. She pinned me down on the floor, grabbed me by the ears and tried to swaller my face. When she was done torturing me, I crawled outside and puked."

Shorty's face said he didn't know whether to laugh or cry. "Your daddy didn't help you?"

"Naw, he thought it was funny, 'til the next time she showed up. She had a ugly toothless grin and she stuck out her big hawg lips and said, 'I'm gonna kiss you a long time, little buddy.'"

I doubled up my fist and shook it at her and said, 'No you ain't. I wouldn't let you kiss my nekid ass.' Then I took off and hid under the house."

Skeeter's look of disgust didn't change while he waited for the men to stop laughing. Then he said, "A while later, she left, and I crawled out. Daddy blistered my butt with a switch, but it was worth it, 'cause she never tried to kiss me again. Ain't no woman that's kissed me since, and that's just the way I like it."

Shorty wrinkled his brow and shook his head. "Do us all a big favor, Skeeter: please don't tell us about the first time you got screwed."

***

Hobos made trips to the kettle, told worn-out jokes, passed around a newspaper, and swapped the latest rumors about jobs. Jobs were always in another town… until the men got there. In Albuquerque, they said the jobs were in Santa Fe. In Santa Fe, they were in Homestead, Florida. When men found work at a new location, it was never enough, and most jobs paid far less than the rumors claimed. The rumor in Homestead said they could find work in Dyersburg. So they came.

Two or three would find day-jobs at the local sawmill or cotton mill. Others might pick beans or corn on a nearby farm for a day or two. At the end of the job, they'd put a few extra pennies in their pockets, and the farm workers would get a pound or two of the harvest to take along, something they could throw in the mulligan pot at the jungle. But most men would find nothing except more rumors. And tonight, a dozen men or more would hop the midnighter out of Dyersburg to chase the good jobs in other towns.

Blue sat on a wooden crate away from the crowd, tuned his guitar, picked a few tunes and hummed along. Then he called out to a man with a pocket watch and asked the time.

"Twelve fifty-six," the man said. Blue stood, leaned his guitar against the crate, and told himself Sherry had a good reason for missing their date. He'd been excited about the picnic and spending time alone with her, and his stomach had been excited about the meal. Now, it appeared he'd spend his afternoon at the camp and settle for more stew.

First thing this morning, Blue had chopped a small bunch of wild green onions he'd gathered, and tossed them into the big steaming pot as other men threw in potatoes, carrots, and beans. One man skinned and butchered a squirrel he caught with a rat trap. Not much meat, but it added bulk and a bit of taste to the mix. Now that the other guys had breakfast and lunch, Blue hoped there'd be enough for him. He started for his sack to retrieve his cup.

A car door shut, and Blue looked toward the road. Sherry waved and walked toward him while mumbles and whispers buzzed through the camp. Every man stood and scanned her up and down as she approached. Blue smiled and tried not to look smug when he took her hand. He led her to his guitar, picked it up, and turned back toward the car while every eye in the jungle followed them.

A long moan came from a man with dark hair and a red beard. “You believe that? Blue really does have a date.” He shook his head. “I’da bet against it.”

The man beside him laughed. “Hell, you ain’t got nothin’ to bet with.”

The crowd laughed as Blue held the driver’s door open for Sherry. A tall hobo near the kettle yelled, “Hey, honey, if I learn to play the guitar, will you take me for a ride?”

Blue’s date didn’t answer. Instead, she caught the back of Blue’s neck, pulled his head down and gave him a big kiss. Then she smiled and waved as she got into the car.

Shorty talked loud enough for the whole jungle to hear. “Now Skeeter, you can’t tell me you wouldn’t like a kiss from that woman.”

From behind Shorty, Skeeter said, “She sure don’t look nothin’ like Josephine.”

Blue moved to the other side of the car and laid his guitar on the back seat. With the door open, he stepped onto the running board, cupped his mouth and yelled across the top of the Model B Ford.

“Don’t stay up and wait for me, fellas. I might be late.” He scrambled in, shut the door, and they were gone.

Chapter Twenty-Eight

Blue had never been alone with Sherry for more than five minutes at a time. He stole a kiss when he could, but now as they drove to the river with the windows up to keep out bugs and dust, he didn't know what to do or say. He would've felt uneasy in a quiet car. But it never was.

Sherry drove too fast and watched the road too little. But she talked full-time about her family and about friends at work. She talked loud to be heard above the clatter of the car on the gravel road and the loud pops when the tires slung gravel against the underside of the fenders.

The noise also drowned out the growls in Blue's gut as the smell of food teased him from the basket in the back seat. After several minutes of noise from the car, from Blue's gut and Sherry's life story, she turned into a field of small trees and tall weeds where a pair of tracks meandered toward the river. After a mile or more over dips, bumps, and scrapes, the tracks ended.

Blue leaned to kiss her as soon as the car stopped. Sherry giggled and drew back.

"Plenty of time for that later," she said. "Let's go eat." She hopped out and lifted the basket off the seat while Blue picked up his scissors and stuck them in his back pocket. As he lifted his guitar, Sherry pointed at the floor. "Grab that old blanket."

They followed a narrow trail to the river and spread the blanket on the bank. From the basket Sherry grabbed a Mason jar filled with lemonade and chipped ice, and poured it into cups while Blue dug out egg-salad sandwiches and pickles wrapped in wax paper. Blue dug the scissors from his pocket and laid them near the blanket as he sat. Sherry made a face.

"How come you carry the scissors everywhere?"

Blue glanced at them. "That's the best tool I got. Never know when I might need them."

Sherry shook her head. "Tool? They look more like a weapon. You could probably kill somebody with those things."

Blue laughed and reached for the food.

Minutes later, they laughed and made faces at each other while they ate.

"Sorry," Sherry said, "I didn't think about it. I guess lemonade doesn't go with sour pickles. But, if I do say so myself, I'm a pretty good cook."

Blue took a big bite and then held up his sandwich and nodded.

Sherry cocked her head. "No, I don't mean sandwiches. I make chicken, biscuits, gravy, mashed potatoes, all kinds of good things. And I make a great breakfast with eggs, bacon, potatoes, biscuits, and gravy. How'd you like to wake up to that every day, Blue? I mean… it's important for a woman to make a man happy."

Blue shifted back and forth and cleared his throat. "I'm already happy and I uh… I like everything." He took another big mouthful and chewed for a long time. As soon as he swallowed, he said, "So how long you been driving?"

"About three years. Dad taught me so I could take my mother to church. She doesn't drive."

"Your daddy won't take her?"

She shook her head and looked down. Her words came out just above a whisper. "Not anymore."

Sherry finished the last of her lunch and took a deep breath. "My parents used to go every Sunday, and took my sister and me to church and Sunday School. Then my sister got rheumatic fever.

"Every night at bedtime, my father got out the Bible, and our family got together by my sister's bed and we prayed really hard that she would be healed. The church even held a special prayer service just for her, and everybody came and prayed out loud for a long time."

Sherry crossed her arms over her chest. Her eyes lost focus as she stared down. "My sister never got to grow up, to have a boyfriend, to get married and have kids. To have her own house or yard. None of that. She was younger than me, only thirteen when she died." Sherry took a long breath and shook her head. "I don't think Daddy ever forgave God for that. He ain't been to church since."

Like Sherry, Blue looked down at the blanket. "My sister died too. But it's not God's fault. It's cause my daddy was drunk. He always was."

"How old was she?"

"Two. And then my mama died a few weeks ago. That was my daddy's fault too. But I don't want to talk about it no more."

Sherry leaned and hugged him. "I'm sorry."

After a minute of silence, she started to clean up and put things into the basket. Finished, she sat in front of him, her eyes now sparkling, and searched his face while he stuffed the last of the sandwich into his mouth. Her face changed as she talked.

"Blue, when we first met, I asked you how

you got your name. You said it was an old Indian custom. The first thing your daddy saw after you were born was a blue-tick hound dog. He didn't like the name tick or hound dog, so he said your name was Blue. When I thought about it later, I figured out that was a lie. And then I got mad because you made me feel stupid."

Blue covered his mouth and laughed at Sherry's ruby face and hard stare. He looked away, and the harder he tried to stop, the harder he laughed. When his eyes grew wet from laughing, Sherry jerked his hand away from his mouth and leaned forward. "I'm glad you think it's funny, but I don't want any more bullshit. Just tell me the truth."

The laughter died. Blue had never heard her talk that way. He wiped his eyes on his sleeve and cleared his throat.

"Okay, here's the truth according to my dear mother. She said the night I was born, it was just too hot to give birth in the house. So the woman who was with her helped her outside, and Mama laid down on a tow sack under a big oak tree. When I came out, the woman cut the cord and cleaned me up. That naked little boy kicked and squalled, and she held him toward the sky and said, 'I yanked a lotta babies into this world, but this is the first child I ever pulled out during a blue moon.' Mama said, 'I think that's a good sign. We'll call him Blue Moon Bailey.'"

Sherry sat with her arms across her chest and her head lowered, and rolled her eyes up at him.

"Blue Moon? Now you're telling me your name is Blue Moon? If you're lying to me again, it's not funny. I'm going to—"

"That's my real name. I swear. That story?" He shrugged. "I don't know, but it's what my mother told me."

Her eyes softened and a weak smile formed. "Actually, I kinda like it."

"I'm glad you like it, but don't ever tell anybody what my middle name is." When Sherry didn't respond, he stuck his face in front of her. "Never."

She looked up, startled. "Okay, I promise." She sat without speaking, lost in thought while she checked her fingernails, and then said, "Blue, I want to ask you something. You can tell me it's none of my business if you want to, because it's not. But uh… have you ever… you know… done it?"

He stared at her. "Done it?"

"Yeah, you know, like… with a girl?" When he didn't answer, she touched his arm. "It's okay if you never did. I mean… a woman has to ask questions. But you don't have to tell me if—"

"I'm nineteen. Not twelve."

"Of course. I'm sorry, Blue. I should have never even—"

"Two times."

"Oh. I didn't mean to pry, I just…"

Blue drained his cup of lemonade and wiped his mouth with the back of his hand. "When I was fourteen."

Sherry rolled her eyes. "Two times? When you were fourteen? Are you kidding me?"

"I'm not kidding. It's just that I never told anybody before."

"I thought boys like to brag about their girlfriends. But of course she said, 'Don't ever tell anybody.' And you didn't. That's very sweet of you, Blue."

"She didn't say that."

"No?"

"It was not my girlfriend." He looked away from her. "It was my mother's cousin. Her name is Lyla."

"Oh no. I mean... really? Your mother's cousin?"

"Now you know why I never told."

"It's getting hot out here." Sherry held the hair off the back of her neck to let it dry, and looked up. "How old was the girl?"

Blue looked at her for a few seconds before he answered. "Fifteen. She showed up at our house one Sunday and asked me if I wanted to walk to church with her. She said her friend was gonna get married after church was over, and they'd have cake and stuff. So I went. And then on the way back we took a shortcut through the cornfield and she said, 'Well, I guess we know what they're gonna be doing tonight.' We both laughed, and then the next thing that happened was she just stopped and looked at me and said, 'Blue, you wanna do it?'"

Sherry covered her grin. After a minute of silence, she took his hand. "Don't you want to ask about me?"

He shook his head. "It's none of my business."

"You're being too sweet. But I'll tell you anyways." She looked away and said, "I never have. I always wanted to wait for the right man. You understand?"

Blue didn't understand, but he nodded.

When she turned back, he was pulling something from his left shoe. He held it out to her.

"What's this all about?" She unfolded a two-dollar bill. Blue had written *Sherry* above the portrait. She smiled. "So you think I look like Thomas Jefferson?"

"Ha. No. I just want to give you something from me. Two-dollar bills bring good luck when you give them to someone you love."

Tears popped into her eyes. "Oh, Blue, this is really special." She leaned and kissed him. "I'll give you two one-dollar bills because you need this money. I know you do."

"No. If you pay for it then it wouldn't be a gift. It'd break the good luck part. It might even be bad luck."

She held it next to her heart. "I'll keep it forever." She dragged her purse next to her and tucked the bill into a small pocket. "Blue, does this mean you're serious about this?"

"About *what?*"

"You know. About us. Do you ever think about things?"

"What things?"

"Things like where you'll be five years from now. Who you'll be with. Things like getting married. That kind of stuff." She looked up at him.

His face was a big smile. "Married? Me? No, I never really thought about that. Do you?"

"A lot. Having a good man who loves me, a couple of kids, maybe. A little house a mile or two from town with a picket fence, chickens in the yard scratching up the flowers I worked so hard to plant. And I want a covered front porch where we can sit in the rockers and talk while some old hound dog snoozes beside us. I see me standing on that porch waiting for the dust to settle after the mail truck comes by, then walking out to my own mailbox and finding a catalogue with my name on it, or a letter from a friend who lives out of town. And I imagine my husband sitting at the kitchen table reading the funnies in the newspaper while I'm cooking breakfast for him, and watching him smile when the eggs are just right, and listen to him brag about how good the coffee is." She smiled and her face glowed pink. "And feeling him slap me on my bottom when I turn around to get him some more coffee."

She giggled, and then turned serious again. "Is that too much to ask for, Blue?"

Blue wagged his head and grinned. "I'd slap your bottom anytime you like."

Sherry didn't smile. "You know what I mean. Don't you have dreams and wishes like that too? They're not just for women, you know."

Blue squirmed and rubbed his chin. At last, he looked up at her and shrugged. "I guess I don't. At least not the same way."

She stuck her face close to his and whispered, "Why not?"

"Well, you know. I'm not a man that a woman would say is a good catch. I don't even have a steady job. I'm just a hobo, remember?"

"You don't have to stay one."

They sat without talking while she dug a handkerchief and a small mirror out of her purse and dabbed at her face. Finished, she returned the items, snapped the purse closed and looked at him again. "There's a difference between a hobo and a vagabond, you know."

"A vagabond? What's that supposed to mean?"

"Vagabonds are just bums. They don't want to work. Hobos do. You know my father's the boss at the sawmill."

"I know. A man came to the jungle this morning in a truck. Said he worked for Mister Wolfe. He picked up three men to work at the sawmill." Blue's eyebrows arched and he leaned close. "I would've gone, but I had a date."

She caught his arm. "You see what I mean? You could work there too."

"That was just day jobs. They'll bring the men back by suppertime and they might not work again for two weeks."

"Yeah, but if we got married, I'd bet Daddy would give you a full-time job."

"Uh… married?" Blue fidgeted and looked away. "I uh… I don't know if that would work."

"Why not? You're a man. I'm a woman. You said you love me. It's not complicated."

Blue tried to stifle a nervous laugh but couldn't. "Sherry, I uh… I mean… what if your daddy didn't give me a job? What if he didn't even like me?"

She leaned back and stared. "Why wouldn't he? You'd be his son-in-law. He wouldn't want his daughter's husband to be without a job."

Blue stood and took a deep breath. He looked into the tall trees across the river. "I been to a lot a places and everywhere's the same. First time you go someplace, you might find work for a few days. Next time you go, there's nothing. No work, no factory, no business, no store, no people, because nobody's got any money to buy the stuff the businesses used to make or sell. When people can't buy lumber, nobody's gonna pay a man to just stand around and make sawdust."

"Well, if you didn't work at the sawmill, you could work *somewhere*. Maybe at the cotton gin. My father knows a lot of important people around here. Ask anybody if they know John Wolfe. You'll see. How do you think I got my job at the Red Cross?"

Blue turned and looked down at her. "Why

would you even want somebody like me? I got nothing. Maybe I'm just that vagabond you talked about."

She stood, leaned close, and pulled up his chin. Her voice rose. "No you're not. You're a good man, decent and kind. And I don't see you for what you have or don't have. I see you for what you can be… if you want to." Her words grew slow and soft. "But most of all, it's because I love you, Blue. I didn't plan for that to happen. It just… it just did. I'd be a good wife for you. I know I would. That is… if you really love me like you said."

"I do, Sherry. I meant that. It's just that all this stuff… it seems like it's moving too fast. I need to think about it for a few days." He turned his head again and stared across the river. "Besides, who ever heard of a hobo getting married? It's hard to make sense out of things sometimes."

She sat beside him and shook her head. "Sense? Love's not about sense. It's not numbers or arithmetic. You can't measure it with a yardstick. It's not about what you think or plan or try to figure out. It's about feelings, Blue. It's about what makes you happy or sad. It's what guides you through life, helps you make decisions about people who are important to you."

A light smile formed as she leaned close and placed her hand on Blue's arm. She looked into his eyes, and spoke just above a whisper.

"When you make a decision based on love… it's always the right decision."

Sherry stood, crossed her arms again and spoke slower. "Sorry, Blue. I didn't mean to preach." She grew quiet, looked around and took in everything. A mockingbird on a bare tree branch showed off its talent as it mimicked the calls of other birds. A small log bobbed and drifted down the river, and Sherry picked up a stone and threw it at the log. The bird flew away when the rock splashed in the water.

She walked among scattered wildflowers along the bank and picked a small white flower. Blue sat cross-legged on the blanket and chewed on a stem of grass as he watched her. Sherry brought the flower back, stopped next to him and held it out. She caught a deep breath when he dropped the grass and took the flower. He smiled big, caught her hand and sat her down in front of him. Blue sniffed the flower and then held it under her nose. She jerked back and shook her head.

"What's wrong, Sherry? You don't like the smell of flowers?"

She shook her head again.

Blue frowned. "I never heard of a woman that didn't like flowers."

"Well, I think they're pretty. It's just that… at my sister's funeral, the church was so full of flowers they almost didn't have enough room for the people. When the funeral man led our family into the church, everybody else was already seated, and they started crying when they saw us. My knees got weak and I was hurting so much inside I could hardly stand. And the smell of flowers was so strong I thought I was gonna pass out. I guess it sounds crazy, but I just don't like the smell of them anymore."

Blue kissed her on the cheek and held her close. After a minute, Sherry pulled loose and leaned back. She spun around, lifted something from the basket, and unwrapped the towel that covered it. "You didn't see this in there, did you?"

"A bottle of wine. Where did you get that?"

"Well… let's just say my daddy knows a man…" She squeezed the bottle between her legs, popped out the cork, and held the bottle in front of his face. "How about it?"

When Blue leaned back and shook his head, Sherry laughed. "Just drink out of the bottle. It's okay."

"I uh… I don't drink."

"Nothing? Never?"

"I tried a couple of things. Some moonshine once, and tequila, but I didn't like it."

"This ain't like that. Just try it."

Blue tasted the wine. His throat didn't burn, and he tasted again. "Mmmmm." He took a large swallow and smiled as it went down. He nodded and they both grinned as he handed Sherry the bottle.

Sherry gulped, swallowed, and laughed. She returned the bottle to Blue and wiped wine from her chin with her hand. Blue took her wrist, pulled her hand to his mouth, and sucked the wine from her fingers. Sherry's mouth hung open. She licked her bottom lip. Her eyes grew wide.

The bottle changed hands a dozen times while they laughed and kissed, and laughed again. When the bottle was empty, Sherry's face grew serious. She looked down at the blanket and then up at Blue. She opened her mouth to speak, but didn't. She dropped her head, took a deep breath and looked up again.

"Blue, I'm sorry about, uh… about what I told you a few minutes ago. Because it's not true."

"What's not true?"

She lowered her head. "I'm twenty years old, Blue. I'm not a little girl anymore. I'm a grown woman." She cleared her throat, and dropped her head again. "And I'm uh… I'm not a virgin." She bit her bottom lip. When Blue did not reply, she looked up with a long face and a hint of fear behind her large eyes. "Well?"

"Well… truth is, I uh… I already knew how old you are." He smiled and looked away.

She straightened her back and brushed a tear from her cheek. "Please, Blue, don't make fun of me. Didn't you hear what I said? I'm trying to tell you something important."

He caught her arm, leaned and kissed the tears on her cheek. "I heard you, Sherry, and I'm not making fun. I'm trying to tell *you* something that's important. It's all right."

After a ragged breath, she spun around and stared at the river. "I had a boyfriend when I was eighteen and… a couple of times, we uh…" She shook her head. "I'm sorry."

"Did you love him?"

"I thought I did at first. But I didn't really. Once or twice he said he loved me but I could never say it back."

"Does he live around here?"

She shook her head. "Not anymore. He got a job in Rogers Springs and I never heard from him again. Which is good because I don't want to anyway."

Blue leaned close behind her and put his mouth to her ear. "It's okay, Sherry," he whispered. "It's okay. But I don't want to hear any more."

She turned her head to see his face. "You're not mad? You're really not mad? You don't think I'm awful? I was afraid that…"

"I'm not mad. I just… need to know… that you love me."

"I do love you." When she spun around, her

knee bumped his guitar. She picked it up. Her face glowed, her eyes smiled big. "Play a song for me, Blue. Play one that tells me how you feel about me. Please."

For a few seconds, he stared into the distance, brushing his open hand over the strings. Then he said, "How about one with my name in it?" With an easy strum on the guitar, his eyes locked on hers, and he sang.

What would I do
If you left me all alone
And I was so blue
What would I do?

Sherry bit her upper lip. Her eyes grew misty as Blue leaned closer.

What would I do
If I learned your love
Just wasn't true
What would I do?

Her eyes never left his as she clamped her hand around the neck of the guitar, eased it away from him, and laid it aside. "I love you more than anything," she whispered.

He touched his lips and whispered back. "Kiss me right here."

She wrapped her arms around him and pressed her lips to his with a kiss that grew long, passionate, and intense, with low moans, racing hearts, and *oh-baby* whispers—a kiss that left them fighting for air. Their lips separated and they leaned with their foreheads touching, her breath blending with his.

Blue's body ached for hers. But he feared Sherry's preacher had killed any chance for a blanket party. When Sherry and Blue sat in church during the Sunday night sermon, the man held up the Bible, shook it at them, and repeated the same scripture so many times that Blue remembered every word.

Walk in the Spirit, and ye shall not fulfill the lust of the flesh.

Now the works of the flesh are manifest, which are these; Adultery, fornication...

When they left the church, Blue told Sherry the preacher would have a hell of a time making friends if he keeps saying that stuff. Sherry shot Blue a hard look, but didn't reply.

Now, she spoke.

"I love you," she whispered into his mouth and then kissed him again. She took his hand, pushed it under her blouse and placed it on her breast. Blue's mind raced... *the lust of the flesh.* He moaned as she spread her hand over his and squeezed his fingers, and then moved her mouth to his ear. Her words were slow, soft, and deliberate.

"Make love to me, Blue."

Racing hearts and ragged breath shut out the world around them. They saw only lips and eyes and private places. Felt only need and desire. Heard only the music of rippling water and the heated passion of making love on the riverbank.

Blue's mind raced. *Was it the wine that made her want him? Would he have to save up for another bottle? A case?*

***

They sat side by side, held hands and watched the river. Then Blue listened while Sherry told him about her life—school, church, family, and growing up in Dyersburg. It was more of what he'd heard in the car, but Blue was glad she talked. It filled the awkward silence after their first time together. After they'd done it.

He thought of how hobos talked all the time about women. Blue believed some of what they said, but only some. One thing they seemed to agree on was that nothing's as good as your first time. They were wrong. Maybe it was about being in love. He didn't know. But he knew making love with Sherry on the riverbank beat the hell out of humping Mama's cousin in the cornfield.

Sherry stood and caught Blue's hand. She pulled him to his feet and led him along the shaded bank. Across the river, a raccoon doused his lunch in the water. A squirrel scampered up a tree in front of them, ran out on a limb and complained about their intrusion.

Sherry stopped, pulled Blue close and kissed him. "I loved your song. You said, 'What would I do if you left me all alone, and I was so blue? What would I do?' Well, you don't have to be alone, you know". She ran her fingers through his hair. "We never have to be apart again."

Blue did not reply. She turned and walked into the wildflowers like before. This time she walked farther where flowers grew taller in thick bunches along the bank. Blue waited and watched. He could see only her head as she got farther away. Then he could see only weeds and flowers moving, but didn't know if she made them move or if it was only the breeze.

A splash in the river got his attention, but he saw no cause for the splash. A branch fell from a tree, he guessed, though he saw no branch in the water. He looked back at the wildflowers.

They did not move. Sherry was gone.

He stood on his toes and craned his neck, but didn't see her. He walked toward the flowers and called her, but got no answer.

"Sherry," he called again, and walked faster. He ran into the flowers, calling her name. He stopped and looked in all directions as he spun around.

"Sherry, answer me, please." He waited and listened, and then ran in all directions through the maze of colors. "Say something, Sherry. You're scaring me, dammit."

"Sherry, I love you." His voice quivered when he thought again about the splash. His heart drummed in his ears. A lump grew in his throat and he started back toward the river. "Sherry, where the hell…" He stopped and stared and tried to catch his breath. Twenty feet away Sherry sat on a stump near the bank.

Blue took a step toward her, then another. "Sherry, are you all right?"

With a deadpan face, she looked up at him. "I'm fine."

"Didn't you hear me?" He stood in front of her. "That was not funny. I was worried sick. Why are you doing this?"

"Well, Blue, now you know how it feels."

"How *what* feels? You're not making sense."

"How it feels when someone you love suddenly disappears." Her head dropped, her eyebrows arched as she looked up at him. "Twice before, you took off without saying a word." She stared at him without blinking. "But you didn't show up five minutes later. Oh no. You stayed gone for months. I didn't hear from you and I didn't know if I'd ever see you again, or if you were dead or alive. Then you show up in Dyersburg whenever you feel like it and you think we can just pick up where we left off."

Blue sat down a few steps in front of her with his legs crossed, and shrugged. An unwelcome grin crossed his face as he rolled his eyes. "What happened a few minutes ago? That ain't exactly where we left off last time I was in town." Before he finished the last few words, he knew he'd said the wrong thing. But the grin left him stranded.

Her face distorted. "Is that what I am? Just someone for you to take advantage of?"

Blue's back stiffened. "Take advantage? You're the one who said, 'Make love to me, Blue.'"

"Oh yes, and you didn't exactly turn me down, did you?"

"I thought this was about me leaving. You got it figured wrong. Both times I left because I had a chance to get work. And when a hobo learns about someplace he can work, he's gotta jump and run, get there before the job's gone. I couldn't wait. I couldn't come and say goodbye. I had to catch the first train going in the right direction. That's just the way my life is."

"You call that a life?"

"Call it anything you want. But don't say I take you for granted. I keep coming back because I care about you, Sherry. You're warm and sweet and wonderful. You do things for me and you make me smile and feel good all inside. You make me want to be a better man and… besides all that, you uh… you make love like… like every teenage boy's dream. And I thought you liked it too." He breathed deep, his eyes grew misty, his voice low. "You're just… the most wonderful and the most beautiful woman I ever met. Sometimes, I can't believe I was lucky enough to find you."

He stared at the ground and waited for her to

reply, but she didn't speak. A minute later, he heard her moving but he did not look up until something dropped. Her shoes and socks lay beside the stump.

Her eyes never wandered from his while her fingers eased down to loosen the top button of her blouse. She watched Blue's eyes grow wild and wide as her fingers moved in slow motion, released the next button, paused for a few seconds, and then moved down to the next.

Blue felt his chest rise and fall, but his eyes never left *her* chest as her fingers worked painfully slow on each button. When all buttons were free, she leaned forward with her shoulders pulled back, and opened the blouse. His eyes grew wider still as she peeled off the blouse, held it above her shoes for a few seconds and then released her fingers and let it fall.

Blue sat up straight, speechless. His mouth dropped open. His breath came in shallow puffs as his bug-eyed stare absorbed her. A primal need coursed through every part of him. He started to push himself up, but she held out her hand and shook her head.

A silent gasp escaped his mouth when she stood, unfastened a button at her waist, and stepped out of the skirt. Blue felt his entire body responding as he watched Sherry drop the skirt on the pile and hook her thumbs in the waistband of her last article of clothing. A slight smile crossed her lips.

Blue slapped his face. "Oh my God."

He sprang to his feet as the delicate pink article slid to her knees and then to the ground. She lifted one foot, stepped out of the pink ruffle, and kicked it away with her other foot.

When he started toward her, she held out her hand again to stop him. Her eyes moved from the top of his head to his boots and back again. Then she licked her lips and cocked her head.

“Your turn.”

Chapter Twenty-Nine

His first picnic turned out to be the greatest day he'd ever had, Blue told himself. A better day than he'd ever imagined, a day when the world came back into focus while he lay on his back… in the grass… on the riverbank. He pulled her bare body tight against his and said, "I used to not believe in heaven."

She smiled. "And now you do?"

"You just took me there. I never dreamed anything could be that good."

She whispered into his ear. "If we got married, we could do this any time you want. Think about that."

"I will," he promised. "A lot."

Sherry kissed him again and rolled off. She turned her head to watch him behind her while she wiggled her bare butt and walked back to the stump where she'd left her clothes. Then she shrieked.

"Oh shit."

Blue jerked and sat up. Sherry grabbed at her clothes and covered herself as she stared at the river. A man sat in a canoe and stared back. While Blue scrambled for his own clothes, the man glanced at him, and then turned his head away and paddled downstream. Seconds later, he disappeared around a bend where trees hid the river.

Sherry shivered, her eyes tearing, embarrassment showing all over as she dressed. Blue thought again about the splash he'd heard in the river, and wondered how long the man watched from the canoe. How much did he see? How much did he hear before Sherry noticed him?

Blue finished dressing with his back turned to her. He told himself the situation was not funny. But he didn't convince his grinning face, and that was the last thing he wanted Sherry to see.

When Sherry began rolling up the blanket, Blue caught her hand. He pulled her to him and hugged her for a long time as he thought about the man in the canoe. He was a big man. He looked Indian, and wore a Robin Hood hat that had a short, red feather. He let Sherry go.

"Do you know that man in the canoe?"

She shook her head. "No. Thank God, I don't."

As the sun escaped behind the horizon, Sherry took the long way back to the jungle, and talked nonstop about what life might be like if they were married.

"Who knows?" she said. "In a couple of years, we could have some kids."

Blue smiled and nodded. "Maybe a little girl just as pretty as her mother."

Sherry looked at him and grinned. "Maybe a son who looks just like his daddy. Of course, you'd have to teach him to play the guitar." She laughed and then turned serious. "Blue, remember that day at the Red Cross station when you bought a candy bar for that little girl?"

His eyes grew wide. "How did you know?"

"I watched you through the window. What you did was the sweetest thing I ever saw in my life." She wiped a tear and looked at him. "I know you'd be a really good father, and our kids would be so proud to call you Daddy."

Sherry took deep breaths, and drove without talking. Blue had never seen that, but he watched her face, and knew she was not finished. An easy smile covered her face as she looked at him again, and he told himself she was the prettiest woman he'd ever seen. But his mind wouldn't let go of the man in the canoe. Sherry didn't know him. Blue had seen him before but thought better of telling her. He did not want her to worry, but he could not help feeling uneasy. He wanted her to talk, to lead his mind in another direction. She smiled, and turned to look at him.

"Not everything would be smooth and easy," she said. "But you know what they say… love conquers all."

Blue believed her, and the more they talked and planned and dreamed, the better it all sounded.

She would pick him up again tomorrow after she got off work. They would have dinner at her home and tell her parents about the wedding plans. Sherry said she'd be happy with a small ceremony, but she wanted to marry within a couple of weeks.

"I'll tell my parents you're coming," she said as she stopped the car at the jungle. They enjoyed a long goodnight kiss and then another. When Blue opened the door to leave, she squeezed his hand.

"You're a real charmer, Blue. Mom and Dad are gonna like you. I know they will." She brought a bottle of wine from the back seat. "Share this with your friends when you tell them the news."

***

Men sipped coffee and mulligan stew, smoked or chewed tobacco, talked low, and moved without noise. Smoke drifted with the breeze while glowing chunks of wood popped, and sank to the bottom of the pile. Firelight danced on tin cups and in the eyes of the half-dozen hobos who sat in the dark on logs around the campfire and solved everybody's problems. One man summed it up. "Gov'ment's the biggest pain in the ass we got. We'd be better off without no gov'ment anyhow."

A few men still moved about the jungle. The rest had turned in for the night. Some were promised jobs for tomorrow, and would be up by daybreak. Others would be up early to look for work. They lay on their backs or sides in bedrolls, stretched out on the ground or curled up with dirty blankets, rags, and newspapers in tiny shacks made of wood scraps, pieces of tin, cardboard, canvas, cotton sacks, and anything else they could find.

Blue tiptoed around the neighborhood, past grunts, groans, snores, and rumbling sounds of sleep to find his bindle. He dug out his cup, filled it with the hours-old coffee still warm in the pot, and sat on a log near a tree apart from the other men, where the fire cast just enough light for a man to find his way around.

His face distorted when he sipped the coffee—thicker than the mulligan stew, and bitter. He'd drink it anyway to stay awake, to sort out the day. Only now did he begin to realize all the plans he and Sherry made in a single afternoon. Tomorrow, the two of them would tell the world, and his life would change forever.

Blue sat, rested his head in his hands, and tried to shut out everything around him. But moments later, he heard feet shuffling nearby. Two hobos stopped in front of him. He'd seen them before. The one in a ragged cowboy hat always stood with his hands in his pockets. The other wore a goofy grin, and nodded every time someone spoke. Both men moved so slow Blue couldn't imagine how either could ever catch a train. He lowered his head again, hoping they would go away.

"Hey, Blue, we gonna catch out tomorrow, bout noon. You coming?"

"Not this time, boys." Blue did not look up, but he knew who asked the question. Cowboy's real name was Loman. The men called him Slowman. He was the slowest talker Blue ever heard.

"You… find… work… here?"

"Not yet. Maybe in a day or two." Blue stood and shook hands with them. "Where ya headed?"

Cowboy angled his head toward the tracks. "Ever been to Georgia?"

Goofy Grin nodded. "There's work in the peach orchards. Don't pay much, but dinner's free. That is… if you like peaches."

Cowboy added, "You really ought to think about coming with us, Blue. You'd be good company."

As slow as these guys moved, Blue couldn't imagine either one earning more than fifty cents a day picking peaches, or anything else.

"Been through there a couple of times. Never worked there. But there's something I gotta do tomorrow." He wished them luck, and the two men left.

An hour later, while he wrapped himself in his bedroll, an uneasy feeling gnawed at Blue. So many things had happened in the space of an afternoon and now he was afraid he'd overlooked something important. Maybe a sip or two of wine would help him sleep.

With his scissors, he persuaded the cork to free itself from the bottle Sherry gave him, took a sip, and then a gulp. He looked around. Everybody was asleep. They wouldn't appreciate it if he woke them just to share his wine. He took another sip, and another gulp, and realized he could not put a mangled cork back in the bottle. By morning, the wine would be no good, wasted. Unless…

***

The world was fuzzy, and sleep was too stubborn to leave him. But all around, men grunted and grumbled, yawned and groaned, cleared throats, blew noses, coughed, talked, and laughed. How could anyone sleep through all the noise?

Blue rubbed his face, shook his head, and sat up. After a trip to the pee tree just outside the jungle, he grabbed his cup and spoon. On his way to the kettle, he heard a truck, and he glanced at the road.

A pickup truck stopped on the roadside where Sherry parked her car the night before. A tanned arm hung out the window, and when Blue looked at the driver, the man extended his arm and motioned for him. Blue waited and stared. The driver motioned again. Blue walked toward him. When he got close, the man stepped out and left the truck running.

Blue stopped. His mouth went dry. This was the same man who came to the jungle yesterday to pick up dayworkers for the sawmill. Big. Tall. Long, black hair. Robin Hood hat. One red feather. The man's dark eyes did not blink. His gaze did not waver. His deep voice left no doubt about his meaning.

"Stay away from Mister Wolfe's daughter."

Blue's chin dropped. He watched the man take a pipe from his pocket, and press his finger into the bowl to pack the tobacco, or whatever he smoked.

"Stay away? Says who?"

The giant's eyes never left Blue as the man struck a match on the truck fender and lit the pipe.

"Says Mister Wolfe."

Blue's face paled. "What did you tell him?"

"I told Mister Wolfe you two had a picnic on the riverbank." He smiled and made a slight nod. Then he turned, slid into the truck, and poked his head through the window.

"Stay away from Mister Wolfe's daughter."

Blue rested his hands on his hips, and felt the scissors behind him. "And what if I don't?"

The Indian took a long draw from his pipe and blew the smoke toward Blue.

"I will tell Mister Wolfe everything I saw. And… I saw everything." As the smoke cleared, he said, "Then… I will do what Mister Wolfe wishes."

Morning sun flashed on the blade of a large knife in the man's hand.

Robin Hood drove away.

Chapter Thirty

Blue ran alongside the 11:45 bound for Atlanta, and handed up his guitar to Cowboy. He latched onto a board near the door, and swung inside. He'd seen these cars many times. They looked like big cages, or a rail fence with a roof. He'd never considered riding in one, and now he hated himself for letting Cowboy and Goofy talk him into making a trip in a damn cattle wagon.

"They're a lot cooler," they told him.

"Maybe so, but they gotta stink to high heaven."

"Naw," they said. "Lots of fresh air comes through. It's better than a boxcar." Goofy shrugged. "'Cept when it's raining."

Well, now he was in. He'd make the best of it. Blue grabbed a shovel that hung on a nail at one end of the car. He scooped dried cow manure and pushed it across the floor to the edge of the car, where it fell outside. Goofy and Cowboy sat against the back wall on hay bales, and watched. Neither offered to help. Goofy snickered.

"You won't even smell that stuff when the train's moving faster."

Blue ignored them, finished his job, and sat on a bale beside them.

"Well, boys, I had a feeling this damn cattle toilet was gonna stink like hell. But if you stink more than the manure, I guess you don't smell it. And you two ride in them all the time."

They looked at each other. Goofy wrinkled his forehead. "How many times we hitched a ride in one of these?"

Cowboy wagged his head. "We ain't never."

Blue frowned. "Never? But you said—"

Cowboy raised his hand. "No. We just figured out stuff."

Blue leaned toward them. "Figured out stuff?"

Goofy nodded. "That's what we do."

Blue pushed the hay bale against the wall, and leaned back. "Okay, tell me about picking peaches in Georgia. What is it, a half-day's ride from here?"

They looked at each other again. Goofy nodded. Cowboy answered.

"Figured you'd know far it is."

"Me?"

"Yeah. We ain't never been there."

"You ain't never…" Blue sat up. "Last night you said—"

Cowboy's head wagged. "We didn't say nothin'. We just, uhm…"

"I see," Blue said. "You just figured it out?"

Goofy nodded. "That's what we do. We wanted to try it. And we wanted you to come with us."

Cowboy grinned. "And here we are."

Blue leaned back again. "Okay, boys. Figure out how far it is, and wake me up when we get there."

***

While the cattle wagon rocked, Blue watched Sherry as she sat on that stump near the riverbank. He moved closer, and her fingers were on the buttons of her blouse while the wildflowers swayed in the breeze. He couldn't see her face right now, but she really was a beautiful woman. And she loved him.

Why did he have to leave her there? He wanted to be there with Sherry. He ran through the flowers with a bottle of wine, and called her name while something splashed in the river. That man in the canoe—was that her old boyfriend? Sherry's father is a wolf, and Robin Hood is his friend.

His face felt wet. Tears? Sweat? Water dripped from somewhere.

Blue jerked awake and sat up. Rain gushed in and drenched his clothes. Cowboy and Goofy ran around in the car and yelped while they tried to escape the soaking. The car had a solid roof but the rain blew through the sides. Neither man found a dry spot, but Cowboy's feet found a smudge of manure on the wet floor of the moving cattle wagon. He went down butt first. Hard. Cowboy yelled. Loud. Goofy watched and nodded. Blue hugged his hay bale, and again felt like an idiot for letting those other two idiots talk him into this trip.

In less than five minutes, the train moved out of the rain cloud, but the cloud had managed to soak everything except the hay bale Blue covered with his body.

The bright sun now turned the cattle car into a steam kettle. Blue moved near the side so he could breathe, and watched the countryside through the doorway while the sun and the breeze dried his clothes. Moments later he moved his guitar and bindle close to the door. He wanted them dry when he left the car, and the train was slowing. He glanced at the two men who leaned against the wall and out of the wind at the front of the car, and lit their pipes.

Cowboy and Goofy watched him and laughed. Cowboy said, "Hey, Blue. You don't have to jump. You can step out when it stops. Them railroad bulls don't come near this car."

Blue grinned. "You boys know about that? Or you just figured it out?" He knew it could have been the glow from the pipes that made their faces look red. Regardless, neither man spoke.

The car jerked as it slowed. The floor and hay bales had dried, but the manure under Cowboy's boot had not. He went down again. He yelled again, and his corncob pipe clattered to the floor. Ashes and sparks, caught in the breeze, scattered toward the rear of the car. And a glowing chunk of tobacco tumbled from the pipe and rolled headlong toward the hay bales.

Cowboy picked himself off the floor and snatched up his pipe as the car jerked again. He kept his balance, but swore at the car as he glared at his pipe.

"At's the last hunk o' tobakker I had." He eyed Goofy's pipe. "Now I can't even smoke."

Blue motioned toward the other end of the car. "Speaking of smoke, you'd better grab that bale and throw it out."

Cowboy looked up, shrugged, and ambled toward the bale. Goofy yelled behind him.

"Hey, Cowboy, I'm gonna tell your buddies you run outa tobakker and started smokin' hay."

While Goofy laughed, Cowboy grabbed the smoking bale and headed toward the door. The car jerked again. Cowboy tripped and dropped the bale. Blue started toward it, but Goofy raced to the scene and smacked the bale with the shovel. While Cowboy scrambled to get out of his way, Goofy beat the bale apart. It scattered across the floor, and the breeze carried it back to the other bales. Goofy chased the flaming stalks, still believing he could beat out the fire with the shovel.

"Get the hell out of here," Blue yelled. He strapped his guitar on his back, and grabbed his bindle. Cowboy rushed to pick up the bindles he and Goofy left near the bales. Seconds later, the bales exploded with flame, and Goofy's shirt was now on fire.

Blue could see only a cloud of smoke as the wooden side rails began to burn, and wondered if the other men could find their way to the door. He screamed again. "Over here. Over here. Get the hell out." He turned toward the door and leaped, hoping they would follow.

For several minutes, the train had been slowing. Blue knew it was still moving too fast for a safe jump, but he had little choice. His chin bounced on his knee as he landed, and his elbows plowed gravel. Blue raised his head and watched the cloud of smoke that surrounded the cattle wagon as the train clunked to a stop a quarter-mile ahead. He saw no sign of Goofy or Cowboy. But three bulls ran toward the car.

***

"That fuzz gets all over you," the farmer told him. "And it itches. But it gets a lot worse when you scratch it."

Blue scratched, and found out the farmer was right. But now after a week of picking peaches, the fuzz bothered him less while he pulled the peaches from the trees and lowered them into the canvas bag that hung on his chest. Besides, he was making almost a dollar a day, and he had his own hut.

Farmer Jess patrolled the orchard in his striped overalls, his cap tilted back on his head, and always a toothpick sticking from one corner of his mouth. The toothpick kept a beat while he talked with the pickers and checked on them. He made sure they didn't overlook good peaches when they moved from one tree to the next. And he wanted only good peaches, no slugs, leaves, or twigs when the pickers emptied their bags into the wooden bushel baskets.

Blue liked the man. He was friendly, always said "good morning" on his first round of the day, and yesterday after the workday, Farmer Jess asked Blue where he was from and how he wound up here. They sat on wooden crates in the orchard and talked for a half-hour.

The farmer laughed about Cowboy and Goofy when Blue told him about the trip from Dyersburg. Blue shared the story of how he wound up in a place called Villa Rica, Georgia, when he left the burning cattle wagon.

"I walked across the tracks, jerked my thumb up, and got a ride from the first truck I saw. I asked the man where I could get a job picking peaches, and he brought me straight here. You can't beat that."

Jess nodded. "Thay's a lot of good people around Villa Rica, and here in Carrollton too."

After a minute of silence, Blue looked up.

"I was never good buddies with them other guys, but I feel bad. I don't know what happened to them."

Farmer Jess held up his finger. "You know, my wife was reading the Times Georgian just last night, and I think there was something in there about that. When I get back to the house, I'll ask her."

Next afternoon, Blue sat half-asleep on a

wooden box in his hut, and rested from a long, tiring day. The knock on his door startled him, and he jumped up to open it.

Farmer Jess and his wife, both with big smiles, stared at him. Jess carried a rolled newspaper. She stood with her hands behind her.

He leaned his head toward her. "I believe you met my wife, Maudie?"

"Hey, Mister Green." The lady nodded.

Jess cleared his throat. "No, dear. His name's Blue."

Her face glowed pink. "I'm mighty sorry."

Blue beckoned for them to step in. "It's quite alright, Ma'am. I been called things a lot worse than Green."

She drew back her head, her face paled, and her eyes grew wide. She looked at her husband as if she feared Blue was about to say something indecent. The farmer shook his head, and motioned her to step inside. She stood her ground.

"Well now, we ain't got no time to stay. We just felt like bringing you something." She nodded her head at the newspaper, and Jess held it out.

"This here's the story I was telling you about yesterday; them two men you was with on the train. Maudie wanted you to have it."

Maudie kept one hand behind her as she held out a small bundle wrapped in butcher paper and tied with twine. "This here is some homemade, whole-hawg pork sausage I just cooked. Everybody says it's real good."

Blue nodded and blushed as he took the package. She brought her other hand around and handed him a bottle.

"This peach wine helps you wash down the sausage. Makes it even better."

His company left as abruptly as they came. Blue sat, ate sausage, drank wine, and read the newspaper.

Police and firemen were summoned to a burning train car, and found two men inside. Both were treated at a local clinic for burns and smoke inhalation, and released.

An hour later, Blue fell asleep, empty bottle in hand, and dreamed of Sherry.

Chapter Thirty-One

Sherry just had to see *Every Girl Should be Married.* The movie wouldn't stay at the Liberty Theater much longer, and she needed the laughs. She also needed to see Cary Grant, the best-looking man on the planet, and his image stuck in her mind as she left the theater. But the image couldn't compete with the noise on the sidewalk, with blaring car horns, and the high-pitched hum of tires on busy brick streets.

She left open her long wool coat, bought a copy of the News Palladium from a sidewalk newspaper vendor, and started for the corner, telling herself that going to the movies alone worked out best. Besides, the matinee was cheap, and this was a rare Saturday off work.

Fifteen years ago, the Red Cross promoted her to management with a transfer from Tennessee to southwest Michigan. She grew accustomed to the cold, to Benton Harbor's heavy, lake-effect snow and long winters. But with overcast skies for weeks on end, winters seemed to drag on forever. Bitter winds off Lake Michigan numbed her chin and made it hard to talk. Coal-fired furnaces dumped clouds of brown smoke into the gray skies and added to doubts that spring would ever arrive.

But this was a rare January day. A bright sun warmed Sherry's face, and most of the snow had melted. Today, residents ventured out to enjoy a day off work, soak up the sunshine, and catch a breath of fresh air.

A crowd formed at the corner to catch the city bus, and Sherry hurried to get in line. She skimmed through her newspaper while she waited, and wondered if she'd wasted a nickel. News about President Truman didn't interest her. Ads for clothes and shoes always caught her eye, but today, car ads dominated the pages. The new '49 Fords were handsome. They were also beyond her reach. What caught her eye today was a picture of the local train station and a story about hobos.

Her mind shut out the crowd as she leaned against a streetlight pole and lost herself in the story. A reporter felt sorry for hobos, and told how most didn't hang around here through the winter. But a few did, and during most winters, at least one died from exposure.

The green-and-white city bus made a noisy stop at the curb and treated the waiting line to exhaust from its big diesel engine. The line filed past Sherry to board the bus, but a minute later, a young man came back.

"Excuse me, Ma'am, the driver wants to know if you're getting on the bus."

She looked up. "Oh, sorry. I've changed my mind." The young man turned back, shook his head and said something about women as he stepped on board.

While the bus rumbled away, Sherry stopped reading and rolled up the newspaper. She walked back past the theater with the paper in her fist and with no destination in mind, just a chance to walk down Main Street lost in the crowd and lost in her thoughts. Her head always seemed to sort out things best when she was riding or walking.

From her first summer in Michigan, Sherry found friendly people, a variety of entertainment, interesting places, and the House of David—a fascinating religious cult that appeared to own half of Benton Harbor.

The twin cities of Benton Harbor and Saint Joseph were divided by the Saint Joe River that spilled into Lake Michigan, and the cities were connected by a drawbridge that spanned the river. Large ships docked at the harbor, and sailors in uniform were a common sight on the docks and streets and at the bars. A picturesque lighthouse attracted photographers, and when fog hung over the lake, a deep-bass foghorn sounded a long, low moan with a force that could rattle your insides from a hundred yards away.

Benton Harbor was also the heart of the fruit belt. Local farmers grew strawberries, cherries, pears, plums, apples, grapes, and other crops. The area sponsored an annual Blossomtime Parade that drew thousands of people, and the town boasted the world's largest open-air fruit market. The market spread over many acres, its streets lined on both sides by farmers and merchants selling their finest from bins, bags, baskets, boxes, and stacked wooden crates.

From long distances, buyers, sellers, and sightseers came to the Benton Harbor market, an energetic, fast-paced world of its own in spring, summer, and fall. During the season, Sherry rode the bus there almost every week to buy fresh fruit and vegetables, and talk to merchants and customers. She loved the huge variety of colors, and breathed deep as she wandered through the market streets to take in all the wonderful smells of berries, grapes, apples, and other fruits, and the earthy aroma of fresh produce.

Somewhere in the back of her mind lay another reason for her trips to the market. The businesses there offered lots of temporary jobs, jobs that attracted hobos. And somewhere in a sanctuary for broken dreams hidden deep inside her, lived a need that would not be denied, a need to find a hobo who played the guitar, the hobo she fell in love with so long ago.

Yet, the last time she saw Blue still hung in her mind—the picnic lunch and making love on a river bank in Dyersburg. They would announce their engagement to her parents the following night. That was the plan. But Blue disappeared. Now, that day seemed like a lifetime ago in another world.

For twelve years after, Sherry tried to convince herself Blue was dead. That notion seemed easier to handle than any other she could imagine. In spite of that, she looked for him at every train yard, hobo jungle, and rescue mission she saw in her limited travels. She talked with mission workers, hobos, railroad employees, and anyone who would listen.

"Do you know a man named Blue who plays a guitar?"

She began to wonder if her growing sense of desperation showed on her face. Many hobos claimed to know him but asked for money before they talked. She sighed and shook her head as she thought about how many quarters she gambled on information, most of it phony. None of it paid off.

Today, here on Main Street, the tantalizing smell from Popcorn John's did not stir the usual cravings in her gut as she walked past. Today, the familiar billboard ads for Coca Cola and Camel cigarettes did not register. Today, the noise of the traffic was muted. Sherry's mind blocked all of it as she walked with the newspaper still in her fist and the half-read hobo story still in her head.

She recalled a similar story in the paper

about a year ago. Before that story appeared, Sherry thought she'd given up looking for Blue. Instead, she caught a cab outside her apartment and rode to the train station where she talked to every hobo she could find. But that day, she said nothing about his guitar.

When two men claimed to know him, she asked for a description before offering money. They tried, and they lied. She left them muttering, turned and waved her hand to summon a cab. Then someone called out behind her.

"I beg ya pardon, Ma'am, I know the man you lookin' for."

Sherry stopped, dropped her head and waited, but didn't turn around. When she started away, he talked louder.

"Ain't seen him in a while, though. Plays a guitar and sings. A good man."

Sherry spun around. A tall black man with a wide nose and narrow-set eyes stood with his hands resting in the pockets of a worn-out jacket. She walked toward him knowing he could have heard about Blue without ever meeting him. But when she stopped in front of the man and looked up, his dark eyes seemed honest and kind.

"I been knowin' Blue for quite a spell. Eight or ten years, I reckon, maybe a bit longer."

Sherry drew her hand from her pocket. "I know this is not much, but would you mind telling me what you know?"

His thick lips made a half smile as he looked at the two quarters in her open palm. He shook his head.

"I don't want your money, Ma'am. Besides, what I know ain't likely worth nothin' anyway."

"When was the last time you saw him?"

His shoulders rose until they hid his neck while he squinted at the ground. "Don't rightly know. Could be a year, maybe more. Dyersburg, Tennessee, near as I recollect."

Sherry felt her heartbeat in her throat. "Dyersburg?"

He nodded. "You ever been there?"

"I have." She took a deep breath. "Do you know if he ever comes here?"

His shoulders dropped. "I been in this jungle half a dozen times, but I never seen Blue here."

"Any idea where he is now or where he might be headed?"

"I don't know that about nobody. Don't know where I'll be tomorrow myself. All I know is I heard Blue sing and play a few times in different jungles. A few years back, he put on a show for a bunch of us in a boxcar. We was on our way to Wisconsin to pick apples. He's good. When he's playin' I always want him to sing Hobo's Lullaby. And he always does. Do you know it?"

Sherry shook her head. The man cleared his throat and a mist formed in his eyes as he began to sing, his voice deep, soft, and smooth.

He sang a simple, comforting lullaby of an exhausted hobo sleeping in a boxcar while the towns drift slowly by, and the rhythm of humming rails that lulled the hobo to sleep. He is safe from wind and snow, and can sleep in peace by thinking only of today, and let tomorrow take care of itself.

Sherry swallowed past the lump in her throat, and wiped her eyes. She took an envelope from her pocket and folded it.

"If you see Blue, whether it's next week, next month or three years from now, would you give him this note? Tell him he can find me in

Benton Harbor. He can just ask for me at the Red Cross station. They'll let me know."

He held out his hand. "I'd be happy to, Ma'am. Blue's a good man." Sherry pressed the envelope and her two quarters into an oversized hand rough with calluses. With her other hand she closed his fingers around the bundle. With a shy grin he stuffed the bundle into his pocket.

"Must be real important," he said.

"Yes it is. I want to talk to him. Thank you, Mr…?

"Soda Pop. That's what everbody calls me."

On the way home in a cab, ,Sherry rested her head in her hands and called herself an idiot. Soda Pop would open the envelope. He would find not just a note, but the two-dollar bill Blue gave her years ago with her name written above the portrait of Thomas Jefferson. Below the portrait, he'd see the words, *Benton Harbor*, that Sherry added minutes before she gave it away. How long would a hobo hold on to a two-dollar bill when he got hungry? Maybe Soda Pop was hungry when she talked to him, and maybe she was a fool, she told herself. But she searched for Blue for many years and got nowhere. She had to try something.

***

A man's voice brought Sherry back to the present, back to the sunny January day and back to the sidewalk on Main Street. She stopped and looked toward the voice. A cab waited at the curb, and the driver called to her through the open window. "You need a taxi, Ma'am?"

"Oh, uh, no thank you." She turned and started back. Fatigue began to settle in like so many times before when she searched for Blue for days on end without a lead. When she read everything she could find about hobos. When she lied to herself that she would find him and talk to him once more.

Her worry and frustration about a man she knew many years ago had worn her down. Too many times her stomach churned because of him. Too many nights she'd been robbed of sleep. Too many days she spent chasing the ghost of Blue Moon Bailey.

More than a year had gone by since she left the two-dollar bill with Soda Pop. She would never again trust a hobo. No more trips to the jungles, no visits to rescue missions, no more quarters spent on useless information, lies, and promises.

She walked faster, breathed deeper, held her head higher. "Enough is enough," she said aloud, surprising herself. She also surprised the man coming toward her on the sidewalk. As he got near, she said, "Today's news. No charge." Without slowing down, she pushed the rolled newspaper at him. His eyes widened and his chin dropped, but he took the paper. Sherry heard a mumbled "thanks" behind her as she walked past, but she did not turn around.

She would not finish the story and she vowed never to read another sentence about hobos, bums, vagrants, vagabonds—whatever they were. But she couldn't shake a nagging fear. If Blue came to see her, would she tell him to go to hell? Or throw her arms around him and sob like a heartbroken child?

Chapter Thirty-Two

Sherry was convinced June and September were the only decent months of the year in southwest Michigan. And September couldn't be trusted. Winter often wore out its welcome and hung around past the end of March. When the spring thaw finally elbowed its way in, it exposed all the new potholes in the streets—winter's parting shot. The leftover snow and ice turned to an ugly brown slush, splattered onto sidewalks and pedestrians by passing cars, and tracked into shops, stores, and homes by shoes, boots, and pets.

April brought an overdose of rain. Cold rain. Good for the farmers, maybe, but often miserable for everyone else. July and August were just too hot, with humidity that rivaled a rain forest. Damp sheets did not make for restful sleep.

She could think of disagreeable conditions for the rest of the year too, but didn't bother because today, Sherry was happy. Three months ago, the Red Cross gave her a big promotion and she moved to a new apartment almost twice as large as the old one. The new one, too, was upstairs. But it was warmer in the winter, cooled by giant maple trees in the summer, and the rooms had a fresh coat of paint and new linoleum floors.

Besides all that, the best month of the year was finally here, and on a Sunday morning in June, Sherry raised the windows to enjoy the fresh air.

Someone shut a car door, and Sherry stuck her head out the living room window. Cindy Linn, a friend from work, stepped out of a cab on the street below. Sherry called to her and waved. Cindy looked up, her face pale.

"Hi, Sherry. Okay if I come up? Got something to show you."

"Of course." Sherry smiled big as she waved her up, but something seemed not quite right. She'd invited Cindy here a few times, but her friend had never dropped by on her own. A knot began to form in Sherry's stomach as she stood at the door and held it open while her guest climbed the stairs.

Cindy stopped before stepping in, leaned her head to look past Sherry and whispered, "You alone?"

Sherry wrinkled her brow. "Yep, just me. Why?" Cindy stepped inside. Sherry shut the door and turned toward her. "Is everything okay?"

They stood in the living room facing each other while Cindy held up a rolled newspaper. "Did you see yesterday's News Palladium?"

Sherry's eyes narrowed and her head moved in a slow wag. "I didn't buy one. Why?"

"Sherry, you have to read this. I'm sorry, but you just have to." Cindy unrolled the paper and pointed at a headline: *Hobo Tragedy in Benton Harbor*.

Sherry parked her hands on her hips. "No. I don't have to and I don't want to."

"But, Sherry, a man was killed and…"

Sherry shook her head and pushed her open palm toward Cindy, the only friend Sherry had confided in about her past life and about Blue.

"I'm done with it, Cindy. I promised myself—no more hobo stories. Thanks for thinking of me, but… no."

Cindy shook her head and started for the door, but paused. She traced the story with her finger and then held the finger in place as she turned back. "Just read this one paragraph, please."

"Why, Cindy? Tell me why?"

"Because… because… it's about Blue." She drew another long breath and shivered. Tears flooded her face and her mouth drooped as she choked out her words. "Sherry, I'm so sorry. I think Blue's been killed."

Color drained from Sherry's face as she took the paper and placed her finger where her friend's had been.

A single teardrop splattered on the paper as Sherry tried to read. She finished the paragraph, drew a ragged breath, and turned toward the open window, handing the paper back to Cindy.

Cindy touched her arm. "Sherry, are you all right? You uh… you don't seem too surprised."

"Oh, but I am." Sherry moved to the window and stared out. Her breath came in small quakes, but she refused to cry. "I thought Blue was dead a long time ago." Her eyes grew misty, and she wiped them with the back of her hand. In the yard next door, happy birds in a tree seemed to mock her grief while they chirped, and hopped from limb to limb.

"Birds… they're hobos." Sherry said the words aloud, more for herself than the woman behind her. "No permanent home. Eat when they find food. Come and go whenever they want…" she shook her head, "… like no one else exists and tomorrow will never happen."

Cindy whispered from across the room. "You think they'd ever be happy in a cage?"

Sherry pulled away from the window and stared at a picture of a freight train she hung on her wall years ago, a picture she had moved from one home to the next and stared at a thousand times.

The churning in her gut, gone for months, was back.

Over the years Blue's life impacted hers in ways he could not have known. The man she loved for so many years lied to her, left her stranded, broke her heart. The man she envied for his freedom was the man she tried so hard to catch—a wild bird always just beyond reach.

A part of her felt relief. Another part made a place for guilt. Her biggest regret was that she had no chance to talk to him just once more. Could she begin a new life now that his had ended?

Cindy interrupted her thoughts when she moved up behind her. "Sherry, I should go now. But I'll leave the paper here if you want to read the rest of the story."

Sherry turned without looking at her. "How about if you read it to me?"

They sat on the couch. Cindy spread the newspaper on her lap, and cleared her throat. "I'll just tell you what it says. I read it three times already. The police broke up a robbery Friday night in the alley behind the Red Cross blood station on Territorial Road." Sherry caught Cindy's arm, turned and stared at her, wide-eyed. But she didn't speak. Cindy waited. When Sherry released her arm, Cindy glanced at the paper and started again.

"They found the body of a man that they think was a hobo. And uh… they said he had no ID, but another hobo came forward and said the dead man's name was Blue. That's all he knows. And it says the police are asking anybody who might know him to go to the morgue and identify the body."

Cindy stood and rolled the paper. She left it on the couch and walked to the door. With her hand on the knob, she turned back to look at her friend. "Which is worse—loving a man you can't have, or having a man you can't love?"

***

At the city police station, Sherry sat in a straight-back wooden chair at the end of the sergeant's desk and waited for him to come back with the report. He had introduced himself as Sergeant Curtis and told her he was a detective. *He'd have to be a good one*, she told herself, *to find anything on his desk.* Sloppy stacks of papers covered the desk with sheets of carbon paper between the pages. At one end, an overloaded ashtray sat wedged between the stacks. A dirty coffee mug, two Snickers candy wrappers, and a half-empty bottle of Pepsi fought for space at the end where Sherry sat.

"Tell me how you know this man," the sergeant said as he came back to his desk. He plopped down on his chair with more papers in his hand and looked up at her. "You a relative?"

Sherry straightened in her chair. "No, sir. I uh… I don't know him."

The sergeant looked down at the paper and then back at her. "But it says here you know a hobo named Blue. You went to the morgue yesterday, viewed the body, and filled out this form. It says you know a hobo named…" he wrinkled his forehead, "… Blue Moon Bailey. Is that correct?"

"Yes sir." She took a deep breath. "I met him when I lived in Dyersburg, Tennessee, back in thirty-three. I worked at the Red Cross blood bank there and Blue came in with a friend. They were both hobos."

"And you were positive that the body is not the man you know?"

"Positive."

"From what you told me earlier, I assume

you've met thousands of people in your line of work."

"Yes sir, I have, but only one named Blue. And the man I saw is not him."

"I see." The sergeant waited, but Sherry shook her head. He looked at the papers again. "The man you know? Blue Moon Bailey? What can you tell us about him or his family?"

"He grew up in Possum Trot, Missouri. Well, what he really said was he didn't get a chance to grow up; he was *yanked up*. I never met any of his family, but he said his little sister died when she was two, and I think his mother died the year we met, in thirty-three. And his father was a useless drunk and a lazy bastard." Sherry cleared her throat. "Sorry, that's what Blue said."

The sergeant chuckled. "That's it? Do you know any of their names?"

"That's all he ever told me." Sherry blushed as she remembered Blue's story about *doing it* with his mother's cousin, but it didn't seem the kind of family information the police needed to know.

Sergeant Curtis laid the papers on one of the stacks. "Did you ever see Blue with a pair of large scissors?"

Sherry jerked her head toward him. "He uh… he carried them everywhere. Did you find some?"

The sergeant nodded. "In the dead man's chest."

Sherry gasped and covered her mouth. "Oh no."

Without looking up, the cop said, "Do you know if Blue ever had a guitar?"

Sherry straightened her back and licked a tear from her upper lip. "It's what he was known for. He played it for me a few times. The one he had then was called a Martin."

The cop nodded as he studied the papers again. "That's what we found. I think a man, maybe two men, followed Blue to rob him of his guitar." He watched Sherry as if waiting for her to comment. When she didn't reply, he continued.

"When they attacked him in the alley behind the Red Cross station, your friend, Blue, tried to defend himself with the scissors. But one man took them away from him and stabbed Blue in the chest. One man grabbed the guitar. That's when our patrol officer showed up. The man saw him, dropped the guitar, and took off running."

Sergeant Curtis held the report in front of him as he shrugged. "Everything seems to fit—the scissors, the guitar. It appears that our dead man is Blue Bailey." He looked at Sherry and waited.

Sherry looked down and shook her head. "The whole thing is just so awful."

"So…" he held up the coroner's report and turned it toward her, "… you met this man years ago at your workplace and you still can say for certain that this is not him?"

Sherry glared at the cop. "What makes you think it is him? Who told you that man's name is Blue?"

"We drove to the local jungle and asked if any of them knew a hobo who owned a guitar. Only one man would talk to us. He rode to the morgue with me and identified the body. He said, 'I've known him for a long time. His name is Blue Moon Bailey.'"

Sherry stiffened and stood up. "He actually said, *Blue Moon*?"

Sergeant Curtis rocked back and forth to nod

his head while he stared at the report. “That’s exactly what he said. And then you come here and say you know a man with that same name, but this is not him. What am I supposed to believe?”

Sherry walked to the window and looked out. “I can’t tell you who the dead man is. I can only tell you who it’s not.” She turned and looked at the sergeant. “The man I saw is not Blue Moon Bailey.”

The detective stroked his chin and watched her. After a moment of silence, he said, “Should I assume you saw Blue Bailey close-up more than once?”

Sherry turned back to the window, folded her arms across her chest, and stood up straight. Her words carried no emotion. “Blue and I have a son. He’s almost sixteen.”

Sergeant Curtis coughed. The Chesterfield he was lighting shot from his mouth, bounced off his leg, hit the edge of the chair, and rolled off. He scrambled to pick it up, stomped at sparks on the floor and then puffed on the cigarette until the fire came back to life.

“Sorry,” he said. Color flooded his cheeks, and he fumbled again with the papers.

Sherry paced back and forth, looking at nothing. “We went out on dates. We got along well and then… we uh…” she walked to the chair, pulled a handkerchief from her purse and dabbed at her eyes, “… we fell in love.” She turned again and stared out the window. “Or at least… I did.”

“If you’ll pardon me for saying so, miss, I don’t meet many women who want to marry a hobo.”

She looked at the sergeant. “I never met another hobo like Blue.”

"The two of you were never married?"

"We got engaged but the wedding never happened." She took a deep breath and leaned toward Sergeant Curtis. "So, what happened to the guitar?"

Curtis angled his head toward a door. "In the storage room. I don't know if I can let you have it without you being a relative. But… well, I uh… I guess your son is entitled to it as much as anybody if you want it."

Sherry sat down again and nodded. "My son takes lessons but he doesn't have his own guitar. And I…" she looked away, "… I can't afford to buy him a good one." She looked back as Sergeant Curtis nodded, and smiled without showing his teeth.

He wadded the candy bar wrappers and tossed them into the metal trash can beside his desk, retrieved a half-empty bag of Planters Peanuts hidden under the wrappers, and stuffed it into his shirt pocket. After a swallow of Pepsi, he set the bottle atop a stack of notebooks on the shelf behind him and then set the dirty coffee mug beside it.

Now he had room on his desk, and he pulled a Receipt-of-Merchandise form from a drawer and laid it in the only clear spot. "I'll just need you to sign for the guitar. You can take it, but you have to bring it back if we ever need it for evidence." He drew a fountain pen from its holder, handed it to her, and pointed at the signature line. "I'll be right back."

A minute later he laid a battered guitar case on the chair next to her and opened it. Sherry stood and stared, relieved that the guitar was not damaged, and rested her hand on the strings. She swallowed hard.

"It's the same one and…" The lump in her throat would not let her talk. She recalled the song Blue sang to her that day on the river bank, and fought back tears as the words came to mind.

What'll I do
When you are far away
And I am blue

"I'd like to go now." Sherry closed the case, picked it up, and started out. She stopped at the door and turned. "Thank you, Sergeant, for… well… for everything."

He crushed out his cigarette, walked to her and rested his hand on her shoulder. "I wish you all the luck in the world, miss. Seems to me you might need some. I uh, I know how it feels… not being with someone you love. My wife died almost three years ago. Nothing's been the same since." He reached to open the door for her, and Sherry squeezed his arm.

"I'm so sorry, Sergeant Curtis. You seem like such a good man." She started out.

"Wait," he said, and drew an envelope from his pocket. "I almost forgot. We found this in the guitar." He placed it in her free hand and opened the door. Then he gestured at the guitar. "I'll carry that to your car if you like."

"Thanks, but I don't have a car."

"I'd drive you home, but I'm the only one here and I can't leave the station."

Sherry looked into his eyes. They seemed kind, but sad. She nodded and smiled, and walked out.

Outside, she beckoned for a taxi. The bus would be cheaper but the fast-moving clouds could bring rain before the bus arrived. And she wasn't sure about handling the guitar on the city bus.

The driver loaded the guitar into the taxi and asked Sherry how long she'd been playing. She couldn't tell if he really cared, if he was just being social, or making a pass. She told him the guitar belonged to someone she had not seen in many years.

"O-o-oh," was all he said.

Lost in her thoughts, Sherry was glad the driver didn't talk while he drove her home. But he jerked his head around when she gasped. The envelope from Sergeant Curtis held the two-dollar bill she gave to Soda Pop two years ago.

Chapter Thirty-Three

She looked at the price on the pump. Nineteen cents a gallon was no bargain, but she needed fuel, and the young man with *Conoco* on the left side of his shirt, and *Billy* on the right, looked eager and ready to serve. She smiled. "Fill 'er up."

"Yes, Ma'am."

Sherry hated to be called ma'am. The term was for women over forty, not her. But she ignored it. Her chest puffed out as she waited. She'd driven from Benton Harbor to Effingham, Illinois, in her own car. Alone.

Billy stood with a constant grin while the bell on the gas pump dinged and the tank filled. He leaned and looked at the rear of the car and then straightened up. "Nice-lookin' Ford, Ma'am. A forty-eight?"

"Yes, it is."

"You get it new, Ma'am?"

"No, I got it six months ago. It's three years old but it's in good shape. New battery, new tires and tubes and a good spare. And it had a tune-up just last week."

He nodded. "Wish I could buy one like this."

"I set a goal," Sherry said, "and saved money for more than two years. Now, it's all mine and I'm proud of it."

Billy topped off the tank and checked the oil and tires, and whistled while he cleaned the windshield.

"That'll be three dollars even, Ma'am."

She tipped Billy an extra quarter, glanced at

her watch, and pulled out of the filling station. Benton Harbor to Dyersburg could be a long, two-day drive, maybe three, Sherry figured. But the first day of her trip was done and she was eager to start the second.

Yesterday, she sorted through the rough spots in her life and relived the past. The car ate up the miles. The hours flew by. And the radio and signs entertained her.

He lit a match
to check gas tank
Now they call him
Skinless Hank
Burma Shave

Her last trip to Dyersburg was four years ago on a bus, when she and her son went to see her parents. Sherry told them about the visit in a letter she sent a month before. Still, they acted surprised when she showed up.

Mealtimes were quiet and awkward in spite of how hard Sherry tried to liven up the occasion and make people talk. She hoped evenings would be family time. Instead, her father worked late, her mother preferred her radio shows, and they went to bed early. After three days, Sherry paid the extra charge to trade her bus tickets for new ones, and she and her son left two days early. She apologized to him all the way back to Michigan.

Now she was on her way back to Dyersburg. But this time, her parents didn't know she was coming. She would talk to them about their cold-hearted treatment of her son over the years, treatment that started before he was born. Mom didn't hide her anger or disappointment when she learned her daughter was pregnant. But the two of them talked, cried together, and talked again. Sherry believed Mom would have accepted an illegitimate grandchild, but Mom had to keep peace with Dad.

After her son was born, Sherry and baby moved in with an older lady who cared for him while Sherry worked. The arrangement seemed to suit everyone, especially her parents. They never came to visit, and she seldom saw them. Life was routine, functional. When the Red Cross offered her a management job with a transfer to Michigan, her decision came easy. Later, Sherry wondered if her father had arranged the transfer to get her out of Dyersburg. If so, he did her a favor. The move to Michigan was a good one for mother and son.

Tears came as Sherry thought of her boy, and she stopped the car on the roadside and dug out her handkerchief. "Maybe I just need some rest," she said aloud. Last night brought little sleep. The first motel seemed nice enough, and clean, but the sleepy-headed clerk shook her head when she learned Sherry was alone.

"Sorry, we don't rent to no woman that's by herself. That's our policy. But you might try the place down the road."

Gray's Getaway, the place down the road, was half the price of the first motel, and struck Sherry as a business that never turned away a customer. But she was exhausted. Tonya, the night clerk, offered a choice of rates. Sherry chose the all-night rate instead of the hourly rate for the room, and discovered the lumpy bed may have served a purpose for some things, but sleep was not one of them.

***

Covel's Carbondale Café served a tasty lunch. Sherry relaxed with an extra coffee after the meal, and stared at the Seeburg jukebox that hogged one corner of the dining room. Its lights and chrome cabinet reflected off the polished hardwood floor, and the machine seemed as gaudy and overdone as a Buick Roadmaster. The manager said it was a late model that played the new 45 rpm records. But while Sherry waited, the big beast sat silent like the few customers who came before noon to avoid the crowd.

She glanced through a local paper. But her mind was neither on news, nor ads, nor the man at the table across from her staring at her breasts. Sherry paid her bill and stood beside the table. When the man looked again, she stuck out her chest, flashed a big smile, turned and walked out. She thought she heard him chuckle just before the screen door slapped shut behind her. She wore a red-faced grin all the way to her car. Breast man stood in the doorway of the café and watched. Sherry waved goodbye and giggled as she drove onto the road.

Now, serious thoughts filled her head, and she fought with herself for turning the wrong way, for going to the hobo jungle she passed a few miles back. Her chest tightened. Concerns about her son always lingered in the back of her mind—questions waiting for answers, decisions that must be made.

On the morning he turned sixteen, Sherry gave her son the guitar his father had owned, along with a new case, new strings, picks, and songbooks. Martins were expensive, high-quality guitars, and her son was excited. He promised to be home by six o'clock for his birthday cake, and left to show his treasure to his best friend and guitar teacher for more than three years. When he came home he'd find a surprise party with a houseful of friends.

Sherry drew a ragged breath while her mind turned the next thoughts into silent words that caught in her throat. The party was a big surprise for everyone except the birthday boy. The guests waited till nine o'clock. Her son didn't show.

Days and nights became a blur, with days spent looking for him and nights filled with worry instead of sleep. With no evidence of foul play, Sergeant Curtis was reluctant to get involved, but Sherry pleaded. Two weeks later, he delivered a report to her apartment, a three-page list of places the police checked and the people they interviewed. "Sorry," the sergeant told her, "there's nothing conclusive."

Two years had crawled by since her son disappeared. It seemed like twenty. Now, her hands shook on the steering wheel while her father's words came back to haunt her once again. And they hurt now more than ever.

Three weeks before her son was born, a crowing rooster woke Sherry in the gray dawn of early morning, the same multi-colored boss of the yard that woke her every day. The same one that strutted in his iridescent feathers and crowed as if he was responsible for the sunrise. But that day, Pretty Boy's wake-up call came earlier and seemed to echo off her bedroom window as if it was meant just for her. She sat up, her mind still fuzzy, heart racing, breath coming in short gasps as her father yelled at her mother in their bedroom.

"How the hell am I supposed to feel? Do you know how ashamed it makes me when every man at the sawmill knows my daughter was knocked up by a damn hobo? And then the lazy sumbitch took off and left her. And how do we know her little bastard won't turn out to be just like its daddy?"

***

Sherry parked near the train yard. As she turned off the car, a sudden thought flashed through her mind, and she relived the day she sat at the police station and talked with Sergeant Curtis. She knew the dead man was not Blue, but the sergeant said a man from the local jungle identified the body as Blue Moon Bailey. Now she knew why, and who.

Blue had always been embarrassed about his middle name. He told no one except Sherry, and made her promise to never tell. The only one at that jungle who knew Blue's middle name was Blue. Maybe he was ashamed of the man he'd become and wanted people to think he was dead. What better way than to go to the morgue and identify someone else as himself?

Sherry wiped her eyes, grabbed her purse, and stepped out of the car. Hobos stood with their arms crossed, their heads cocked, and their eyes fixed on the attractive young woman while she walked toward them. They shifted their feet as she drew closer.

"My name is Sherry Wolfe." She stopped and held up a dollar bill, and they crowded around. She asked direct questions but got no direct answers. After parting with three dollars and getting worthless information, Sherry sighed and turned to go. "Déjà vu," she muttered and walked toward her car. Then someone called out behind her.

"I know the lad you lookin' for."

Sherry stopped and spun around. A tall

black man stood apart from the others in the shade of a large tree. In spite of the warm day, he wore a worn-out jacket, his hands in the pockets. A slight smile found his lips as she hurried toward him.

"Soda Pop," she yelled. "I never thought I'd see you again." He lifted a huge hand from a pocket and she grabbed it with both of hers, her eyes wet again. "Thank you. Thank you, you dear, sweet man. Thanks for delivering that note to Blue."

"Took a while. But it was the least I could do." He put his hand back in his pocket, leaned his head and wrinkled his face as if to apologize. "I delivered another message too. I uh… I told Blue that you and him had a child." He drew up his chin and dropped his head, exposing the large stain on the top of his denim cap as he stared at the ground.

"What?" Sherry stooped to see his face. "You told him what?"

"That uh… that you two had a child." He raised his head and looked at her. "Was I wrong?"

"How could you know? I never said anything about that. I didn't even—"

"I just knew, Ma'am. The way you acted that day. The look in your eyes. And you trusted a hobo you didn't even know with a two-dollar bill. Couldn't a been nothin' else. Forgive me?"

"Forgive you? It's the greatest thing you could have done. That's why Blue came to Benton Harbor. It must've been." Sherry lowered her voice. "He uh… I mean… I don't know if you heard about Blue getting mugged, but…"

He nodded. "I heard." He pulled the big, callused paw from his pocket again and gave her hand a gentle squeeze.

Sherry straightened and smiled. "So you know my son, Grey?"

The big man nodded again. "I know Grey. Been a few months since I seen him, but, yeah. Dark wavy hair, bright blue eyes. Looks just like his daddy." He was silent for a moment and then added, "He's a good lad. Plays guitar too and sings." He shrugged. "Don't play all the same songs his daddy did. But he knows Hobo's Lullaby."

Sherry unzipped a pocket inside her purse, pulled out the two-dollar bill and placed it in his hand.

"Would you give this note to Grey next time you see him?"

Chapter Thirty-Four

He leaned hard on a cane that thumped on the wood floor as he stumbled to a wicker chair on the back porch. A rusted spring creaked and struggled to shut the screen door behind him, but gave up four inches from closing. He sat down hard, looked up and studied his guest from hat to boots, his voice raspy but strong when he spoke.

"Now, what did you say your name was, young man?"

"Grey Wolfe, sir."

The man pushed white hair away from his earlobe and wiggled a finger in his ear. "My hearin' ain't what it was." He chuckled. "At the door, I thought you said you was a son of Blue Bailey."

"Yes, sir."

"Yeah, you're the spittin' image of him, all right. But you ain't got his name."

"It's a long story, sir."

"Well…" the man nodded at the chair across from him, "… park right there and tell me the best part." He yanked a dirty handkerchief from the bib pocket of his overalls and blew his nose.

Grey sat and tried to be patient. Until now, he'd talked about his father only to hobos. They knew Blue Bailey, but none had seen him in a long time and knew nothing of his family. Yesterday, at the Possum Trot jungle, Shorty said, "I ain't seen Blue for a long spell and don't know if he's dead or still kickin'. But I'll help you find your daddy." He cocked his head. "If that's possible."

Shorty told Grey more about his father than his mother ever had. Maybe more than she knew.

And now, maybe this old dairy farmer could tell him even more. When the man wadded the handkerchief and stuck it back into place, Grey stood.

"I'm trying to find my father, and—"

The older man held up his hand, and then dropped it and lowered his head. "Sorry, son. He ain't here."

"I know, sir. But Shorty at the jungle told me to find a dairy farmer out here, a Mister Rodman. I followed the trail through the woods and found your house. I hope you're Mister Rodman."

"Nope."

Grey's chin dropped. "No?"

"I'm Johnny Rodman. My father's been gone more years than most people been alive. And this ain't no dairy farm no more. I worked it fifty-five years. Never had me a son to take over. Sold the cows."

Grey took a deep breath and sat again. He crossed one leg over the other, laced his fingers over his knee, and leaned toward the man.

"Did you know my father's mother?"

The farmer's face brightened as he raised his head. "Bonnie?"

"I don't know her name."

"Blue's mama?" He nodded. "That'd be your grammaw. Knowed her all her life. Worked for me when she was just a kid. Her daddy died when she was twelve, and her mama was bad sick. I wanted to help. Offered her a job."

He nodded while he imitated milking a cow. "Best milkmaid I ever had." After a deep breath, he blew it out hard and said, "Died right here on my land when she was thirty-three… or four." His chin quivered. He wiped his eyes on a sleeve and shook his head. "Choppin' wood."

The man sat silent, shaking his head. A minute later, his face glowed, and he chuckled. “That girl could make you laugh. Always fun to be around. Of course, she was one of them Irish, and they have some strange ways. She growed up thinking that a two-dollar bill was good luck. Every time she said that, I’d tease her and say, ‘yeah, if you got two dollars you’re lucky to have it.’”

While the older gentleman cleared his throat, Grey shifted on the chair and waited. “Any idea where my father might be?”

Rodman struggled off the chair and stood. “Well now, Bonnie’s buried over by the Nazarene church.” He fumbled with the handkerchief and blew his nose again. “But I ain’t seen hide nor hair o’ Blue since we planted his mother.”

The man left his cane behind and dragged his feet across the porch to reach a water bucket on the rail. He stared into the bucket and shook his head as he lowered the dipper. A frown covered his face while he scooped the top of the water and dumped a dead fly over the rail. Chickens across the yard clucked and flapped, and scrambled toward the splash. A reddish-brown hen won the race and gobbled up the prize. The rest of the flock grumbled and fussed while they rambled away.

His hand shook when he refilled the dipper, and he held the bottom with his other hand as he brought it to his mouth. While he drank, tobacco juice oozed down the outside of the dipper. He stopped short and looked at Grey.

“Sorry about my manners. I ain’t had to use ’em in a while. My wife passed on nine years back, and I ain’t got nobody to keep me in line.” He offered the dipper to his guest. “You need a drink o’ water, young man?”

The young man frowned and shook his head. "Oh no, sir." He gripped the canteen on his belt. "I mean uh… I brought my own water. Thank you."

Rodman downed another swallow and dropped the dipper into the bucket. He wiped his mouth with his sleeve, and then turned and leaned toward Grey.

"Now, I'd like to tell you just where your grammaw is buried out there." He shook his head. "I'd like to, son, but I just can't recollect."

***

The few headstones the young man found among the weeds were interesting, but dated too far back to be helpful. Side-by-side stones marked the graves of two men who shared a family name, born the same day, died the same day in 1864. Both stones read: *Murdered by Sherman in the War of Northern Aggression.*

Mister Rodman said Bonnie's grave, like most graves out here, was identified only by a ledger, which he explained was a small stone laid flat on the ground with nothing more than a plot number and the name of the deceased. And sometimes, the year of birth and death. Grey brushed years of dust from a dozen or more stones but didn't see what he hoped to find.

He took off the hat, wiped his forehead with the back of his hand, and wiped the hand on his pants. The breeze cooled his head until the sun dried his hair. He replaced the hat to shade his face. June was a lot hotter in Missouri than in Michigan.

Another hour. Still nothing. He scratched his back with a twig and tried to remember what his mother had told him about his father. Not much. And he had to pry it from her each time he asked.

He knew he was the son of Blue Bailey, a hobo who played guitar and sang. And when Grey met Soda Pop, the man bragged on Blue's talent and said, "You sure look like your daddy." Then he nodded and said, "And sound like him too."

Grey believed he'd never really know himself until he knew more about his family. But Mom told him nothing except, "Your father's mother died in Possum Trot in 1933. At least, that's what he told me."

Now, as the afternoon sun bore down on the cemetery, the heat sapped Grey's energy. A pine tree offered a small shade, and he sat and massaged his sore fingers. But not for long. After a drink from his canteen, he found a branch that made a good broom, broke it off, and swept the dust from more ledgers. He'd look at every stone here if he had to, but there was little time for rest. The trail back to the jungle might be hard to follow after dark.

He straightened his back, took a long breath, and counted eleven stones left to sweep. His eyes caught a reflection when he looked back and forth at the markers. On a small stone, three gravesites from the fence, the letter B defied the dust.

Grey dropped the broom and rushed to the site. He knelt and wiped the stone with his hand, uncovered the name Bailey, and blew away the loose dust. His heart beat faster while his hands worked harder until he found, *Bonnie Bailey 1899 – 1933*.

Grey swept the remaining stones but found no Blue Bailey in the cemetery. It did not prove his father was alive, but it renewed his hope as he hung the bindle on his shoulder and blew his grandmother a goodbye kiss.

On his way to the cemetery, he'd seen the

sign, faded and falling apart, for the Nazarene Baptist Church. The roof sagged. The front door hung open as if the faithful abandoned the building long ago.

On his way back, Grey took off his hat as he walked by, thinking the little church may have been the place of his grandmother's funeral. Maybe for his grandfather too. The sudden thought of his grandfather seemed strange. He might still be alive. When Grey asked his mother about the man, she told him, "Your dad mentioned his father only once, and said the man was a worthless drunk."

The landmarks between the cemetery and the hobo jungle made Grey wish he had more time. But the sun would not wait.

***

Tall weeds stood like sentries around the big barn as if to protect its heritage from strangers. Above faded planks on the walls, and above a dilapidated tin roof, a lightning rod stuck up near each end while a rusted windcock posed between them as if to spite the passing of time, and creaked in the afternoon breeze.

If walls could talk came to Grey's mind. How many stories would the barn tell from its days of shelter and service? Would it brag about a million gallons of milk? Things it had seen? People it had known?

Johnny Rodman said Grey's grandmother had worked there, and a light pang in his heart made him wish she was still around to share the stories of her life. He didn't know why, but he liked old barns, and this one stayed in his mind as he walked through the sunshine over the rolling hills of tall grass.

Back on the trail that led through the woods, Grey stopped by a stream and dropped his bindle on the bank. He filled the canteen and took a short rest. When he hoisted the bindle back to his shoulder, he heard something drop. He smiled as he picked it up, and walked back to the trail with the whistle in his hand. When he held it to his mouth and blew, the sound took him to Dyersburg.

Before he came to Possum Trot, Grey spent three days in Dyersburg, and met a man in charge of the events at the square. Grey played and sang in the square, got a few tips, and lots of compliments. He spent the night at the hobo jungle where his father had stayed. The next afternoon he waded across a nearby field of weeds to find an old barn where he planned to spend a couple of hours to look it over, hear its secrets, feel its presence, and spend the night. According to Shorty, it was nothing more than an old barn surrounded by weeds, but Blue thought it was the best sleeping spot on the planet. Shorty doubted the barn was still there.

It was.

Grey's first glimpse of the old building brought a sense of wonder. It was just like he'd pictured, as if he'd seen it before. Like the barn where his grandmother once worked, this one earned an instant home in that feel-good place at the back of his mind. Maybe, just maybe, he told himself, his fascination for old barns came from his father. He liked to think so.

Reverence stirred in his chest as Grey approached the back of the barn. The feeling changed when he stepped around the corner. Instead of weeds, a well-kept lawn stretched from the barn to an impressive brick home where a man sat on the steps of a covered back porch. Chips and shavings flew off his knife as he whittled a stick. He blew dust from the masterpiece and held it up for inspection.

Grey took an easy step back. Some people despised hobos, and he'd heard about hobos getting shot at. After a slow nod and a smile of satisfaction, the man moved the carved stick toward his mouth as he lifted his chin. Grey started back another step when the whittler saw him. The man stood, tucked the stick into his shirt pocket, and shaded his eyes.

"Who goes there?"

Grey didn't answer, and the man yelled, "Who is that on my property?"

Grey waved. "Sorry, sir. I'm leaving."

"Come here, young man."

Grey started to turn and run, but waited as the whittler closed his knife and dropped it into his pocket. He sat again on the edge of the porch and rested his feet on the steps. When the man beckoned, Grey hung the bindle strap on his shoulder and started forward, now glad he left his guitar with Shorty.

The man on the porch wore an expensive suit and shoes, and initials *HL* were embroidered on the tie that hung loose around his neck. Grey stopped in front of him, looked down at the wood shavings on the steps, and smiled.

An easy laugh came from the man's throat while he pulled his creation from the shirt pocket and looked it over again.

"I was carving a train whistle." He stared at Grey and held it out. "I think this one's done. Give it a try."

Grey hesitated, but put the whistle to his lips and blew two short blasts and one long, like he'd heard from a train engineer more than a hundred times. They both laughed when he offered the whistle back to the man.

Grey shook his head. "Sounds just like a train. How'd you do that?"

"When I was a lad, my stepfather made them for me. Then he showed me how. I was always crazy about trains. Still am, I guess." He pointed at Grey. "You like it, you keep it."

"But I don't want to take—"

"No, no. It's yours. I make them just to whittle. Gives my mind a rest." He stood, walked across the porch, and sat on a swing. "Get out of the sun. Come on up and rest your bones." He motioned to a chair across from him. Grey dropped his bindle beside the steps, stuck the whistle in his pocket, and joined him on the porch.

From inside the home, the aroma of cooking meat came through an open window. Grey sat, leaned back and took a deep breath. His gut rumbled. "Sorry."

The man laughed. "I've got a pot roast on the stove. When I hear the bell, she'll be ready. I don't get interesting company here very often. Stay and have supper with me, and we can talk."

Grey's eyes brightened. "I really like pot roast, but…" He looked at his shoes and clothes.

"Nonsense. Your clothes don't matter. I'm an attorney now, a lawyer. But believe it or not, I was a hobo for a few years."

Grey's face paled. "You? A hobo?"

The man nodded. "I was. Traveled a lot, but stayed at the local jungle a few times. I got to know Dyersburg, and moved here when I opened my practice." His chest expanded and his unfocused eyes looked into the distance. "I fell in love with the town. Or at least, the town square."

Grey's eyes brightened. "I been there. It's kinda strange. First time there, I felt like I belonged. I just wanted to sit around and watch everything that happened. It's amazing how much you can learn about people that way."

The man nodded. "You're a bright young man… and you're right. Been there many times, and I keep going back." His eyes wandered into the distance, and he sat without talking, his face changing expressions. He breathed deep and shook his head.

"Met a nice, young woman, a pretty little thing, who worked near the square. But… she left a long time ago. And it seems nobody knows what happened to her."

His eyes came back to the porch, and he looked at his guest. "Sorry. Sometimes I get lost in my own head." He stood and stuck out his hand. "I'm Harry Logan."

Grey stood. "I'm Grey." They shook hands, and sat again.

From a small table beside the swing, the lawyer picked up a pipe, dipped it into a tall can of Flying Dutchman tobacco and packed the bowl with his finger while he stared at Grey, looked away, and then back. He took a match from a box on the table, and again looked away and back while he lit the pipe.

"You look like somebody I know. Can't think of who… but it'll come to me. Where you from?"

"Michigan."

The lawyer squinted. "Don't know a soul up there. What brings you here?"

"Looking for my father. You used to be a hobo. You might know him."

Logan wagged his head and blew a ring of smoke that spread and hovered over him.

"Don't know any of them anymore, son. The ones I used to know?" He shrugged. "Most of them are probably dead. And I have no idea where the others could be. So what's your father's name?"

"Blue Bailey."

The man's head jerked back, and he stared wide-eyed, smoke rolling from his mouth and nose as he spoke. "No-o-o! I'll be damned." He stood, turned away, and then back, color flooding his face. He leaned forward and looked at Grey up close.

"My God, I should've known. You're Blue's boy, all right. You look just like him. I suppose next you're gonna tell me you play the guitar."

Grey grinned. "I do."

Logan took another pull on the pipe, and the smoke flew again from his mouth and nose as he laughed.

"So your father is Blue and you're Grey? Your daddy gave you that name, didn't he? What a sense of humor."

"No sir. My mother picked it out. Said she liked the name and it had nothing to do with my dad or his name."

The lawyer leaned close, his eyes wide. "No offense. I like it." He sat up, and stroked his beard. "Born in Michigan? So Blue met a woman up there and married her. Good for him."

"Well, not exactly. They, uh, they never actually got married." He looked at the porch floor. "Truth is… I've never seen my father."

A low grunt escaped from Logan, and a silent moment passed. Grey kept his head down but he could feel the man staring.

"My mother moved to Michigan when I was

a baby." Grey looked up. "But I was born here."

"Here? Dyersburg?"

"Yes sir. My mother worked at the Red Cross. My father was broke, and he showed up there once with a friend to sell blood. That's how my parents met."

Harry Logan grabbed for the pipe as it clattered to the floor. He shook his hand and coughed, touched a burned finger with his tongue, and then blew on the blister. After a long, ragged breath, Harry gathered up the pipe, and stood silent. His forehead wrinkled, his eyes bulged. His face grew hard. Yet his controlled voice sounded sympathetic as his head made a slow nod, and he spoke without looking at Grey.

"You're Blue Bailey's bastard son?"

Grey hung his head as the man turned toward him. Logan's eyes widened and he spat out his words.

"Let me guess… your mother's name is Sherry."

Grey stiffened and looked up. "You know her?"

Logan jerked his head from side to side and looked down at him. "No."

"But sir, you—"

"No. I thought I knew her. But I never did."

A bell sounded in the kitchen. Logan hooked a finger on a chain and pulled a railroad watch from its pocket.

"I just remembered an appointment." He glared at Grey. "You can go now."

Chapter Thirty-Five

Grey took another drink from his canteen and realized he'd been standing in the same spot in the woods for ten minutes. He blew the train whistle again, dropped it into his pocket, and started forward.

"Hey," someone yelled behind him.

The hair stood up on the back of his neck as Grey jumped and turned. He saw no one, and said, "Hey yourself."

"Drive that train over here." The voice came from near the creek.

Grey started toward the voice, but stopped. "You a train robber?"

A man laughed as he stepped into sight on the trail, his legs unsteady. Clothes, torn and filthy, hung on his skinny frame like rags. His finger clutched a ceramic jug, and he held it out. Grey stepped back, wrinkled his face and shook his head.

A rat's nest of black hair poured over the man's ears and forehead, and a scraggly beard covered his face. Yet, he looked strangely familiar. Grey did not offer a handshake, but greeted him with a slight nod.

"Hello, mister. My name's Grey. I think you might be my grandfather."

The man laughed again and took a swig. He swallowed hard, wiped his chin with the back of his hand, and shook his head.

"I got no grandkids. My name's Blue."

Grey stared at the ground, his face puzzled. His mind did not accept what he had just heard. The man rocked back and forth and stared. When he stopped, a single tear clung to his cheek. Grey looked at the jug again. In spite of the afternoon heat, a cold chill crawled over him when he gazed into the strange man's eyes.

"Blue?" Grey swallowed hard. "I've been looking for you for two years. You're… you're my… my father." As the words left his mouth, Grey saw his first sober expression on Blue's face.

Blue nodded. "Oh God." He combed the beard with his fingers, and ran the same comb through his hair. He looked down at his clothes and slapped dust from his britches. His eyes drooped as he looked up.

"I'm sorry."

The two looked at each other, looked away, and back again. Then Grey brought something from his shirt pocket, and his eyes locked on Blue as he held it in his closed hand.

"You know a hobo named Soda Pop?"

Blue nodded. His eyes widened. "One of the best."

Grey extended his hand and opened it. "He gave me this. I think Mama would like you to have it."

Blue set the jug on the ground, unfolded the two-dollar bill, and stared. Tears now ran down both cheeks.

"I'm sorry, Grey. I'm sorry, my son."

***

On a hot night in June, a scarce ration of moonlight filtered through the treetops. Darkness saturated the night while crickets chirped and frogs croaked along the creek bank outside Blue's brush hut in Possum Trot, Missouri. Inside, Blue lay awake.

He lay awake with a mind half-dulled by guilt and cheap whiskey, with memories of a life as a hobo. He'd wanted to travel. Some travel memories brought good feelings, and reminded him of happy times. Not all. Now, the places he'd been and the people he met played through his mind like a series of photographs.

Martin - lost. Mother - died. Halo - lost a friend. Railroad watch - gone.

Sledge, El Paso jail. Belle Glade sugar cane.

He told himself he did it all, looking for… freedom. Was it just another word for nothing left to lose?

Grey—Blue's chest swelled with pride. He and Sherry made a son who now slept only two feet away. The lad's peaceful breathing assured Blue that his own son was really here, not just a dream.

His father—that one hit home. Last time he saw him was the day of his mother's funeral. The man was not at the funeral, but here, in a hut made of sticks, with a jug…

Silent tears wet the ground near Blue's face till sleep rescued him from his memories.

Chapter Thirty-Six

The old boxcar offered a rough, noisy ride for the nineteen men on board as it shook, rattled, and creaked. Some slept. Others complained nonstop. A hobo called Limey by his friends sat silent till he could take no more. His eyes grew large. His face distorted. His voice and sarcasm rose as he spoke.

"You knobbers are gobsmacked by the ride? It's a bloody freight train." He shook his head. "And it's a short squat to Dyersburg. So stifle your bitchin'. Just tell the conductor you expect a refund, or fetch a barrister and sue the bloomin' railroad." The men had a big laugh. Limey heard no more complaints.

The men in the boxcar were on their way to Dyersburg to watch Grey perform in the square. He played there two weeks ago, and got a standing ovation from the afternoon crowd of visitors. While he put away his guitar, a man who looked too warm in a suit stopped to talk.

"You sure know how to please a crowd. You got lots of jobs lined up?"

Grey shook his head. "Not yet. I'm working on it."

The man loosened his tie, stepped into the shade beside Grey, and stuck out his hand. "I'm Joe Taylor, Events Planner for the city. Our July 4th celebration is coming up. We're gonna build a stage out here, and we need entertainment from two till five p.m. But it only pays fifty dollars. Interested?"

Grey was interested. Now he slept in a corner of the boxcar on the way to his first gig.

Blue sat alone in another corner, wide

awake, excited and anxious about the coming days. Life had changed in so many ways since Grey showed up at his stick hut two days ago. Blue woke early that next morning, bathed in the creek, and apologized for having no food to offer his guest. But the hour-long trail to the Possum Trot jungle let them get acquainted, and talk of their passion for music. They enjoyed a breakfast of mulligan stew at the jungle, saw old friends and met new ones.

Blue got rid of his beard with a borrowed razor. Grey paid a hobo thirty-five cents to cut Blue's hair with large scissors that reminded Blue of the pair he owned for years, the pair he left in Benton Harbor, which also brought back the memory of his guitar. After the haircut, he told Grey about his precious Martin. Grey looked at him and smiled.

"Let's go talk to Shorty."

Minutes later, Shorty brought out Blue's long-lost friend. While Grey explained how he got the guitar, Blue stood speechless and wagged his head. When he told the men the story of how he got the guitar, Grey hugged his father. One man cried. Blue wanted to cry with him but would not. Word had spread through the jungle, and every hobo there had gathered to watch.

Most hobos in the jungle that day had never met Blue Bailey. Still, many knew of his travels and his music. Years ago, on a trip somewhere in Georgia, he performed with a borrowed guitar in a boxcar that carried fifteen men. That happened only once, unless a man believed what dozens of others told about attending one of Blue Bailey's boxcar concerts. And the exaggerated tales grew bigger as they passed from one hobo to another. Every man wanted to know someone famous, so they turned

Blue Bailey into a celebrity hobo. When word spread that he was here, a crowd gathered.

Blue hung his head, his face flushed with color, while hobos around him told stories about his fame. And when Grey gave Martin back to his father, the whole jungle stood, clapped, and cheered. But his surprise was not complete.

Shorty held a small wooden box sealed with several layers of tape wrapped over the lid. He held it up as he spoke to Blue.

"Quite a while back, maybe two years ago, a man showed up here looking for you. He said he was from Mexico." Shorty looked down at the box. "I ain't got even a half idea what's in here, but he said this belongs to you, and he knowed you wanted it back."

Blue's hands shook as he took the box. He struggled to open it till Grey brought out a knife and cut the tape. Every man in the jungle stood with his head held high and pushed forward, and gazed at the box.

Blue handed the lid to Grey, dug out a wad of newspaper, and then a note.

Señor Blue

Sorry to say Sledge died at my home. I found this in his pocket.

Your amigo, Pablo.

Blue took more paper from the box and began to unwrap whatever it held. His breath caught when he saw the chain, and a loud gasp escaped when he pulled out the watch.

***

On July 2nd, Blue and Grey spent most of the day in downtown Dyersburg. Blue sold his watch to a jeweler, and went to a clothing store. When he started into the fitting room, Grey said, "I'll meet you at the square in two hours."

At Uncle Marvin's Music Store, Grey walked out with a Gibson guitar after he convinced the owner to lend it for the show. Grey would plug Uncle Marvin's at least twice during the performance. Then he found Joe Taylor's office and talked the man into hanging a large banner over the stage to advertise the performance.

***

On the afternoon of Independence Day, hundreds of people flooded into the town square, a crowd much larger than city officials expected. Joe Taylor, dressed in red, white, and blue, beamed while he worked his way through the crowd of excited people.

A few dozen hobos stood in the crowd, for they were true patriots who loved their country. They came to pay tribute, to watch the fireworks and enjoy the concert. And this year, they felt a closer connection to the celebration. The man on the stage right now who plugged Uncle Marvin's Music Store was one of their own. The other man on the stage had been one of their own for many years.

When the music started again, it reached the ears of two women who left a car in a no-parking zone and hurried toward the square. The women were longtime friends who once worked together at the local Red Cross station. After many years, they had reconnected. Now, they stared wide-eyed at each other.

"No wonder we couldn't find a place to park," Sherry said. "Live music."

Wanda shook her head. "I didn't know either, but they sound good from here."

For ten minutes, the two women wormed their way through the crowd to get closer to the music. Sherry began to feel light-headed but did not know why. The music sounded somehow familiar, yet she could not remember ever hearing the song now playing.

Still several feet from the stage, Sherry sighed, and stopped pushing. The crowd ahead was too tight to penetrate.

She'd lost track of Wanda. Sherry didn't care. On her tiptoes, she now had occasional glimpses of the performers when the tall man in front of her moved his head to one side. She prayed the singers would turn and look her way when her next glimpse came.

As the whispered prayer left her lips—it happened. The one closer to her looked her way.

Grey?—Grey?

Sherry's mind did not accept what her eyes had seen, what her heart now knew, what her gut tried to tell her all along. Her stomach fluttered while she leaped as high as she could and screamed, "Oh, my God."

Half the crowd turned and stared. The man who had blocked her view turned and leaned toward her, concern on his face.

Sherry now had a clear view of both men on the stage while they looked her way. And... suspended between trees, a large red-white-and-blue banner flapped in the breeze above the men.

Drink Coca-Cola,
and enjoy Blue and Grey on July 4th

When Blue and Grey ended the song, Grey stepped to the microphone.

"Ladies and gentlemen, our next song is to honor a special request."

Sherry sobbed, weak in the knees and still shaking, as her son and his father began *Hobo's Lullaby*.

Annoyed, people turned again, and glared when Sherry cried out, "Oh, Grey. I love you, son."

But she forced herself to turn and look back when she heard a smooth, deep voice somewhere behind her, and she gazed at the big, black man in the crowd while he sang along. At the end of the song, he smiled and nodded at her. He cupped his hands around his mouth, and his strong, rich voice rang out.

"Ain't it a miracle… what you can get these days with a two-dollar bill?"

About Frank Allan Rogers

"I put characters in conflict with each other, and sometimes with themselves, because I want them to become a part of the reader's life, and remain long after the story ends – not just to make an impression, but to make the story feel real and worthwhile. My goal is to be known not as a great writer, but a great storyteller."

Frank Allan Rogers and his wife, Mary Rogers, an award-winning oil artist, enjoy extensive travels to the American Southwest, where she finds inspiration for her paintings and he finds a story down every trail.

Acknowledgements

I try always to make my fiction stories authentic. My readers deserve that. But I could never do it alone, and I owe a debt of gratitude to several people.

A special thanks to my darling wife, Mary – for your encouraging words, understanding and patience while I write. And for your honesty when you read those occasional paragraphs to see if they made sense – some yes, some no. I couldn't do it without you.

Glenn Laing, a longtime friend – for your patience and guidance from the time I started my first novel. Thanks for believing in me, and for the body-slam critiques that made me improve much faster than I could have otherwise.

Dr. Robert C. Covel, a trusted friend and kindred spirit – for sharing your knowledge of literature, and for our never-long-enough conversations on creative writing.

Carrollton Writers Guild – for all the read-and-critique sessions, for your comments and suggestions that improve my work and help me stay focused.

Denise Wellman – for research advice and encouragement.

John Van Binsbergen – for eagerly sharing your true-life hobo stories. They helped to add realism to the characters as I created them.

Roy Abercrombie – a good friend and voracious reader. Your enthusiasm for a good tale inspires me to create new stories and to write at the top of my game.

To the kind and generous staff at the Herald Palladium, formerly News Palladium, and to the supportive people at the Benton Harbor Public Library, who helped with my research of 1940's Benton Harbor.

A special thanks to Brandy Moody Box of Dyersburg, TN – for your time and knowledge of the 1930's Dyersburg Red Cross facility, the downtown square, and the history of Dyersburg and Dyer County, the principle setting for this novel.

References

The Great Depression – America in the 1930's, by T.H. Watkins

Big Sugar – Seasons in the Cane Fields of Florida, by Alec Wilkinson

1934 Montgomery Ward catalog – for styles and prices of clothes, shoes, and household items of the time period.

If you enjoyed this story, check out these other Solstice Publishing books by Frank Allan Rogers:

Upon a Crazy Horse

Frank Allan Rogers

When Jack Brannigan signed on for the week-long, 135-mile horseback ride to chase the ghost of Billy the Kid over the mountains and across the desert of New Mexico, he expected new demands on his wits, his strength, and his stamina. But no man could have expected what Brannigan encountered.

The brochure offered a mild caution about *elements*. For Jack, those elements tested the limits of human endurance. But the brochure said nothing about kidnapping. Nothing about murder. Nothing about a sadistic rancher who held a beautiful young woman as a slave on a remote desert ranch. No one told

Jack Brannigan his ride upon a crazy horse could be the last ride of his life.

Heartbreaking Compelling Suspenseful
Rewarding Funny

~ Nominated for Georgia Author of the Year Award ~

Available online at
www.solsticepublishing.com
www.amazon.com

Find Frank Allan Rogers on Facebook and on Twitter @frankarogers
For autographed copies, email
franktheauthor@yahoo.com

"If hell lay in the west, Americans would trample across heaven to get there."

Can a man from the 21st century survive in 1847?

Murdered on his 57th birthday, August Myles finds *crossing over* is nothing like he'd ever heard, read, or imagined, and learns he has not earned a ticket to Paradise.

In a grand experiment, the members of the Divine Council gave August another chance. Or did they?

With all the limitations of a mortal, he is sent

back in time to rescue an 11-year-old orphan girl, to get her safely from Missouri to Oregon. An impossible mission. An adventure filled with death and danger, courage and fear, love and hate, happiness and heartbreak – a grueling journey on the world's longest graveyard – with Bonner's Disciples on the Oregon Trail.